HIGHLAND SISTERS

A Selection of Recent Titles by Anne Douglas

CATHERINE'S LAND
AS THE YEARS GO BY
BRIDGE OF HOPE
THE BUTTERFLY GIRLS
GINGER STREET
A HIGHLAND ENGAGEMENT
THE ROAD TO THE SANDS
THE EDINBURGH BRIDE
THE GIRL FROM WISH LANE ★
A SONG IN THE AIR ★
THE KILT MAKER ★
STARLIGHT ★
THE MELODY GIRLS ★
THE WARDEN'S DAUGHTERS ★
PRIMROSE SQUARE ★
THE HANDKERCHIEF TREE ★
TENEMENT GIRL ★
DREAMS TO SELL ★
A SILVER LINING ★
NOTHING VENTURED ★

★ *available from Severn House*

HIGHLAND SISTERS

Anne Douglas

This first world edition published 2017
in Great Britain and the USA by
SEVERN HOUSE PUBLISHERS LTD of
19 Cedar Road, Sutton, Surrey, England, SM2 5DA.
Trade paperback edition first published
in Great Britain and the USA 2018 by
SEVERN HOUSE PUBLISHERS LTD

British Library Cataloguing in Publication Data
A CIP catalogue record for this title is available from the British Library.

ISBN-13: 978-0-7278-8750-4 (cased)
ISBN-13: 978-1-84751-864-4 (trade paper)
ISBN-13: 978-1-78010-927-5 (e-book)

This is a work of fiction. Names, characters, places and incidents
are either the product of the author's imagination or are used fictitiously.
Except where actual historical events and characters are being described
for the storyline of this novel, all situations in this publication are
fictitious and any resemblance to actual persons, living or dead,
business establishments, events or locales is purely coincidental.

All Severn House titles are printed on acid-free paper.

Severn House Publishers support the Forest Stewardship Council™ [FSC™],
the leading international forest certification organisation.
All our titles that are printed on FSC certified paper carry the FSC logo.

Typeset by Palimpsest Book Production Ltd.,
Falkirk, Stirlingshire, Scotland.
Printed and bound in Great Britain by
TJ International, Padstow, Cornwall.

Part One

One

Rosa Malcolm, sister of the bride, was up early on the morning of the wedding, 2 April, 1910. This was the special day.

Of course she would be up early on such a day, even if she wasn't used to being up with the larks anyway, which, as a housemaid, she was. All domestic servants had to be up early. It was part of the job, even when your mistress, like Rosa's in Inverness, was so kind she had actually given Rosa three whole days off to return to Carron, her home village some miles beyond Nairn, for her sister's wedding. That same sister who was lying sleeping now in the rickety bed next to Rosa's, her face lovely in repose, her yellow hair fanned out like a halo on her pillow, her breathing so peaceful it could scarcely be heard.

How like Lorne to be still sleeping on the morning of her wedding to Daniel MacNeil! Rosa was certain that had she had been marrying Daniel she would not have been sleeping on her wedding morning. So handsome, wasn't he? So much the most desirable man in the village, even if he did have a mother who was possessive to the extent that she must at times feel to him like a ball and chain round his neck. But who wouldn't endure Mrs MacNeil for the sake of a man like Daniel? Too late now to hope, and Rosa had never hoped, for he had given his heart to Lorne, who was here sleeping away her wedding morning like the calm and unworried girl she was. At eighteen, two years younger than Rosa, she'd always been known for her ease in facing the world, letting nothing bother her. Was it because she was so pretty she felt she needn't worry, then?

Some folk said Rosa herself was pretty, with her rich, dark hair and luminous dark eyes, but she knew it was the wrong word for her. Attractive, perhaps. Striking, even. But however she looked, she'd never get away with things as Lorne always could.

'Lorne!' she whispered, shaking her sister's shoulder. 'Lorne, be waking up now! It's your wedding day! And a fine one it is, too!'

Slowly, Lorne opened her eyes, green and narrow, fringed with dark lashes, and as a smile lit her kittenish face, she stretched her arms high and raised herself in her narrow bed. 'Rosa, do you think I don't know what day it is?'

'Sure, I know you know.' Rosa was tying an apron over her working dress. 'But we've things to do – first, make some porridge.'

'Porridge!' groaned Lorne. 'Not for me.'

'We'll need something, Lorne. The wedding's not till two o'clock and we'll not be having much before then, seeing as Mrs Guthrie is doing us all a meal afterwards. So, we'd best have the porridge and then tidy up in case anyone looks in.'

'Why, who's to look in? There's no need for anyone to come here.' Lorne's smile had faded. 'And I am not spending my wedding morning cleaning this cottage. What's to clean, anyway? A few mats, a table and four chairs? It will not be taking five minutes, I reckon.'

'You might have done it before, then,' Rosa snapped. 'I couldn't get here until yesterday, but you've had a week since you gave in your notice at Bluff House – plenty of time to tidy up.'

'For these folk who probably won't be coming? Rosa, just stop your nagging, eh?'

Lorne, who was wearing a cotton shift dress instead of a night-gown, threw back her bedclothes and sat up, pushing back her long hair. 'Though maybe I will do a bit of cleaning when I've done my packing, if you'll do me a favour, Rosa.'

'A favour?' Rosa's expression was dubious. 'What sort of favour?'

'Will you go up to Mrs MacKay's and ask her for the flowers she promised me? You know, Da's got nothing in his garden to suit and I wasn't going to bother about a bouquet, but then Mrs MacKay said she'd have some grand spring stuff ready if I came round. Thing is I have to do my packing.'

'Another thing you could have done before.' Rosa shook her head. 'How you do put off doing things, Lorne!'

'But will you go? I'd really like the flowers.' Lorne's tone was wheedling, at which Rosa sighed with exasperation.

'Mrs MacKay's just past the end of the village – it'll take an age to get to her. And when did you see her, anyway?'

'It was on my afternoon off. I was buying ribbon at Jennie Doune's shop and Mrs MacKay came in and we got to chatting. That was when she said I could have the flowers if I came for them.'

'And now it's me who has to get them?' Rosa sighed again. 'All right, I'll go round later, if you'll promise to sweep the cottage out and get Da into his suit.'

'Thanks, I promise!' Lorne relaxed, yawning. 'Suppose I should get up now.'

'It'd be a help.'

'Thought I might press Ma's dress later on. Want me to do yours as well?'

'No, it doesn't need it, thanks. Look, you can see – no creases! They all came out overnight.'

As Lorne, still yawning, crossed the chilly, canvas-covered floor to join her, Rosa stood gazing at the wedding garments hanging on the back of the door. Hers was the simple blue dress she had made herself, while Lorne's was the classic white wedding dress beside it, which, twenty-one years before, had been their mother's. Yes, twenty-one years had passed since she'd worn it and for all that time it had lain in a trunk in Da's room, safe from the light of day. Until now.

'Poor Ma,' whispered Rosa, thinking of the mother she still missed though eight years had passed since Martha's death from consumption. 'She was so proud of that dress, you know. Not many girls were lucky enough to have anything like it. Strange to think she was a maid at Bluff House, just like you, Lorne, when Mrs Thain gave her the material as a wedding present.' Rosa sighed. 'And now they're both gone, eh?'

'Oh, don't talk of death on my wedding day!' cried Lorne, turning away. 'There's another Mrs Thain at the house now, and Mr Hamish and Mr Rory have a nice stepmother. For heaven's sake, let's not be brooding on the past!'

'Sorry, I didn't mean to be gloomy on your special day.' Rosa moved to the door. 'Will you get dressed now, then, and I'll give Da a shout and start the porridge.'

But Lorne, looking in the cupboard to find something to wear just for the morning, was too preoccupied to reply.

Two

The Malcolms' cottage was the same as all the others in Mariner Street, the best street in Carron in Rosa's opinion, because it faced the Moray Firth. Each small house had two rooms upstairs and a living room and scullery with sink downstairs. Water for washing had to be brought in from a well, there being no piped water in Carron, which meant that the only hot water came from kettles boiled on the living-room range, and weekly baths were, as Greg Malcolm put it, the Devil's own job to provide. When the sisters were away in service, gladly using proper bathrooms, it was not known what their father did without the two of them urging him on to fill the old tin bath for himself. 'Best not to ask,' advised Rosa.

At least on the wedding morning Greg was shining with cleanliness, having washed himself and his yellow hair in cold water in the scullery, and now, feeling virtuous, was adding wood to the living-room stove to get the heat up for the breakfast porridge. Still a handsome man in his late forties, he had given his looks to his younger daughter, though it was dark-eyed Rosa, so like her mother, that he missed most when both his lassies were away – not that he ever said.

'Why, Da, you're up – I never heard you!' Rosa cried now, coming down the steep stairs. 'And you've got the range going? Oh, that's grand!'

'Knew you'd want a good start today,' he said, standing back proudly as she took a pan and began to prepare the porridge. 'This day of all days, eh, when I'm losing a daughter?'

'You are not losing a daughter, Da, just gaining a son-in-law. And when Lorne comes back from her honeymoon she'll only be up the road in Kinlaine – that's no distance at all.'

'Need the carrier, though, to get there.' Greg pulled a chair up to the kitchen table already set by Rosa the night before and sat down. 'Still, I'm not complaining. Daniel MacNeil is a fine young man and a grand joiner. He will provide well for Lorne and thinks the sun shines for her, which is as it should be, is that not right?'

'Oh, I'm sure,' murmured Rosa, stirring the porridge very fast. 'But give Lorne a shout, will you? She should be down by now.'

'So, I am down, then!' cried Lorne herself, tripping down the stairs and looking a picture, even in a faded work dress and with her hair only loosely pinned. 'And do not be giving me any of that stuff you've got there, Rosa. I'll have bread and butter, unless you're frying Da some bacon afterwards. Mrs MacRitchie brought some in before you came. Did you see it in the meat safe?'

'I did; I thought I might keep it for tonight.'

'No, no, there's plenty; let's have it now!' ordered Greg, leaping up to fetch in the gift of bacon as the sisters exchanged glances, for everyone knew that Mrs MacRitchie, the widow next door, had been setting her cap at their father for years without the slightest success. Much to the relief of his daughters, who were grateful, even so, that the widow kept an eye on their father when they were away.

'I think I am deserving of a rasher of bacon,' Greg remarked as Rosa served up the porridge. 'After all, did I not catch that grand fish we had last night, when I went out in Will Crawford's boat? I may only be a crofter, but I am as good a fisherman as the Crawford lads, and that's the truth.'

'A crofter?' echoed Lorne, buttering herself some bread. 'Since when were you a crofter, Da? You live in a cottage, you grow a few vegetables – how can you call yourself a crofter?'

'You need animals to be a crofter,' Rosa put in. 'Where are your cows, then?'

'I make some money from my vegetables,' Greg retorted, looking hurt. 'You lassies never give me credit for what I do. Remember, if I did not turn my hand to do so much, there'd be nothing on this table. Do I not even manage repairs for folk that need 'em? Was I not up at the manse last week, mending window frames for Mrs Guthrie? Jack of all trades, you might call me, but I say I just do what I can!'

'Sure you do, then, Da!' Rosa cried, touching his hand swiftly. 'We are very grateful for all you do for us, is that not so, Lorne?'

'It is,' Lorne replied, rising to put a frying pan on the stove. 'Shall we fry that bacon now, then?'

When breakfast was over and they had washed up and cleared away, the sisters, Rosa with energy, Lorne with reluctance, tied dusters over their hair and set to work on the one main room of the cottage, polishing the stove, washing the windows and shaking the mats outside, until they were quite out of breath and had to sit down for

a cup of tea. Meanwhile, Greg, who had been sent out of the way
to tidy up the garden, was brought back in to put on his good suit
for his daughters' inspection.

'You know well what I look like in it,' he groaned as he came
stiffly down the stairs, wearing the dark blue suit that rarely received
an airing. 'Twas Uncle Joe's and always too tight for me. Is it not
at this minute giving me palpitations?'

'It's fine,' Rosa told him, jerking down the jacket and turning
him round to see it from the back. 'You'll need to put on a clean
shirt, though – there's one on the back of your door – and then
see if there's anything in the garden you can use for a buttonhole.'

'Why, he can have one of Mrs MacKay's flowers,' Lorne put in.
'You'll be going there now, Rosa, eh? Time's getting on.'

'You're right, for I have to get ready when I come back,' said
Rosa, following her father up the stairs. 'I'll just get my jacket. If
you're going to press Ma's dress, Lorne, you had better be putting
the irons to heat. Watch you don't scorch the dress, now.'

'As though I would!' Lorne answered smartly.

But when Rosa came down, ready to go, it seemed to her that
Lorne was suddenly looking pale. She had taken off the duster she'd
tied round her head and freed her hair from its pins so that it fell
around her face, giving her a strange, woebegone look that was not
naturally hers. Rosa, surprised, put her arm around her.

'Why, Lorne, what is it? Are you getting wedding nerves, then?
They say some brides do but I never thought you'd be one!'

'Oh, I'm not,' said Lorne quickly. 'I expect I am just a bit tired.
And hoping, you know, it will all go well.'

'Of course it will go well! Everything's arranged and all we have
to do is walk up to Saint Luke's where Daniel will be waiting and,
before you know it, you will be Mrs MacNeil!'

'Rosa, you're very good,' Lorne said quietly. 'I may not say much,
but I know that is true.'

'Whatever's got into you?' Rosa, buttoning up her jacket, was
even blushing a little as she turned for the door, this sort of talk
from her sister being so rare she didn't know how to respond. 'I
think I'd better get off to Mrs MacKay's. See you soon, then.'

'Soon,' Lorne agreed.

And with some relief, Rosa hurried on her way.

Three

Outside the cottage in Mariner Street, she halted, taking deeps breaths of the sea air and pleasure as she always did in looking out over the wide expanse of the Moray Firth. How lucky she had been, she often thought, to have been brought up in a place like this, even if there was so little money about. Maybe money was all some folk would care about, but for Rosa, to be close to the sea, so fascinating in all its moods under the great empty sky, was all she wanted.

The trouble was, being in service, she was so rarely able to see either sea or sky, for her work kept her indoors, and even when she was free to go out on her afternoon off, being in a city, even a port like Inverness, was not the same as being in Carron, which she still missed so much.

Her father's cottage had first been rented from Mr Thain, the local landowner, by Rosa's grandfather, who had been a real fisherman, unlike Da, who only fitted in fishing around all his other jobs, but Rosa had never known her grandfather or his wife. They and her mother's folk had died young and were buried, like Martha herself, in the graveyard outside the kirk in the High Street, the only busy street in Carron. It would be past its little shops and the village school that Lorne and her wedding party would soon be walking, up to the kirk itself and, thinking of that and of how she mustn't be late back, Rosa began to hurry on her way to Mrs MacKay's.

Her cottage, as Rosa knew, was quite a step from the main village – no wonder Lorne had not wanted to go for the flowers herself that morning! Of course, if she'd gone yesterday she'd have saved Rosa a trip, but she hadn't thought of that. More than likely, she'd just done what she usually did and put off doing something until the last minute. Lord, how annoying she could be! Yet Rosa was more patient than usual in thinking of her sister, for she was still concerned by Lorne's out-of-character behaviour. Was she really suffering from nerves? No, Rosa decided, that wasn't likely. Yet, if there were some other reason for her manner, Rosa couldn't think what it might be, and gradually put her worry from her mind.

Her way out of the village took her past Seal Point, where Bluff House, the 'big' house of the area, was home to the Thain family and where Lorne had worked as a housemaid, like her mother before her, until giving notice last week. Rosa herself had never seen the inside of the house, though she'd heard of its fine rooms and grand furniture and, of course, she'd seen members of the Thain family around the village, driving their carriages or riding their horses, even occasionally visiting the sick – at least, that was what the second Mrs Thain did when she remembered.

Attractive and young – much younger than her husband – she was said to get on very well with her stepsons, Hugo and Rory, both now young men, tall, fair, English looking, Rosa thought, with longish faces and high-bridged noses. Was it true that they were somewhat wild? There were rumours, but Lorne said she didn't know if they were true. Staff at Bluff House didn't really know much about the lives of the Thain boys away from home.

Best get on, Rosa told herself but, quickening her pace, she began to feel the warmth of the April day as hot as summer, making her clothes and the thick knot of hair on her neck feel unpleasantly sticky, while the sweat rolled down her back. Taking off her hat, she stopped to wipe her brow, which brought no relief, but at last, when she'd turned the next curve of the road, she saw the little cottage that was home to Mrs MacKay and thanked God for that. Trust Lorne to want flowers at the last minute from this place at the back of beyond, but now, Rosa supposed, she'd have to help Mrs MacKay pick them. Not that she could see any in the tiny front garden except a few daffodils wilting in the heat, but maybe they were at the back? She would soon see.

Replacing her hat, Rosa rapped on the front door, calling, 'Mrs MacKay, are you there?'

All was silent, except for a bird singing, until at last there came the sound of footsteps and the front door slowly swung open, revealing a plump little woman whose round brown eyes opened wide in surprise on seeing Rosa. She wore a blue cotton dress with a white apron and a white cap over tight grey curls, and looked to Rosa to be quite elderly. Over fifty, at least.

'Who is it?' she asked, her hand shading her face from the sun. 'Who's there? I am not expecting anyone.'

'It's Rosa Malcolm, Mrs MacKay. You remember me? Martha Malcolm's daughter. We live in the village.'

'Oh, I remember Martha,' Mrs MacKay said at once. 'A sweet lassie she was, too. And you're her daughter – Rosa? I am sure I do not know why you've come to my house but you'd best come in. 'Tis hot out there.'

Drawing Rosa into the shadowy interior of her spotless little cottage, Mrs MacKay bustled about, settling her into a chair with a woollen cushion and insisting on pouring her a cup of tea.

'No, really, you needn't bother—' Rosa was beginning, but Mrs Mackay only set the cup before her, together with an oatcake, and shook her head.

'Why, lassie, you're fit to melt! Now you drink that – it's got two sugars, it'll do you good. And then you can tell me why you've come a-calling out of the blue!'

'I'm sorry I don't get to see you these days,' Rosa answered, gratefully drinking the tea in spite of the fact that she usually took no sugar. 'It's just that I'm in service, over in Inverness, and don't often come home. My sister, Lorne, saw more of the village than me, she being at Bluff House, but of course she's just left.'

'Lorne?' Mrs MacKay repeated. 'That's your sister?'

'Why, yes.' Rosa raised her dark brows. 'My sister who's getting married. As you know, it's her wedding day today and she's asked me—'

'Her wedding day's today? No, I did not know that. My Dinah never said. She's my daughter, you know, and tells me what she hears but she's out o' the village now, like me – got a wee house in Kinlaine so doesn't keep up so much with Carron gossip.' Mrs MacKay leaned forward to fill up Rosa's cup. 'But whatever are you doing here, then, on your sister's wedding day?'

'Well, the ceremony's not till the afternoon and I've come to collect the flowers you said you'd let Lorne have. She should have come herself, 'tis true, but she's not had the time.'

'Flowers?' Mrs MacKay's eyes were wide, her face quivering with surprise. 'What flowers? I never said I'd any flowers for your sister! I declare, I've never set eyes on her for years and I've no flowers anyway, 'cept a few daffodils, and what bride wants them? Rosa, I do not know what you are talking about!'

Something dark seemed to be enveloping Rosa as she sat listening to Mrs MacKay's words repeating themselves in her head, over and over again, over and over again . . . *I never said I'd any flowers for your sister . . . I never said I'd any flowers for your sister . . .*

No flowers for Lorne. No need for Rosa to come to Mrs MacKay's, then. No need for her to be away from the house in Mariner Street, except, clearly, it was what Lorne had wanted. The darkness around Rosa was fading now but a sharp little pain was taking over in her chest, so that she began to feel she could scarcely breathe. The cottage was too small, its kitchen range too big. She must get out, into the fresh air and run, run, run back home to find— Oh, God, find what? What had Lorne been up to?

'Lorne never asked you for any flowers?' Rosa whispered through dry lips, struggling to her feet, her eyes on Mrs MacKay deep and dark.

'I'm telling you! I've never even seen the girl, did not even know she was getting wed! There must be some mistake, Rosa, is all I can say.'

'No,' said Rosa, turning away her head. 'There's no mistake. Mrs MacKay, I shall have to go now. Thank you for the tea.'

'No, no, sit down again, lassie! You look so pale, you're not well – there isn't a bit o' colour in your face. Have another cup o' tea and rest yourself. Have something to eat—'

'You're very kind, but I must get home.'

Rosa was at the door, opening it and taking deep breaths of air while Mrs MacKay fussed around her, exclaiming and clucking yet failing to stop her when she wanted to go.

'Put your hat on, lassie, so you don't get the sun!' she called at last to Rosa's fast-retreating back. 'Don't be hurrying now, 'twill do you no good, but wish your sister all the best from me and say I'm sorry I did not have any flowers for her. Do not forget now!'

'I won't forget,' Rosa called over her shoulder and was gone, leaving Mrs MacKay to turn back into her house, shaking her head and wondering, what had all that been about, then?

'I'll ask Dinah,' she decided. 'Dinah will find out, to be sure.'

In the meantime, she would boil up the kettle and have another cup of tea.

Four

Run, run, run, Rosa had told herself, and run she did, so fast, still in the unseasonable heat, that by the time she reached Mariner Street she was exhausted.

Pray God, may Lorne be here, she whispered, letting herself into the house. May she be here, may she tell me why she sent me for flowers that'd never been promised. Oh, may she just be here!

But the living room was empty. No sign of Lorne. No sign of her father. There were no irons by the range, no feeling that the house was alive, preparing for a great event. Only a silence that was so strange, Rosa put her hand to her side where a stitch was acutely aching and tried to hear something, anything, that would mean Lorne had not left.

But why should she leave, anyway? She was due to be married; where would she go? To meet Daniel? She'd never do that before the wedding. Perhaps she was, after all, upstairs, getting ready, finishing her packing? Go upstairs, then, and see. True, from upstairs there was no sound, but Lorne could be lying on her bed, resting, sleeping, even, as she could so easily do . . .

Rosa, breathing hard, threw aside her jacket and hat and set her foot on the lowest step. Why not go upstairs? Because she was afraid of what she would find. Or, rather, not find, and that would be Lorne. Something was going on. Rosa could not understand what but she knew she did not want to go upstairs and find her sister not there.

Moments passed, long moments of dread, until at last Rosa found the breath to call: 'Lorne, I'm back. Are you there? Lorne, answer me!'

But there came no answer, and with a sudden, desperate rush of energy, Rosa ran up the stairs and into the little room she'd always shared with her sister.

'Lorne!' she cried again, but there was no point. The room was empty.

No Lorne. No honeymoon case. No brush or comb on the chest of drawers, except for Rosa's. No clothes of Lorne's except the oldest in the hanging cupboard. But from the back of the door to the room, as Rosa saw with a pang of hope denied, there still dangled next to her own outfit their mother's wedding dress – the dress Lorne was due so soon to wear for her marriage to Daniel MacNeil.

So she hadn't taken it. Her other clothes, yes, her wedding dress, no. Yet if for some strange reason she had gone to meet Daniel before the wedding, wouldn't she have taken it? No, she wouldn't. No, it was nonsense even to think that Lorne had gone to meet Daniel before the wedding. What bride would do such a thing? Give up the drama of arriving at the kirk, walking up the aisle, being the centre of attention, seeing the special love and admiration in her bridegroom's eyes as she joined him for their marriage?

No, no, Lorne had not gone to see Daniel, but she'd taken her case and her clothes and must have gone somewhere. But where? Where could she possibly have gone?

Her head reeling as she stood, trying to make sense of what had happened, Rosa suddenly heard her father's voice calling from below, and with wild hope that he might know something, she ran down the stairs to throw her arms around him.

'Hey, hey, what is all this?' he asked, laughing as he put her aside. 'Did you think I had gone missing, or what? I've only been next door with Mrs MacRitchie. Lorne sent me round to borrow some milk and we got to talking, you know how it is—'

'Lorne sent you round?' Rosa's great eyes searched his face. 'When? When did she send you round?'

'Why, soon after you went off for the flowers she wanted. Did you get them? Where are they?'

'She didn't want any flowers, Da. It was just a ruse to get rid of me, like she got rid of you.' Rosa shook her head. 'She's gone, Da. Lorne's gone. She's taken her case and her clothes and she's gone.'

'Rosa, what are you talking about? How could she have gone? She's getting married! We'll be going to the kirk, Daniel will be waiting – how can she have gone?'

'I don't know, Da, I wish I did. But she's nowhere in the house and all her things are gone – except for Ma's wedding dress.'

Rosa, trying to control the sobs that were threatening to overcome her, turned to take out her handkerchief and from the corner of her eye saw something white over the clock on the shelf above the range – an envelope – that had not been there before.

'Da,' she said quietly, 'I think she's left a note.'

'Where?' His eyes were everywhere. 'I see no note.'

'Over the clock.'

With a couple of steps, Rosa reached the range and, stretching up her hand, snatched down the envelope that she could now see bore her name and her father's in Lorne's sloping hand.

'It's a note, all right,' she whispered, handing the envelope to Greg. 'Open it, Da.'

Five

The time it took her father to draw out the one sheet the envelope contained seemed to Rosa to be endless, and when he then said he couldn't read it as he hadn't got his reading glasses, she snatched it from him and said she'd read it herself.

'Aloud,' he ordered. 'Read it to me aloud!'

'Da, I don't know if I can.'

The lines were dancing before her eyes. She couldn't make out their sense, or if they had any sense anyway, but she began to read: '"Dear Da and Rosa—"'

'Speak up!' her father ordered. 'Your voice is too faint; I cannot hear you!'

'"Dear Da and Rosa,"' she began again, '"I have to tell you that I am going away—"'

'Of course she's going away, soon as she's wed!' Greg cried. 'What's she on about?'

'"I am going away,"' Rosa read again, '"but not with Daniel."'

At these words, she lowered the page and met her father's eyes, wide, disbelieving, the same as her own, then shook her head as though she could shake away what she had just read aloud.

'"Not with Daniel"? What does she mean?' she asked her father. 'Who, then? Who can she be going with if not Daniel?'

'Maybe . . .' Greg was hesitant, his gaze now wavering, wandering, away from Rosa. 'Maybe she's got the wedding nerves folk talk about, maybe felt she had to run away?'

Rosa slowly shook her head. 'No, Da, no. That's not it.'

'Well, read on, then!' he cried. 'Read what Lorne tells us!'

'All right, listen, this is what she says, though I can hardly bear to read it. How can she have written it?'

'Just read it,' groaned Greg.

'"I know you will be angry with me and I'm sorry, but I can't help it. There is someone else who loves me and I love him like I never loved Daniel. I never should have agreed to marry him. I feel bad I let it go so far, not telling him, but I couldn't face it. He will hate me, I know, but what can I do? Rory says we must think of our own happiness; that is why we are leaving Carron. By the time you read this, we will be on our way."'

'On their way where?' cried Greg as Rosa paused and sighed. 'And who's the man she running off with? I don't understand . . . I don't understand what's happening – what my own daughter is doing! Is that it? Is that all she says?'

'That's all, except that she asks for our forgiveness.'

'Forgiveness!'

'"Da and Rosa, please try to forgive me,"' Rosa read, '"and wish me well in my new life. I am not much for writing – it has taken me hours to write this – but I will write to you, I promise."'

Rosa raised her eyes to Greg's.

'And then she sends her love – if you can believe it.'

For a moment, she stood without speaking and then suddenly leaped to her feet, her face colder than Greg had ever seen it but her eyes alive with passionate feeling.

'Her love she sends, as though we'd want it after what she's done to Daniel! How can she write a letter like that, full of herself and her new life when his life is shattered, the stupid, stupid girl! Can she not see that if she's ruined his life she's ruined hers too, for how long is Rory Thain going to stay with her? He'll never marry her, never, and then what will she do?'

'Rory Thain?' cried Greg. 'You mean one o' the lads from the big house? Lorne's gone off with him?'

'Did you not hear me read out his name just then? How many men called Rory are there in this village? Only him, and he's one of the few men she sees, eh? I was racking my brain to think where she might have met a man we didn't know, but I never thought in my wildest nightmares that she would have thrown in her lot with one of the Thains!'

'One of the Thains . . .' Greg put his hand to his brow. 'And his father is my landlord! What will he do, Rosa? I mean Mr Thain? He could throw me out, eh? As a punishment for letting my girl run away with his son?'

'Da, don't be foolish,' Rosa said tiredly. 'How could you have known what Lorne would do? Anyway, Rory Thain must take his share of the blame – she couldn't have done what she's done if he hadn't asked her. But it's Daniel I'm thinking of. What must he be suffering? Jilted on his wedding day, made to look a fool before all the village.'

Rising to her feet, Rosa took up her jacket from the chair where she had thrown it and shrugged herself into it before cramming on her hat and fixing her father with glittering eyes. 'I'm going to his house, Da. I'll speak to him, tell him we knew nothing of what's happened or we'd have stopped it. I'll try to do something to help – anything—'

'There's nothing you can do.' Greg rose heavily to his feet. 'And his mother'll be there, don't forget. Best leave it, Rosa. You're not to blame, so leave well alone.'

'No, I will not, Da! I tell you, I'm going to speak to Daniel. And you'd better get yourself away to the minister at the kirk to find out if he knows the wedding's off. And tell Mrs Guthrie I'll be coming to see her about all the food and everything—'

Suddenly Rosa held her hands against her eyes like a child beginning to cry yet no tears fell, while her father stood by, bending his head against the rush of thoughts that consumed him.

'How could Lorne have done it, Da?' Rosa whispered, letting her hands fall. 'I know she likes her own way but there's no bad in her – she wouldn't want to hurt anyone. Yet when you think of all Mrs Guthrie's done, and what others have done as well, and the service all arranged and the organ booked, folk in their best clothes – Da, how could she have let everybody down?' Rosa's eyes fell. 'And that's not counting breaking Daniel's heart!'

'Lorne is Lorne,' Greg answered in a low voice. 'She doesn't want to hurt folk, it's true, but if she wants something she'll take it. She won't think of anyone else. It's the way she is.'

'But Da, this is something you'd never think even Lorne could do. To run away on her wedding day and leave the bridegroom to pick up the pieces!'

'These things happen, eh? Maybe mostly to women but to men and all. Folk can change their minds, everyone knows that.' He shook his head. 'But it's a terrible thing my own daughter's done, I cannot deny. It hurts, eh?'

'It hurts,' Rosa agreed.

They were both silent for a few moments until Greg said he must be away. And Rosa should go to Daniel's, if she was going.

'Oh, I am!' cried Rosa. 'I am going now!'

Six

When she spoke of going to Daniel's house, of course Rosa meant his mother's, for Daniel's only house was one he rented in Kinlaine, the nearest big village that was almost a town, from where he conducted his joinery business and worked on his real love, which was carving and making furniture. It was to that house he'd planned to take Lorne as a bride, which she'd been quite happy about, believing that living in a town must be more exciting than in a village, but where now, of course, she would never go.

Oh, poor Daniel, Rosa groaned as she hurried towards Mrs MacNeil's cottage, which was some way from Mariner Street and not so attractive, having no view of the sea. Not that that worried Mrs MacNeil, who cared nothing for something that could cause so much trouble: great, salty drops always being blown on to good paintwork and shining windows – who would want it?

Rushing round with her duster, it was her belief that all who cleaned their houses as she did would be much happier in a street like hers, well away from the dangerous elements of wind and rising water, where everything could be controlled. And to have control of people as well as things was certainly Mrs MacNeil's aim; she even made Daniel leave his shoes at the door to save marking her floors, just as she'd made his father before him – though he'd been dead now for many years, out of reach of his wife's control for ever.

It was well known in the village that Daniel had had a tough life with his mother. Not so much because of her being so house-proud, but because she did so dote upon him, always telling him he was all she had, she couldn't do without him, clinging to him on every occasion. But the time came, nevertheless, when he'd rented a place of his own elsewhere and, to her chagrin, she'd had to make the best of it. Oh, the scenes, the tears! Everyone knew about them but Daniel had not given in, and when, later, his mother declared she'd never get over it if he married Lorne Malcolm, he did not waver, simply saying that it was up to her what she did. If she wanted to see him, she must accept Lorne. It would be a case of 'those whom God hath joined together, let no man put asunder', he quoted to her and, after more tears and more hysterics, it was Mrs MacNeil who gave in and the wedding was planned.

But, oh God, what would she be saying now? Rosa scarcely dared to wonder as she arrived at Mrs MacNeil's immaculate front door. She didn't know but she could certainly guess, and only the thought of seeing Daniel, who'd been staying at his mother's before the wedding, made her lift her hand to knock. For whatever Mrs MacNeil said about Lorne, it could only be what Rosa had already thought herself.

'Yes?' cried a voice as the door was flung open by Mrs MacNeil, who appeared on the step, not wearing the wedding outfit she had made herself which everyone had heard about but one of the dark dresses she often wore, which must have seemed to her to be particularly appropriate to that terrible day. For, of course, she must be in a kind of mourning for her son, not because he had lost his bride, for which his mother could only give thanks, but because of how that bride had treated him. Humiliated him before the whole village! Daniel, Mrs MacNeil's son! The cheek of it; how could she have had the nerve?

Even just seeing Mrs MacNeil on the doorstep, Rosa could tell how mortified she was, how she could hardly contain her feelings. It did not help that now on that doorstep she was seeing Rosa Malcolm, sister to the woman who had done all the damage, and as her ice-grey eyes took in the visitor, a great flood of scarlet shot from her throat to her brow, and she had to clutch at her own door to support her in her fury.

'Rosa Malcolm!' she hissed. 'How do you have the face to come here? After what your sister has done to my son! The wicked, wicked girl! I always knew she was not to be trusted, not fit to marry Daniel, and now she's proved it, the wanton, the trollop! And now you come here, knocking on my door, making excuses. How dare you, how dare you?'

'I am not making excuses, Mrs MacNeil,' Rosa answered through dry lips. 'I know my sister has done wrong but she is not what you've called her. She's not wanton, only foolish. She has been led astray—'

'Is that what you are calling it? All I know is Mr Thain's foxy groom came here this morning with a letter for my poor boy from your sister, and stood around so all the neighbours could see him until I sent him packing, the nasty creature! But by then, poor, poor

Daniel was away to shut himself up and not a sign of him have I seen since, but don't ask to see him yourself, for I'll not let you in – away you go, away to your father, and tell him from me he should be ashamed to have such a daughter as your sister! Away, I say, out of my sight!'

And as Mrs MacNeil stood on her step, making shooing gestures as though she were chasing off an unwanted cat, Rosa knew there was nothing she could do. Daniel's mother would never let her near Daniel, and who could blame her? At the thought of him shutting himself away, it was all Rosa could do not to dissolve into tears. But that she would not do in front of Mrs MacNeil, and she was turning slowly away when, amazingly, she heard Daniel's own voice behind her speaking in strange, artificial tones to his mother.

'Is it Rosa there, Ma? Don't be blaming her now, she has done nothing.'

'Of course I am blaming her, Daniel! She's a Malcolm – she is forbidden this house, and that is that.' Mrs MacNeil, almost breathless with rage, had put her hand to her face to cool her cheeks until she looked at her son, standing on the front step, and cried out in new, raw pain. 'Oh, Daniel, oh, dear Lord, your poor face! Oh, what has that girl done to you?'

'My face?'

Oh, yes, his face! Rosa knew at once what Daniel's mother meant, for his face had changed. Still handsome, still with the straight nose, the high cheekbones, the level brows . . . yes, all were still there, but somehow, mysteriously, no longer made up the face that she knew. It was as though all that had made it Daniel's had been wiped away by what Lorne had done, and the beautiful, dark blue eyes that were so expressive had become so blank, so dead, they were like the eyes of no one living.

Oh, Daniel, Daniel – what could Rosa say? What could anyone say? How right her father had been to say that there was nothing anyone could do for him. At least, not then. Time would help, time might work a miracle but maybe only far into the future, and it was clear that after the crushing blow Daniel had received he could not think of any future at all.

'You didn't know, did you?' he asked Rosa now, fixing her with those dead eyes of his. 'She said, in her letter, you didn't know.'

'We didn't know,' Rosa told him, glad to let him have the truth. 'Da and me, we never had an idea. Just this morning, she sent us away so we could not see her leaving the house.' Rosa's mouth was trembling, her eyes filling with tears. 'And now, we do not know where she is—'

'And who cares?' Mrs MacNeil cried. 'If she never comes back to this village, it will be too soon. Daniel, go into the house, away from the neighbours – can you not feel their eyes? Rosa Malcolm, please leave us! Just go.'

'Wait!' ordered Daniel, holding up his hand. 'Rosa, it was good of you to come, I want to thank you. But don't tell me if you . . . hear from her. Don't tell me where she is and where he is, for if I should know—'

He said no more but turned and went into the house, to be followed by his mother, after she had flashed another fierce stare at Rosa, and then the front door was banged shut and Rosa herself was running again, just running, as though speed would take away her thoughts.

Seven

So much to do, so many folk to speak to without knowing what to say . . . For how could anything be said by Greg or Rosa that would make things any better? As they moved around the people they knew, now eating what had been intended for the wedding breakfast, Mrs Guthrie having said it should not go to waste, the father and sister of the girl who had set the whole village buzzing could say nothing, only keep their eyes down and endure what had to be endured.

True, there was some sympathy for them, especially from Mr Guthrie, the minister, and his wife, but as the villagers enjoyed their meal in the hall off the kirk, there was also a certain undercurrent of suspicion of the Malcolms in the air. Could it be certain that they'd had no idea of what Lorne was planning? Had they not had a feeling that she was up to something? And had she never dropped so much as a hint that Mr Rory was in love with her and planning to carry her off right under poor Daniel's nose? Was that not hard to believe?

I'll never get over this, thought Rosa, handing sandwiches and cups of tea. This will be something I'll always remember. Even Da's feeling it – he looks as though he'd just like to crawl away into a corner and curl up till Christmas. And so would I . . .

'Don't blame yourselves,' Mrs Guthrie told them as they prepared to leave the kirk hall. 'You weren't to know what Lorne would do; the minister and I truly believe that.'

''Tis good of you to say so,' Greg muttered, his eyes cast down. 'Plenty are not agreeing with you.'

'Never mind. Hold your heads high, and pray that Lorne will soon come to her senses and return to us.'

'She will never do that,' said Rosa. 'How could she?'

'We must hope that she sees the light and that God guides her to do what is right.'

As Mrs Guthrie shook their hands and wished them well, they were joined by the minister, who showed them the same kindness and understanding as his wife, though it was plain he was having difficulty in finding forgiveness for Lorne. 'God will be her judge,' he said solemnly as they turned to go, but as Lorne had never been one for kirk-going, Greg whispered to Rosa that she would probably never care whether God judged her or not.

'At least that's the worst over,' he added. 'I mean, facing the folk we know. Now we can just go home and shut our door.'

'The worst?' Rosa was staring at her father, her eyes enormous. 'Da, have you forgotten Mr Thain? We've still to face him.'

'Mr Thain . . . Oh, my Lord!' Greg's jaw had dropped. 'What was I thinking of to forget him? Did I not say I was worried before, Rosa, about what he might do? Did I not say we might lose the cottage?'

'And I said we would not. But it's not going to be very pleasant, meeting him. Or Rory's brother. Or his stepmother.'

'I am only thinking of him – Mr Thain. He's the one with the power and it'll be me who gets the blame for what Lorne has done.' Greg passed his hand over his eyes. 'I am thinking I can't face going home now, Rosa, in case the Thains are there.'

'Oh, come, Da, stop talking like that!' cried Rosa, though believing that he might be right. 'We don't know what the Thains will be doing.'

But when they finally reached home, the first thing they saw was an open carriage at their door, in which Rory Thain's father, his stepmother and his brother were sitting – all waiting. Waiting for Rosa and her father, the family of the girl who had snared away one of their own, while Norris, the 'foxy' groom, stood beside the horses, waiting too and failing to conceal a smirk when the Malcolms arrived.

'There you are at last, Malcolm!' cried Mr Thain. 'Where the devil have you been?'

Without waiting for his groom, he opened the carriage door and stepped down to confront Greg immediately, as though he were afraid Greg might run away. Which, of course, he would have liked to do, though with Rosa by his side he managed to meet his landlord's furious blue stare without flinching.

While the groom helped Mrs Thain to descend from the carriage and a bleak-faced young Mr Hugo leaped out himself, Greg cleared his throat and stammered, 'Mr Thain, sir, Mrs Thain, I am sorry we were not in – we've been seeing the minister—'

'I should think you have, though it's myself and my family you should be seeing first,' snapped Mr Thain, a tall, dark-haired, masterful man, rather overweight but elegant in a tweed suit and Homburg hat. In any walk of life he would have been hard to deal with, Rosa thought, but as a prosperous landowner who held his tenants' lives in the palm of his hand, what chance could her father have of making him accept the truth – that they knew nothing of what Lorne and Rory Thain had been planning?

'Still, I am glad you are here now,' Mr Thain went on, 'so please open your door. I have no desire to discuss the present situation on the doorstep.'

'The door's not locked, sir. We never lock the door – there's nothing to steal—'

'Just get on with it, man, and let us in! Priscilla' – Mr Thain put out a hand to his wife – 'let's see if they can find you somewhere to sit down.'

'As though I care about sitting down!'

Still on the doorstep, auburn-haired young Mrs Thain, holding a lace handkerchief to her eyes, appeared grief-stricken and at the same time petulant, shaking off her husband's hand and drawing her fine brows together. In a dark green close-fitting jacket and ankle-length matching skirt, she was as well dressed as usual, but nothing else was usual for her that day, Rosa could tell, and was not surprised to see tears forming in her large blue eyes when she lowered the handkerchief to speak.

'All I care about, Frederick, is having Rory back, though God knows where he could have gone, and why he should have done what he's done to us, his family, is quite . . . is quite . . . beyond me.'

Turning to her stepson, who was staring at the ground, Mrs Thain put her hand on his arm. 'Hugo, you understand, don't you? You feel the same terrible shock as I do?'

'Just come into the cottage, my dear,' Mr Thain said soothingly. 'We can talk inside of what can be done.'

'Of what can be done?' asked Hugo, suddenly looking up. 'I doubt very much that anything can be done. What have you in mind?'

But his father shook his head at him and marshalled everyone except the groom inside the cottage, where only Mrs Thain accepted, in spite of all previous protestations, one of Greg's hard wooden chairs, sinking into it with some relief.

Eight

Rosa, who might once have been grateful that her home had been tidied before this unwelcome visit, now cared not at all how it looked, for other things mattered more. So many things, her head was spinning, but she stayed by her father's side, anxious for him and the nerves he was trying to hide before his formidable landlord, who now turned his gaze on Rosa.

'Malcolm, is this another daughter of yours?' he asked curtly.

'Yes, sir, this is my elder daughter, Rosa. She is in service in Inverness.'

'And sister to the girl who has caused all the trouble. In her confidence, very likely. Am I not right?'

'No, sir!' cried Rosa, her colour rising. 'Lorne told me nothing of her plans.'

'Oh, come! You would be close to her; you would know what she was up to. Please do not tell me she never mentioned my son's name to you. Never boasted about her hold over him?'

'Of course she did!' his wife put in before Rosa could speak. 'I have a sister; I know what sisters are like. Just tell us what she said, Rosa, and I promise no one will be blaming you.'

'Madam, I hardly ever saw her,' Rosa answered desperately. 'I work in Inverness; I only came back for her wedding to Mr MacNeil. And it's the solemn truth that my father and me had no idea what she was going to do. She even found ways to get us out of the house so that we shouldn't see her leave. We couldn't believe it when we read the letter she left us.'

'That's right, sir,' Greg said earnestly. 'It was the shock of our lives when we found out what had happened – we haven't been able to take it in. But we've had to tell folk and see the minister and Rosa here has tried to help young Daniel, but he cannot be helped, he's too upset.'

'Poor man,' sighed Mrs Thain. 'Oh, how could that girl do such a thing to him?'

'You say she left a letter?' Mr Thain asked, ignoring his wife's sympathy for the unknown bridegroom. 'I should like to see it.'

'Papa, you can't!' Hugo exclaimed, fixing his father with outraged eyes. 'That's the Malcolms' letter. It's private!'

'Private?' thundered Mr Thain, a brick-coloured flush rising to his temples as he stared at his son with angry eyes. 'What are you talking about? That letter might be our only hope of getting Rory back and stopping him from making one of the biggest mistakes of his life! Do you want your brother to be the talk of Scotland for being a silly, blind fool?'

'Hugo, your father's right,' chimed Mrs Thain, stretching out to take his hand, which he refused to give. 'Of course the letter is Mr Malcolm's letter, but I'm sure he wants his daughter back as much as we want Rory, and this letter may help. Surely you can see that?'

Before he could answer, it was Rosa who suddenly, surprisingly, spoke next. 'We don't mind Mr Thain seeing my sister's letter, do we?' she asked Greg, who mutely shook his head. 'But it will not help. My sister doesn't say where she's going. I can show you, if you like. I have the letter here.'

Opening her bag, Rosa took out the envelope containing the letter and passed it to Mr Thain, who, after studying her for a moment while his risen colour began to fade, opened the envelope, took out the letter and read it.

'Well?' his wife asked impatiently. 'What does she say? Perhaps I can read it too?'

'That won't be necessary,' Mr Thain replied, folding the letter and returning it to its envelope. 'It's correct what Miss Malcolm says – the girl tells nothing of their plans.' His mouth twisting, he passed the letter back to Rosa. 'Thank you for letting me see it anyway, Miss Malcolm.'

'Very decent of you,' commented Hugo, at which his father nodded but said no more, only stooped to give his wife his hand to help her rise from her chair.

'Seems we are no better off,' Mrs Thain said, sighing again. 'What did Lorne Malcolm actually say, then, in the letter? You should have let me read it, Frederick.'

'It would only have upset you. She claims that she loves Rory and he loves her. Make of that what you will.'

'Might be true,' said Hugo, moving towards the cottage door.

'Oh, no!' cried his stepmother. 'No, no, that cannot be so. Not of Rory, at least. I would have known.'

'We won't argue on that, Priscilla,' her husband said shortly. 'It is time for us to go.'

Turning to Greg and Rosa, who were standing at the door, waiting for what might be said next, Mr Thain addressed Greg. 'I accept your word now, Malcolm, that you had no knowledge of your daughter's plans, and all I can say is that if she gets in touch – which surely she will – I shall expect you to give me any information you have immediately. Is that clear?'

'Oh, yes, sir,' Greg answered, visibly relieved, as Rosa could tell, that nothing was to be said about his giving up his cottage. 'If Lorne gives me any idea of where she might be, I will let you know as soon as I can.'

'Very good. Open the door, then. Miss Malcolm, our thanks again for your help. Hugo, go before us to the carriage. Priscilla, take my arm.'

At long last, thank God, they were off, the groom giving another of his contemptuous smiles as he drove the solemn-faced Thains away, while Rosa and her father watched until the carriage was out of sight.

'What a relief!' cried Greg as soon as they were back in the cottage. 'I'm not to be evicted, Rosa. Is that not good news?'

'Yes, but it doesn't stop us wondering about Lorne, Da.' Rosa was moving the kettle on the stove to bring it up to the boil. 'I mean, what will become of her?'

'It's her own doing, do not forget. And she is not worrying about Daniel, is she?'

As Rosa set out cups, she made no reply and, after a moment, her father smiled.

'I was thinking – you seemed to impress Mr Thain, eh? Calling you "Miss Malcolm" as though you were the quality! And young Mr Hugo was sticking up for us, too, I am sure because of you. Maybe you should apply for Lorne's job at Bluff House, eh? Why not?'

'Why not?' cried Rosa. 'I should think, as Lorne's sister, I'd be the very last person they'd want in her job! No, thanks, I'll stay in Inverness. I go back tomorrow, don't forget.'

And with what a heavy heart she would be travelling, she reflected as she made the tea, compared to the way she'd expected to be returning to work.

For, of course, she would have been happy to see her sister wed, especially to someone like Daniel, even if some might have thought she could only have been envious of Lorne's 'catch' and would have liked to have been Daniel's wife herself. But that was never Rosa's dream. How could it have been, when the only woman for him had been her own sister?

Oh, poor Daniel! Drinking her tea, which she couldn't even taste, all the problems of the day faded from Rosa's mind, as it seemed clear to her that the only thing that mattered in the whole awful nightmare was Daniel's heartache.

Nine

Number twenty-five Wellington Crescent, the fine terraced house in Inverness where Rosa worked, was owned by a Mr Jonathan Fordyce, a young lawyer. It was his pretty wife, Christina, who was remarkable for treating her staff unusually well, believing, as many did not, that they were human beings and not just machines for cleaning and cooking. It followed, of course, that she would have taken an interest in Rosa's sister's wedding and, having given Rosa leave to attend it, would be waiting to hear how it all went.

Just as Mrs Banks, the cook, would also be waiting, along with Hattie, the kitchen maid, Agnes, the parlour maid, and Greta, under housemaid to Rosa, but how Rosa was to tell them what had actually happened was quite beyond her even as she approached the area gate of number twenty-five. How to tell them that there had been no wedding? That her sister had run away with the son of her employer? That the jilted bridegroom was in despair? The whole idea of putting her news into words seemed to Rosa to be quite beyond her.

Whatever would they think of Lorne, for instance? Of Rosa, herself, for that matter? That she was just such another as her sister?

Her dark eyes showing the sorrow she wished she could have kept secret, Rosa bravely moved down the steps of the area and rapped on the heavy back door. Being April, the evening was not yet as dark as she would have liked, so that she might be swallowed up, hidden away from all those waiting eyes. Eyes that, yes, were instantly turned upon her as soon as she stepped through the door opened for her by young Hattie, eyes that at first saw nothing wrong.

'There you are, Rosa!' cried Mrs Banks, who was not like anyone's idea of a plump, comfortable cook, being painfully thin and generally considered 'nervy', given to getting into 'states' when meals were due, only relaxing when the plates came down and it was obvious that the master and mistress had finished everything. Now, with dinner over, she was able to take an interest in Rosa, drawing her nearer to the kitchen range that was throwing out a good heat and telling her to warm herself after being on the terrible train, eh?

'And tell us all about the wedding!' ordered Agnes, the fair-haired parlour maid in her thirties, taking Rosa's coat and giving it to Hattie to hang up. 'We're dying to hear, aren't we, girls?'

'Aye, been thinking o' nothing else,' said Greta, the lanky, easy-going housemaid who worked with Rosa. 'I mean, what's nicer than a wedding?'

'Did you bring us any cake?' asked Hattie, filling the kettle at a nod from Mrs Banks and only widening her eyes when Agnes clicked her tongue and told her not to be so cheeky, as Rosa had had more to think about than bringing back wedding cake.

'Is that not right?' she called to Rosa, smiling, but when she took in Rosa's expression as she sank into a chair at the kitchen table, the gaze of Agnes sharpened.

'My word, Rosa, you look as though that wedding's tired you out. You must have had too much to do.'

Rosa, keeping her eyes down, slowly shook her head. 'The wedding didn't tire me out, Agnes. The truth is' – she looked around at the interested faces – 'there was no wedding.'

No wedding? The silence that met Rosa's words was so long and strange, so filled with the same stunned response, it made everyone feel as one. They knew what they thought but not what to say, for what could they say to poor Rosa? No wedding? Her sister had not become a bride? Had been jilted? Left at the church? Or what? Just what had happened?

As wondering glances were exchanged, still no one spoke as the words sank in ever more deeply: 'There was no wedding . . .'

It was Mrs Banks who at last broke the silence, and no one was surprised that her voice had risen as it did when she thought her cooking had failed or that her eyes were as anxious as when she was working up to one of her 'states'.

'Rosa, whatever do you mean? No wedding, you say, so how can that be? What happened? What could have happened? Was your sister left at the door? That pretty girl we've seen in photos? I cannot believe it, no, no – it's too bad that a man could do such a thing, too cruel to your sister—'

'Mrs Banks, a man didn't do it,' Rosa told her, struggling to be calm. 'It was my sister who left the bridegroom herself. Sent him a note and ran away with someone from the house where she worked. But look, I don't want to talk about it.' Rosa got to her feet. 'I'll go up and unpack my bag.'

'No!' cried Mrs Banks, seizing Rosa's arm with a thin hand. 'No, you cannot do that. The mistress wants to speak to you. She said so particularly, is that not right, Agnes? Did not Mrs Fordyce say if Rosa was back in time to take up her tea – you know she likes a cup of tea at nine o'clock – that she wished to hear all about the wedding? You must go up, Rosa, you cannot say no.'

'It's not my job to take up tea!' Rosa said, pulling away from Mrs Banks' hand. 'How is she to know I'm back, then?'

'Why, if I go up with her tea, she will be sure to ask me,' Agnes declared. 'And what am I to say? You're not, when you are? I am not telling lies for you, Rosa.'

'No, no, I'd never want that, but what am I to say about the wedding when Mrs Fordyce asks me, then? How can I tell her what my sister did? She will think it's too terrible and maybe I'm part of it, that I knew all about it—'

'She will not think that – why should she? Come on, now, let us all have a quiet cup of tea ourselves, and then you and me, Rosa, will get Mrs Fordyce's tray ready and we'll go up together. When the mistress asks about the wedding, you needn't tell her who your sister ran off with, just say she changed her mind and that she has gone away. That's all you need do.'

But Rosa's eyes were dark and tragic; she could not see everything going as smoothly as Agnes had said. What could she do, though? Mrs Fordyce must be told, there was no way round it, and maybe she would, after all, understand, especially as sensible Agnes would be there. Everyone respected Agnes.

After a short pause, during which Rosa's face reflected her scurrying thoughts, she said at last, 'All right, I'll go up. I'll speak to the mistress.'

'Make our tea, then, Hattie,' Agnes ordered. 'You'll feel better when you've had something, Rosa, eh? Then we can go up.'

Ten

Young Mrs Fordyce's drawing room was unusual for its time, being, her critics declared, 'too plain'. Where were the numerous pictures on the walls? The tables full of framed photographs? The cushions, shawls over tables, lace covers over chairs, the mirrors, the rugs, the bowls of artificial flowers, dried leaves and reeds you could usually find in the best reception room of a house in 1910?

True, there were a few of those things – a small selection of pictures and photographs, one or two cushions, a smart hearth rug – but only the flowers were real and there were no covers over chairs or shawls over tables. Who would have thought Mrs Fordyce's husband was a wealthy lawyer when she kept such a poverty-stricken drawing room? the critics would ask. But there were plenty of artists and others who thought Mrs Fordyce's taste to be truly modern and much to be admired. As for her housemaids, they loved it. Less to dust!

On that April evening, when Rosa and Agnes brought in a tray of tea, the room might have seemed to them particularly attractive, with the lamps lit and a fire burning in the grate, except that they had no thoughts for anything other than Mrs Fordyce's questioning. As it was, they set down the tray in silence while the genial Mr Fordyce excused himself for work in his study, wedding talk not being his sort of thing as he explained, while his wife, tall and slim in a bright green evening dress, had a special smile for Rosa.

'There you are then, Rosa, back from the wedding! Did all go well? I'm sure it did. Now you must tell me all about it.'

But only silence fell, for Rosa couldn't begin, and it was Agnes who finally stepped in with her usual confidence.

'We have to tell you, ma'am, that there was a problem with the wedding. Rosa here is very upset – I came with her to help her explain.'

'A problem?' Mrs Fordyce turned her sympathetic gaze on Rosa. 'Oh, I'm so sorry! Was someone taken ill?'

'Nothing like that, ma'am. The fact is Rosa's sister changed her mind. She decided not to marry after all.' Agnes gave Rosa a quick glance, prompting her, as Rosa knew, to enter the conversation herself. 'Everything was cancelled, is that not right, Rosa?'

Meeting Mrs Fordyce's wide grey eyes with her own troubled gaze, Rosa put her shoulders back and stood very straight, willing herself now to find the courage to speak, to discover at last what would be thought of her story that would be so different from anything her mistress might have expected. And of the consequences, if any, for herself.

'It is true, ma'am,' she said quietly. 'There could be no wedding. My sister left a note for the bridegroom and one for my father and me, telling us she was going away with someone else. Then it was left to us to tell the minister. The bridegroom was too upset.'

'Why, I should think so!' cried Mrs Fordyce. 'What a terrible thing to happen! How he must be suffering, the poor man! And you, Rosa, and your father too – you must have had such a shock to have this coming out of the blue?'

'At first, we could not take it in,' Rosa said after a pause. 'It's true my sister has always liked her own way, but she's good at heart, she's never wanted to hurt anyone, so when she . . . did this . . . I couldn't believe it. Still can't,' she added as Mrs Fordyce shook her head.

'How sure she must have been, though, that she knew what she wanted this time. I mean, to be willing to leave her bridegroom.'

'Maybe thought she had found someone better?' asked Agnes, looking at Rosa, whose colour had risen, whose eyes had for a moment flashed, then lost all expression.

'She was wrong, then,' she whispered and turned away to pick up Mrs Fordyce's tea tray. 'It was very good of you to see me, ma'am. I appreciate it.'

'I just wish I could have been able to help.' Mrs Fordyce sighed. 'But what can anyone do?'

As Rosa and Agnes bobbed a small curtsey and made their way slowly from the drawing room, they made no answer. It was true, of course, that there was nothing anyone could do.

Even so, on their way down the back staircase Agnes remarked that Rosa must surely be feeling better, having talked to the mistress, who had been so sympathetic.

'You see, you'd no need to worry about telling her, eh?'

'I do feel a bit easier,' Rosa answered. 'And it was good to talk to the mistress. Seems she doesn't blame me at all for what happened.'

'Of course she doesn't!' cried Agnes, staring at her. 'Why should she? You're not responsible for what your sister does!'

'Well, her employer thought I might be. Or at least thought I knew what Lorne was going to do and didn't try to stop her. I hope Mrs Fordyce doesn't think the same.'

At the foot of the stairs, Rosa stopped to look into Agnes's eyes. 'But I didn't know,' she said quietly. 'I'd never have let her hurt Daniel that way.'

'Daniel?'

'The man she was going to marry.'

'Oh, I see.' For a moment, Agnes studied Rosa's face, taking what she could from her shuttered expression. 'No, I'm sure you'd have done what you could to help him. But people always do what they want to do in the end, you know. Even if you'd known what your sister was planning, you could never have stopped her. So don't go blaming yourself for something you couldn't help.'

'I just wish . . .' Rosa shook her head. 'But it's too late for wishing, eh? Too late for wishing I could have done something.'

'Try not to dwell on it, that's my advice,' Agnes said briskly. 'Get on with your own life and stop worrying.'

At which point, Rosa almost laughed. As though she could!

Eleven

It was work in the end that saved her, and everyone's interest in news that wasn't hers. The sad death of King Edward, for instance, and the succession of his second son, George the Fifth, who wouldn't have succeeded at all if his elder brother hadn't died. No one knew much about him except that he was married to a very serious-looking princess, Mary of Teck, but as Greta said, what had royalty to do with them, anyway? Their lives were so different. When would you catch Queen Mary sweeping and dusting?

'They make life interesting is what I say,' Agnes told her smartly, 'and I wouldn't be without them. Who'd want a president like them Americans? That you'd have to vote for?'

'Seeing as we don't get to vote, maybe you're right!' laughed Greta, but Rosa let the chatter sweep over her. She had personal worries enough to occupy her mind without seeking anything beyond. Over what might happen to her sister, for instance, and also poor Daniel: whether or not he was learning to live with his loss and whether he would one day be really free – free to see others in the world apart from Lorne. But when she got as far as that, Rosa's mind always went blank, as she wanted it to do.

All the time, she was wishing Da would write and give her what news he had, if any. But he was hopeless with a pen, and for Lorne herself to get in touch was probably out of the question. She would want to give no clue to the Thains, who would be desperate to find Rory to make him come home but had no idea where to start looking. Was it possible that he might after all marry Lorne? If he really loved her, perhaps it could happen? But even if he did, Rosa couldn't see the Thains accepting Lorne as a daughter-in-law. All they'd probably do would be to sever ties with Rory, cutting his allowance as well, in which case – oh, heavens, it didn't bear thinking of what might happen then.

Weeks went by, anyway, and the summer was turning to autumn before definite news of Lorne came from Greg enclosing a card she'd sent postmarked Dublin. So she and Rory were in Ireland? Why Ireland? Never mind, it was good to have some idea of where they were at all. Though she was due to begin cleaning the family dining room, Rosa decided to read Lorne's card at once to see if there was any real news of what her sister was doing.

All she said, however, was that she was well, having a heavenly time, and that she and Rory would soon be moving on, so if anyone came looking for them, they'd find 'the birds had flown'. And Rosa could picture her sister laughing over that before she'd sent her love and signed off with a flourish.

What to make of the situation? Rosa could make very little. So far, so good, perhaps, for Lorne, but this was early days and there was always the prospect that Mr Thain would catch up with Rory and make him return home.

'Course, as promised, it was me who had to tell Mr Thain there was news of Lorne, Greg had written in his letter. *And as soon as he heard, he started fixing up to go to Ireland with these men he's taken on – private detectives, like in books. Money no object, anyways, but seems to me they will be looking for needles in a haystack. What good is knowing Lorne and this fellow had gone to Ireland? They could be anywhere now.'*

True enough, thought Rosa, reading her father's final comments, which were about himself.

Do not be worrying about me, Rosa, he wrote in a straggling postscript. *Mrs MacRitchie is very good, for ever giving me things to eat. To cheer me up, she says. Well, I hope you can cheer up too and come back home for a day or two. I am not wanting to lose you like I have lost Lorne. Your loving father, G. Malcolm.*

Do not be worrying about me, he had written. Rosa heaved a sigh. Did he really think she wouldn't be worrying about the prospect of having Mrs MacRitchie as a stepmother? For it looked like the widow was strengthening her hold, providing ever more tasty meals to 'cheer up' her quarry, and maybe succeeding?

Certainly, Da was in a low state after what Lorne had done and could be feeling lonelier than usual, so might this not be the time, having resisted for so long, that he would look on the widow next door not only as a provider of good food but as his special company? Was it wrong not to want that comfort for him?

After all, in the past, Rosa and Lorne, while not wanting their father to marry again, had been relieved that there was someone willing to 'look out for him'. Maybe it was selfish, then, to refuse that someone her just reward, as she would see it? If it was what Da himself wanted as well?

Oh, if only the clock could be put back and Lorne could still be able to come home from Bluff House, ready to meet up with Rosa and laugh over Mrs MacRitchie's plan of attack as they had laughed together in the old days! But of course, Lorne couldn't do that. She had left in terrible circumstances, having broken Daniel's heart, for which she could never be forgiven. The strange thing was, though, that as Rosa stood with Lorne's postcard in her hand, for a fleeting moment she knew that, in spite of all her sister had done, she missed her still.

'Hey, aren't we supposed to be turning out the dining room this morning?' Greta's voice interrupted Rosa's thoughts. 'We'll be in trouble if it's not ready by lunchtime!'

'Well, where've you been, anyway?' asked Rosa. 'I didn't see you around and I wanted you to work with me.'

'I was finishing off upstairs. Thought you'd have made a start.' Greta bustled about, moving dining chairs aside so that she could sweep under the table. 'All right for you, anyway – you've got your afternoon off to look forward to!'

'My afternoon off?'

'Don't say you've forgotten!'

'Of course not!' Rosa – who had, in fact, done just that – was quick to respond. 'Who'd forget their afternoon off?'

Twelve

The weather for Rosa's half day off was perfect – autumn at its best, with a high blue sky, bright sunshine and crisp, pleasant air. So different from Inverness in winter's grip, or even in chill summers that could have been winters anyway. Yes, as Greta had said, things were 'all right' for Rosa, at least for her afternoon off, and she decided to forego shopping and just stroll in the park, breathing the healthy outdoor air she so often missed.

Taking a seat on a bench overlooking a large pond and not minding too much that it wasn't the Moray Firth, she felt relief that she'd put on her pale grey skirt and short jacket which were perfect for the autumn sun. Even so, her thick coil of hair felt too heavy on her neck and she took off her large blue hat to fan herself. At this rate, she might even get sunburnt, though she felt the sun was not quite strong enough, and in any case, she was so starved of sunlight, being indoors so much, she was loath to look for shade. She was thinking that maybe, in a little while, she'd go back to her favourite little café and have a cup of tea – she was, after all, quite thirsty – when a man's voice close by spoke her name.

'Rosa?'

In all the warmth around her, she froze, for she knew that voice, of course she did, though how its owner came to be in Inverness she couldn't imagine. She must respond, though – rise and face the man who had said her name and think what she could say. But, oh, dear Lord, what could she say to someone so damaged by her own sister?

'Daniel?' she whispered at last, rising, hat in hand, to face him, knowing she was right, that it was Daniel MacNeil. Yet so thin it was no wonder she'd been at first taken aback. Not altogether changed, thank God – his good looks had not deserted him – but he seemed like one who'd been ill and not long recovered. Convalescent, perhaps? She couldn't be sure. Better, anyhow, than when she'd seen him six months ago.

'Yes, it's me,' he said gently. 'I know I don't look the same.'

'You do, you do!' she cried hastily. 'I knew you at once! But why ever are you in Inverness?'

'Just to order certain woods I need – came over in my van. It was such a nice day, I left it at the station and thought I'd walk in the park. May I sit down for a minute?'

'Oh, please do.'

As he took his seat next to her on the bench, she noticed that his light jacket and flannels hung so loosely on him they might well have belonged to someone else, but his manner, it seemed to her, was easier than it might have been. Somehow, he must have worked out a way of living with what had happened, which, if it was surprising, at the same time very much relieved her. This meeting might be easier than she had feared.

All the same, under his gaze, she still couldn't think what to say, only fiddled with the hat she'd just taken off and would have put on again, except that Daniel suddenly stayed her hand.

'No, don't cover up your hair, Rosa. It looks so nice, free like that.'

'Trouble is there's too much of it for a warm day like today.' She laughed a little. 'I sometimes wish girls could cut their hair short – I mean, why not?'

'Why shouldn't girls cut their hair?' Daniel smiled. 'I cannot imagine that they ever would. Remember, there was a girl at our school who'd had her hair cut but only because she'd had scarlet fever? Soon grew it again, I think.'

He was talking so easily, she might have thought he was better, quite over what Lorne had done but, looking at his thin face, Rosa somehow knew he was not better at all. He might seem so, but his fine blue eyes, though no longer like the eyes of a dead man, still had a bleakness which gave the lie to his easy manner, and it was clear that the damage wrought on him by Lorne would take a long time to heal. Trying not to think of how he must hate her sister as well as love her, Rosa stood up, finally putting on her hat and smoothing down her long skirts.

'I must go,' she murmured as Daniel leaped to his feet. 'Time's getting on.'

'Oh, surely, not yet! I was hoping we could have a cup of tea together. I mean, if this is your afternoon off, couldn't we have tea somewhere? I know a very good tearoom.'

'It's not the Scottish Harebell, is it?'

'It is. You know it too?'

'My favourite café.'

'Then let's go. What do you say?'

'Well, I usually do have a cup of tea before I go back. Mustn't stay long, though.'

'We'll keep an eye on the time.'

For a moment, they hesitated until, with a good imitation of being relaxed, they left the park together.

Thirteen

When they were seated at a corner table in the café, a pot of tea and toasted teacakes before them, Rosa knew she would have to look into Daniel's eyes again. You couldn't really sit opposite someone without meeting their gaze, but she still wished she needn't, for she had been upset by what Daniel's eyes had told her already and didn't want to think again of what her sister had done.

It helped that she had to pour the tea and add the milk he said he would like but not the sugar, and then pass him his cup with a brief – very brief – glance before offering him the plate of toasted teacakes. Let's hope he eats one, she thought, and after he'd taken one he did look as though he might. But then he only drank his tea, and she was driven to say, 'You should eat something, Daniel. You need to put on weight.'

He raised his eyebrows, no doubt as surprised to hear a personal remark from Rosa as she was herself.

'You think I'm too thin?' he asked. 'Well, maybe I am, but it's only temporary – I did lose my appetite for a while but it's certainly returning now.'

'I'm glad to hear that, then.' Rosa looked down at her plate. 'It's not surprising, after what happened, that you'd be – you know – shaken up. It was a terrible thing that Lorne did.' She raised her eyes to find Daniel's gaze resting on her intently, as though what she had to say was important to him, which was unnerving.

'Da and me,' she struggled on, 'we've felt bad over it all along because – well, we can't forgive her. Any more than you can.'

'I suppose it was the way it was done,' he said slowly, having eaten a little of his teacake. 'I mean, there was no warning, Rosa, it all came out of the blue – and on the wedding day.'

'I know, I know. She did say in her letter that she'd wanted to tell you earlier but couldn't find the courage.'

'Found it in the end, didn't she?'

After that remark, both fell silent, supposedly concentrating on their tea, until Rosa set down her cup and asked, diffidently, if

Daniel minded her talking about what had happened? Maybe she'd stirred things up too much?

'No, not at all. In fact, I think it's done me good to talk to you today. I haven't been able to mention her name, you see, since she left me.' Suddenly, Daniel put his hand to his chest. 'It was all inside me – here, festering – and I knew I should get rid of it, try to get better, but what could I do? I couldn't even talk about her, you see. Until today.'

'It was the right time, then,' Rosa said softly, her dark eyes large with compassion. 'The right time, Daniel, to talk.'

They rose together and, when Daniel had paid the bill, left the café, walking slowly towards a small public garden where they took seats on a bench.

Fourteen

'How long have we got?' Daniel asked. 'When have you to be back?'

'In about an hour or so.'

'An hour. That's good.'

For a moment, he paused, seeming to strengthen his determination to speak, then tried a smile. 'Never thought I'd ask you this, Rosa, but . . . have you heard from her?'

She hesitated, but only for a moment. 'Yes, we have. Da had a letter. She's in Ireland. Or was, anyway. She wouldn't tell us where – didn't want the Thains to know. Said she'd soon be moving on anyway.'

'Ireland? They've gone to Ireland?'

Daniel had stiffened, gazing at Rosa as though she'd said something significant, yet what it could be she had no idea.

'Does it seem a strange choice?' she asked. 'I expect it's just a place they thought Mr Thain wouldn't think of looking for them, but Da has to give him any news Lorne sends. He promised.'

Daniel wasn't listening. 'Ireland is where she wanted us to go for our honeymoon,' he said in a low voice. 'She asked me if we could afford it. I said we could not – I'd just begun renting my van and was short of cash. So we settled on Strathpeffer, as you know. But Ireland was what she fancied – said it was the Emerald Isle, a perfect place.'

'Never mentioned it to me,' remarked Rosa, then was silent, remembering that there were so many things her sister had never mentioned.

'But must have told him, though. The Thain fellow? And of course he could afford it, couldn't he?' Daniel laughed shortly. 'No wonder she chose him. Why did I ever think I had a chance with her? She never really wanted me at all.'

'Daniel, that's not true. I promise you, it's not!'

He shook his head, looking into the distance, seeing only the past; unaware, it seemed, of Rosa by his side, longing to make him believe in Lorne's early love for him, if only to soften his pain.

'Oh, I suppose she was happy when I managed to buy her the

ring,' he said after a pause. 'She was certainly excited about the wedding. Maybe she thought she'd never meet the one she really wanted so she settled for one she didn't want.'

'Don't talk like that, Daniel! I'm sure Lorne did love you! She was led astray by Rory Thain. He turned her head, that's all it was—'

Even as she spoke, Rosa knew it wasn't true. She'd read Lorne's letter where nothing could have been plainer: *There is someone else who loves me and I love him like I never loved Daniel.* That was what Lorne had written. There was the truth, which it seemed Daniel already knew but Rosa wasn't prepared to let him accept it. Somehow, she felt she must salvage something from the intense love he'd lavished on her sister, just to make him feel better. But she was not to succeed.

'No, Rosa. I have to face it,' he told her quietly. 'Have in fact been facing it for some time. The truth is she never loved me.'

There it was: the truth Daniel had reached for himself, perhaps would have reached even if Lorne had never left him, for to love someone as he loved her must have given him a sort of extra sense. If only he had never become involved with her! But what was the use of wishing the impossible?

'I'd better go,' Rosa was beginning tiredly, when he suddenly took her hand.

'Look, I'm sorry, Rosa, about all this talk of what happened to me. Will you forgive me for going on about it?'

'Daniel, you don't have to ask me that. I was glad we talked, you know I was.'

'Well, all I know is I can't tell you how pleased I was to see you sitting on that bench when I walked into the park. It really cheered me – I knew you were a friend, you see. And then we talked and that helped more than I can say. I feel better than I've felt for weeks.'

'That's so good to hear, Daniel.'

For a long moment, they studied each other, his eyes holding a new warmth that made her heart beat faster, even as he released her hand.

'Rosa, I'd like us to meet again. Would you like that?'

Her heart still thumping, her colour rising, she made herself appear calm and said simply, 'Yes, I'd like it, Daniel.'

'That's good, I'm glad. But how shall we arrange it? You can't come over to Carron very often – shall we say I'll come here? Meet you on your afternoon off?'

'That would be best.'

'Maybe we'll go to Loch Ness, see the monster?' He smiled. 'Or just walk again in the park? Shall we say, in two weeks' time we'll meet at the park gates? What time would suit you?'

How quick he was at making arrangements! As though there was no time to be lost? Happy that he should feel that way, she couldn't help wondering why he should be so anxious to see her again. Was it just to talk, to release the floodgates of the feelings he'd been holding back for so long? She supposed that must be it, for it clearly could not be that he wanted to replace Lorne with herself. No, no, that was out of the question – she didn't even consider it. He might hate Lorne now for what she had done, but he was as much in thrall to her as ever, and to be freed would take a long, long time.

'Will two o'clock be all right?' he asked, having waited for her to speak, and she hastily left her thoughts to tell him that two o'clock at the park gates would suit her very well.

'That's wonderful. Depending on the weather, we can decide what we want to do then. Now, may I see you back to where you work?'

'No need, Daniel. You'll be wanting to leave for home. It's been good, though, meeting up, hasn't it?'

'Meant a lot to me. Thank you for agreeing to meet me again. Are you sure you're happy about it, Rosa? Happy to see me again?'

'I'm very happy, Daniel.'

'You're sure? You're looking doubtful—'

'No, no, I'm not. It's just—'

'What? What is it?'

'Just that I'm wondering, you know, if you'd be telling your mother about seeing me?'

'My mother? Why ever have you thought of her? Look, I love her very much but I make my own decisions. She has no say in what I do.'

'If you're sure . . . I don't want to upset her.'

'Leave it all to me. I know what to say to my mother. Now, are you sure I can't see you back to the house?'

'Yes, truly, there's no need. You've a long drive home – better make a start.' Rosa put out her hand, which he took with a quick, firm response and held for some moments until she withdrew it and thanked him for the tea. 'We'll meet again, then, in two weeks?'

'In two weeks. I'll look forward to it, Rosa.'

He put on his hat and stood watching her as she left him until she'd turned a corner and was out of sight, though she, being suddenly too self-conscious to look back, never knew.

'Well, well, you must have had a good time!' Agnes exclaimed when Rosa let herself into the kitchen. 'You look as though you've lost a sixpence and found a shilling!'

'Caught a bit o' sun, I'd say,' Greta remarked. 'Or are you blushing?'

'Better go and change,' Mrs Banks called from the stove. 'I've a dinner party to think about even if you folks have forgotten. Hattie, get on with them vegetables, and Greta, you find a clean apron, eh? That one you're wearing is a disgrace!'

'Oh, Lord,' Agnes murmured to Rosa as she passed. 'Now it starts; we'll have no peace till we've got to the washing-up. Hoist the storm cones!'

What storm cones? Rosa asked herself with a smile. All she hoped to see ahead was calm.

Fifteen

Two weeks before they could meet again. That wasn't so long, was it? Not so long? To Rosa, going about her usual duties with the thought of Daniel colouring all that she did, it seemed an age. Especially as she must keep their meeting to herself.

Not that she minded keeping such a special secret locked in her own head. How could she possibly discuss it even with Agnes, never mind nosy Greta or excitable Hattie? The very idea of how it would be if anyone were to find out about Daniel was so embarrassing she hastily put it from her. It wouldn't happen, she insisted to herself. How could it, when she was the only person who knew about him and she would be saying nothing?

Which was why, when it was time for her half day again, she had no worries that Agnes would make any comment when she saw Rosa getting ready to go out. No more would be said of her looking happy enough to have found a shilling, or anything of that sort, for now all was just back to routine and she was going out for her half day as usual.

'See you later,' she called cheerfully to Agnes, who was alone with her in the kitchen as Mrs Banks was lying down, Hattie had gone to the local shop and Greta was cleaning the staff bathroom. 'It's not so sunny today, I think I'll just do some shopping.'

'Not seeing the young man this time, then?' Agnes remarked, her tone casual as she put away clean dusters.

Standing at the kitchen mirror, settling her hat on her thickly piled hair, Rosa froze. Her eyes went to Agnes in the mirror and she saw that the parlour maid was half smiling, as though pleased to see the reaction to her words.

'Young man?' Rosa repeated slowly, 'What do you mean, Agnes? You know I have no young man.'

'Rosa, no one looks the way you did when you came in the other day if there's no man involved. I'm older than you — I've had some experience of these matters.' Agnes slightly tossed her fair head. 'Some experiences of my own, I don't mind admitting.'

Turning from the mirror, Rosa's face as she gazed at the real

Agnes away from the reflection held so much apprehension that the parlour maid's look softened and she put her hand on Rosa's arm.

'Come on now, no need to look so scared. There's nothing wrong with having a follower – Mrs Fordyce doesn't mind at all. She told me herself if any of us were to meet the right person, she'd be quite happy.'

'He isn't my follower!' Rosa cried. 'He's just a friend. Couldn't be anything more!'

'Look, you can tell me about him, I won't pass it on, but I know you've been nursing a secret ever since you came in last week. Who is he, then, this man who makes you look so happy?'

After a long pause, during which Rosa took off her hat, she said quietly, 'He's Daniel MacNeil, the man my sister was going to marry.'

'What, the poor fellow she left at the church? Oh, my, Rosa, what's he doing here?'

'He's a joiner but he's very talented at making things in wood – has some supplier he sees here. By accident, we met in the park.'

'And you spent the afternoon together?' Agnes seemed surprised. 'Is he wanting a bit o' comfort, then? Can't have got over your sister already.'

'Oh, no, he's not! He just – you know – wanted to talk to somebody who knew what had happened.'

'I see. And are you meeting him again?'

'Next week.' After hesitating for a moment, Rosa replaced her hat and moved towards the door. 'Think I'd better go for my bits of shopping.'

'Yes, but Rosa . . . take care, eh?'

'With my shopping?' Rosa laughed.

'You know what I mean.'

'I don't see why you think I need to take care, Agnes.'

'Just don't get too involved. Might not be wise, if he's still feeling as he does over your sister.'

'Agnes, you don't need to worry about me. I can take care of myself.'

'Now where have I heard that before?' cried Agnes as the back door quietly closed behind Rosa.

Sixteen

When the afternoon came at last for Rosa to meet Daniel, she hurried to their rendezvous, dreading being late, dreading that he might not even be there. Thank God he was, though, standing next to a motor vehicle at the park gates.

'Rosa!' He came swiftly to her and briefly took her hands. 'You're here! I kept wondering if you'd remember . . . what we'd arranged.'

Remember? She couldn't tell him she'd thought of nothing else in the last fortnight, only smiled as she kept her eyes on his, though then her heart gave a little leap, for it seemed to her that there had been a change in his and the coldness she'd seen before had slightly melted. Was she right? She couldn't be sure, for he had turned away, affectionately putting his hand on the side of the vehicle close to him, just as she was asking where they would be going.

'Have a look at the van first.'

'The van?'

For the first time, Rosa paid attention to the vehicle Daniel was standing beside, which was not a motor car but an open-sided, thin-tyre van with a covered top, two seats at the front, one with a steering wheel, and space at the back which held a quantity of wood.

'This is yours, Daniel?' Rosa asked, surprised, but he shook his head.

'No, only rented. I can't afford to buy a van for myself, or a horse and cart, either, but I do need something to get to customers.'

'This must be just the thing.'

Rosa, moving nearer, was impressed to be at such close range to a motor vehicle, for though there were now plenty of motors about the city and Mr Fordyce in fact owned one, she had no real experience of them. But the more she looked at this one, the more she thought it must be very difficult to handle. Much worse than anything pulled by a horse!

'I'm impressed, I really am,' she told Daniel. 'Is it easy to move along? I mean, to drive?'

'Easy to move along?' Daniel smiled. 'I wouldn't say it was, but I taught myself to drive it, anyway, and soon got the hang of it. The good thing is the roads are so empty – not many people can afford motors yet. Doubt if they ever will. But come on, let's be on our way. I think I'm blocking the pavement here, judging by the frowns all round!'

'No, I think folk are just interested,' Rosa told him, accepting his hand to assist her climb into the passenger seat of the van, rather wishing there weren't quite so many people watching and relieved when Daniel said they would soon be away.

'Just got to get the engine started,' he told her from the front of the van.

'You can't start it from inside?'

'No, have to use the outside starting handle. Won't be a second.'

In fact, it was several minutes before the engine roared into life and Daniel could hurry back to his seat, during which the watchers could laugh and offer their advice. 'Get some horses, laddie!' 'Want a hand to push, then?' 'Aye, we always said them contraptions'd never work!'

Eventually, though, they were away, moving noisily from the park gates and following a route through busy streets that would take them to Loch Ness, if Rosa would like to go there.

'Say if you'd prefer to go somewhere else,' Daniel said, briefly turning to glance at Rosa.

'No, I'd like to see Loch Ness if we've time.'

'Oh, I think we have. It's about twenty miles from here. Some years since I saw it – came with my dad. He kept teasing me about the monster – as though there is one!'

'It's all just wishful thinking, Daniel. Brings money to Inverness, that's all. No one's ever seen anything, except a floating log.'

'Wasn't there some saint who said he saw it centuries ago?'

'Like I said, he'd have seen a floating log,' Rosa declared, at which Daniel laughed.

'You're the practical, no-nonsense one, Rosa, aren't you? Anyone'd have thought that would have been me, but I'm the dreamer. I like to think there is a monster in the loch, straight out of a fairy tale!'

'A dreamer?' Rosa repeated softly. 'Is that true, Daniel?'

'It is.' Daniel shook his head as he carefully negotiated a bend in the road. 'And that has its drawbacks, as you might guess.'

'What sort of drawbacks?'

'Don't ask.' Daniel laughed. 'Now, it's next stop for the loch, all twenty-three miles of it. All we'll have time for is a wee walk and a cup of tea.'

Seventeen

Although they'd both seen it before, their fresh sighting of Loch Ness as they left the van filled them with a kind of awe. It was so very long, almost like a sea, seeming to stretch into infinity, and though there were a number of boats on it and people walking along its shores, it was still so silent, so mysterious, it wasn't like any of the other lochs they knew. Certainly, it was no wonder that the legend of the monster had grown up here, for if a monster were to be found in any Scottish loch, Ness, with its length and depth, would surely be the one. How deep was it, though?

As they began to walk by the side of the loch, Rosa asked Daniel if he knew.

'Depth? I don't know for sure. About 700 feet, I should think. Better be careful not to fall into it, eh?'

Daniel, glancing at Rosa's face, suddenly took her arm and held it close.

'But Rosa, isn't this pleasant? The two of us, the best of friends, walking by this great loch?'

The best of friends? Rosa was smiling back but his words were echoing in her mind. The best of friends? Was that all? For him, perhaps. For her . . . oh, better not go into her feelings for him. Just take what came, enjoy the day. It was more than she'd ever hoped for, anyway.

'See, there's the ruin on the opposite bank!' she cried, freeing herself from Daniel's arm and pointing across the shore to distract herself from her own thoughts. 'Castle Urquhart, isn't it?'

'That's it. Ever been round it? What's left, that is? Was mixed up with most of Scottish history, as far as I remember. Why anybody wanted it, I don't know, but pretty well everybody fought over it.' Daniel laughed. 'From Robert the Bruce onwards. So my dad told me.'

'Your father sounds interesting,' Rosa said quietly. 'You must miss him.'

'I do.' Daniel's face was suddenly bleak. 'More than I can say.'

'I'm the same with my mother. Things might have been different for us all, if she'd still been with us.'

Daniel was silent, staring ahead at the loch, lost in his own thoughts, it seemed. Until suddenly he touched Rosa's hand and shook his head.

'Hey, this won't do. We're not supposed to be sad on our afternoon together. Let's go and find some tea, shall we? I believe there's a place not too far away.'

Why doesn't he ask me about Lorne? Rosa thought when they were settled in the café they'd found, and wondered, as she again poured him tea and passed the drop scones, whether she should risk mentioning Lorne herself. After all, she had some news, and interesting news at that.

'Penny for them?' Daniel asked, smiling.

'My thoughts?' She hesitated. 'Just of my sister . . . No, don't look like that!'

'Like what?'

'As though you've put the shutters down.'

He shook his head. 'Rosa, I don't want to talk about her. I don't want to think about her. I have other things in my mind apart from her.'

'I think you should hear my news anyway.' Rosa set down her teacup and leaned forward. 'Because if you want her out of your life, Daniel, I can tell you, she will be. She's going to America.'

'America!'

Daniel might not have wanted to show any interest, but as he made a great play of slicing his scone, he couldn't conceal showing his surprise at Rosa's news.

'Suppose that is unexpected,' he admitted. 'Not that I care where she goes, but at least it's a long way off.'

'We've had another letter,' Rosa told him. 'Seemingly, Lorne now has a passport and everything for America, and Mr Thain will never find her there. Didn't even find her in Ireland, in spite of all his detectives. So . . .' Rosa sat back, her dark eyes glinting. 'You're right; she's going to be far enough away, isn't she? Da's in a state, I can tell you.'

'I daresay. How about you?'

'I don't know what to think. I'm sort of stunned. Plenty of people emigrate to America but I never dreamed Lorne would leave Scotland. Seems so final.'

For a long moment, Daniel was silent, finally asking for more tea, which he drank off quickly, before setting the cup down heavily and fixing Rosa with eyes that told her nothing. Yet he was managing a smile.

'Thanks for giving me that news,' he said quietly. 'I feel the better for it. Ready to give you my own news, in fact.'

'You have news, Daniel?'

She couldn't tell why, but Rosa knew at once that she didn't want to hear his news, whatever it was. Staring at the tea things, she wished with all her heart that he need not tell her what it was. But he was still smiling.

'Good news, in fact. Good for me. I've been offered a job I want away down in Edinburgh. I'll be moving next month.'

Eighteen

Moving next month? To Edinburgh? And he was smiling?

Sitting very still, her cold hands clasped together, Rosa lowered her eyes. Stared at the crumbs on her plate, at the teacups, the teapot, anything except Daniel's radiant face, for what would that tell her? Everything about her own foolishness in expecting something she should never even have considered. Hadn't he earlier that very day described the two of them as 'the best of friends'? How then could she have expected anything else but friendship from him? Especially when she knew that whatever he said about Lorne, he was still under her spell?

How stupid she'd been, then, not to nip in the bud any ideas she might have cherished that there was hope for her to be more than a friend to Daniel. She supposed she'd been hoping that if they'd continued to see each other and taken pleasure in each other's company, as they did, it might have been possible for Daniel's love for Lorne to fade. How different everything might have been then!

But of course it wasn't going to happen. He and Rosa weren't even going to continue seeing each other. How could they when she was in Inverness and he was in Edinburgh, which he appeared to be pleased about? In the words of the old song it seemed that 'the best of friends must part, must part' – but only one of them minded.

Clearing her throat, she finally raised her eyes to Daniel's, and with immense effort managed to say, 'Congratulations. I'm glad you're pleased.'

'Thank you. You'll guess it's what I want – not only for the work, but to get away from Carron where everybody knows me.'

'I know you, Daniel.'

'You're different.'

'Am I?'

'Of course. But I haven't told you about the job.' Daniel sat back in his chair, his face more animated than she'd ever seen it, his eyes, so often showing his sorrow, now so bright in expression, his whole manner appeared changed. 'It's funny the way it all came about,' he told her. 'Quite by accident, really. I always knew there was this first-rate cabinet-maker in Edinburgh, a chap called Frank Lang, but I never thought I'd meet him. Then, one day, a few weeks ago, I happened to be delivering a small table to Doctor MacKenzie – he's one of the few people who know about my real work – and of all people, Mr Lang was there.'

'All the way from Edinburgh?' asked Rosa. 'Why?'

'Seems he's a relative of Mrs MacKenzie's and they have furniture made by him in the house. Things I'd seen – wardrobes and a sideboard – but didn't know where they'd come from. Anyway, that day when Mr Lang was there, the doctor introduced me, said I was a joiner but made furniture when I could and had just delivered an occasional table, as a matter of fact. Well, you can maybe guess the rest!' Daniel's smile was broad, his eyes sparkling.

'Mr Lang liked your table?'

'He did. Had a good look at it. Said I was wasted doing ordinary joinery, and if I wanted a job—'

'And you said you did.'

'And I said I did.' Daniel suddenly took Rosa's hand. 'You don't blame me, do you? I know it means leaving the Highlands, my home, but after what happened, living where I live has been spoiled for me now. This move will give me work I've always wanted to do and at the same time a fresh start. I couldn't turn it down, Rosa, could I?'

When she shook her head, he went on, 'Of course, my mother's in a state, as you'll guess. She can sort of understand why I want to move, she just doesn't want me to do it. But it's my chance to make a better life. You see I have to take it?'

'Yes, I see.' Rosa looked down at her hand still clasped in his. 'It's just – well, I'll miss you, I suppose.'

His eyes, still bright, were fixed on her face. 'There'll be no need for you to miss me, Rosa. You could come with me.'

Go with him? The world spun as she tried to understand him, to read what he wanted of her. It couldn't be what it might be – could it?

'What do you mean, Daniel?' she asked bravely. 'How could I go with you? You want me to find a job in Edinburgh?'

'Of course not! Rosa, listen—'

He was leaning forward, totally concentrating on her, when their waitress came to them, her tray at the ready, her smile fixed.

'Mind if I clear? There's a lady and gentleman waiting for this table.'

'Oh, God – sorry!' Daniel snatched up the bill she had laid down and left a handful of coins beneath a plate. 'Sorry about that, we were just going . . .'

'That's quite all right, sir. Just pay at the door, eh?'

As a sour-faced, sombrely dressed couple took their places, Daniel and Rosa, heads bent, hurried to the cash desk, where, as soon as Daniel had paid the bill, they were able to leave the café with sighs of relief.

'How embarrassing,' Rosa murmured. 'We'd stayed too long.'

'What does it matter? I wanted to get out of there, anyway. Let's walk by the river.'

'I'm worried about the time—'

'This is not a day to be worrying about time.'

Daniel's face was unsmiling as he took Rosa's arm.

'We have things to talk about, you and me. Where no one will be listening.'

Nineteen

'What a relief to be out of there!' Daniel went on fervently as he took Rosa's arm and walked with her again by the loch. 'I was going mad, thinking of what I wanted to say and how I was going to say it, stuck there among the teacups and the gossipers and the waitress hovering—'

'What – what did you want to say, then?'

Rosa, churning with suspense inside, was mystified by the way Daniel seemed to have changed in a few moments, from being full of excitement over his new job to fretting that he hadn't yet said whatever else it was he wanted to say. He'd said something, though, and it didn't make any sense. Suggesting that she should go to Edinburgh but not for another job? How could she do that? What was in his mind?

'We have things to talk about' he had said, and here he was, walking with her, just the two of them as he wanted, yet he was saying nothing while she was on pins, longing to know what he might want to say and trying not to worry about the time and whether she would be late back or not. Well, if she was, she was, and that was all there was to it. Here, on the banks of the Ness, was where she must stay until Daniel told her whatever was in his mind. Or heart.

His heart? Why had she thought of that when there could be nothing in his heart for her? He had given it to Lorne.

'What do I want to say?' he said now, turning his look on her. 'I know what it is, but I'm not sure I dare say it. I mean, I don't know . . . how you'll take it.'

'Try me,' she said breathlessly. 'There's nothing you could say to me that would upset me, Daniel. I know that for sure.'

'Maybe you're worrying, though, about getting back? I don't want that.'

'I'm not worrying. Not really.'

'Let's go back to the van, anyway.'

How he was putting things off, wasn't he? As they made their way to the van and drove off for Inverness, Rosa was almost trembling with anticipation of whatever it was he wanted to say. She would not allow herself to guess, would not face the disappointment of getting it wrong, would prepare herself . . . Oh, but for what?

Suddenly, when he had parked the van, he turned her to face him in their cramped seats, his blue eyes on her seeming dark in the shadows of the van, his hands on her shoulders very firm.

'Rosa, I want to ask you—' He halted and took away his hands. 'Will you . . . marry me?'

There it was. Something she had not had the courage even to imagine. Had not even permitted herself to dream might happen, for even in her dreams she would have thought what he'd just asked was quite impossible. He belonged to someone else, didn't he? Whether that person wanted him or not.

At the look on her face, he laughed uneasily. 'Does it seem as bad as that, Rosa? What I've asked you?'

Keeping her gaze away from him, she shook her head. 'It's just – it's so unexpected.' Not to say, a shock.

'Because we haven't been out together very much? That's what some folk might say. But we've known each other all our lives, haven't we? We lived in the same village, went to the same school. And I have to ask you now because I'm going away and I couldn't bear to go without knowing . . . if you'd consider me.'

His truly handsome face was serious, his eyes searching hers when he added quietly, 'I know we'd be right for each other, Rosa. I know we could be happy.' He put out his hand to take hers but she drew away.

And, before he could speak again, said in a voice she hardly recognized as her own, so clear was it in putting into words what she didn't want to say, 'You shouldn't be asking me to marry you, Daniel. You love someone else. You're not free.'

'But that's it!' he cried eagerly. 'I want to be free! And you could help me, Rosa, if you would accept me as I am, as someone who loves you. In a different way from . . . your sister.'

'A different way? There's only one way, Daniel.'

'No, there's a right and a wrong way, and I love you the right way. I told you we could be happy and I believe that, because we're right for each other in the way Lorne and me never were. Now she's found love elsewhere, she needn't come between us, which means I can build my life with you and forget her.'

Gently, Daniel touched Rosa's face. 'Won't you help me, Rosa? I

knew as soon as I met you again in the park that you were right for
me, the one I should have loved from the start, only I met . . . well,
you know how it was. I met Lorne and became . . . entangled.'

'And still are,' said Rosa, her voice low.

'I am, I admit it. You see, I'm being honest. I'm not free, but I
want to be. I want to be married to you and make you happy. If
you take me, we can make things work, I know we can.'

As she said nothing, he took both her hands and held them fast.
'Please, won't you put me out of my misery? I know it's a lot to ask
and you deserve someone better than me, the sort of man I wish I was
who could come to you with no past to remember. If you say you
don't want me, I'll understand, I will. Only, Rosa, say something!'

What to say? Rosa pulled her hands from his, twisting them
together, her eyes cast down as she tried to gather her thoughts
under his blue stare. If this was truly no daydream and Daniel really
wanted to marry her, shouldn't she have been over the moon, have
been crying, 'Yes, yes, Daniel, I will marry you, I will!'

But she could say nothing. Not while the pretty face she knew
so well danced before her eyes and kept her silent. Its owner might
be in America, might never be seen again by either Daniel or Rosa,
but she would always be there, always be between them. Did Daniel
think he could escape her? Not while he loved her.

He might say he loved Rosa, too, though in a different way, and
she believed he did, but was it what she wanted? To be married
with her sister's image in the background? To have to trust that that
would fade and she and Daniel would be true lovers at last? Would
that happen?

'Daniel, I must go,' she said quietly, putting her hand on the
handle of the van's door. 'Let's not say any more just now.'

'You want us to part, Rosa? Go our separate ways? I thought
we'd be engaged.'

Engaged? The word had such emotional waves about it, carried
such meaning for women who wanted marriage and could see it
on the horizon, Rosa caught her breath. Only a short time ago,
wouldn't she have given all she had to be 'engaged' to Daniel
MacNeil? If she refused him now, turned him down, what would
be left to her? A world without him? Without even hope of happiness? Wasn't it possible instead, that married to her, Daniel would
gradually forget Lorne as he was so desperate to do?

Supposing he didn't?

Rosa turned away her head and sighed a long, painful sigh. 'Daniel, I don't know what to say,' she told him slowly. 'I want to marry you, I do, but maybe not this way. I mean, Lorne would be with us everywhere, even if she doesn't know we're married, because she'll be in your mind.'

'If I forget her, she won't be, and you will be there to help me make it happen, make our marriage strong. Couldn't you do that, Rosa?'

His blue gaze on her was pleading and as she met it and thought again of how her life would be if she let him go, suddenly, with one last sigh, she gave in. Fell into his arms and let him hold her, returned his kisses, never smiling, only taking in the seriousness of what she had chosen for her future – and of the strength she would need to make that future work.

'I'll have to tell Da,' she said, releasing herself at last.

'And I'll have to tell my mother,' said Daniel.

'Whatever will she say?'

'We know what she'll say, but don't worry – she'll have to accept things in the end. And we won't be seeing much of her anyway.'

'I'd like to be on good terms with her.'

'I told you, don't worry.'

They exchanged quick kisses and gazed into each other's faces, finally letting a little radiance shine through before Rosa left the van and Daniel went with her to the gate.

'Let's meet again on your next half day, Rosa, same place, same time, and we'll discuss our plans.'

'Our plans,' she repeated softly, thinking how strange, how amazing it was that suddenly they had them. But then, so much had become amazing in so short a time, it was difficult to take it all in. Whatever would they say, back at number twenty-five, when she told them?

'I hope the folk you work with will approve,' Daniel remarked, perhaps reading her thoughts. 'Don't let them put you off me, will you?'

'Of course they won't do that, Daniel! Why should they? They'll be happy for me.'

'Well, don't forget to hand in your notice.'

With one last kiss, they parted, Rosa to run down the area steps, Daniel to turn back to his van, the thought in both their minds being the same – that their lives had changed for ever.

Twenty

How lightly she ran down those area steps! How radiant was her face as Hattie let her in the back door! The women in the kitchen didn't need to be detectives to see that she had some exciting news, but when she lost no time in telling them what it was and stood back, ready to receive their congratulations, a little smile curving her lips, nothing happened. There were no congratulations, no smiles, no cries of surprise, no hugs or kisses. Only silence.

Looking from one face to another, she couldn't believe they were taking her news in this way, with not a word, not a smile from any one of them. Worst of all, for some time they didn't even look at her – until Mrs Banks, her face twisting with disapproval, did move her gaze to Rosa and began to speak.

'Well, who'd have thought it, Rosa Malcolm! That you'd let yourself get engaged to your sister's cast-off! Whatever were you thinking of? And what sort of a man is he, then, making out he's broken-hearted one minute and the next marrying his sweetheart's sister, eh? Tell us that!'

'Aye, it doesn't bear thinking about,' Agnes put in, staring at Rosa as though she were a stranger. 'After all I said to you, Rosa, about not getting involved, you've just gone ahead and taken on a man like that. It's so upsetting!'

'Why?' cried Rosa, catching her breath. 'Why should it be upsetting? Daniel was very deeply hurt by my sister – he still is hurt – but he thinks I can help, that I'm right for him. Why should we not be married?'

'It's like Mrs Banks says,' Greta declared solemnly.

'He's your sister's cast-off, Rosa. I tell you, I'd want something better than that if I wanted to get engaged.'

'Me too!' cried Hattie, keen to add her piece.

'Why, seems to me, Rosa, your young man just wants somebody to look after him, eh? Anyone'd do!'

'I'm going to get changed,' Rosa said stiffly, thinking she would not, whatever she did, cry in front of these people she'd thought were her friends but who only seemed to want to hurt her. Well, she was going upstairs to see the mistress – just let them all see what she made of her engagement, then! Mrs Fordyce at least would understand!

Yet even Mrs Fordyce was a bitter disappointment to Rosa, for it seemed she was no more approving of the engagement than her staff in her kitchen. Rosa's fiancé must have all too quickly got over his broken heart if he could be offering marriage to the sister of the girl who'd broken it. Had Rosa really seriously considered his proposal? Could she be sure he would be, well, faithful?

'I trust him, ma'am,' Rosa declared, only just preventing her eyes from flashing. 'And I love him. I know he will make me happy.'

Mrs Fordyce sighed heavily. 'Oh, well, if you're sure and your father is happy about it. I suppose the young man has spoken to your father in the correct manner? And is your father happy about the engagement?'

'I'll be writing to him, ma'am, and I know there won't be any problems. He's very fond of Daniel – I mean, Mr MacNeil.'

'You're sure of that, Rosa?'

'Oh, yes, ma'am, very sure. And I'm sure I'm doing the right thing.'

But Mrs Fordyce's young face had not lost its worried expression. 'If that's true, Rosa, we must just wish you every happiness. You will certainly be missed. You've always been an excellent worker, and it has been appreciated. When do you wish to leave?'

'I'd like to give a week's notice, ma'am, and then go back home to see my father and prepare for the wedding.'

'So soon! Surely you should wait, at least have a long engagement?'

'Mr MacNeil has to leave for a new job in Edinburgh at the end of the month. I'd like to go with him.'

'I see. Oh, well, then—'

There seemed to be no more to say and Rosa, having bobbed a curtsey, left her mistress to change reluctantly into her uniform and go downstairs to face those in the kitchen and give as good as she got, as she'd already decided she would. She wouldn't let them say one more word against Daniel!

As it turned out, however, there were shamefaced looks greeting her when she went into the kitchen, and though Mrs Banks said nothing as she began to put out the pans she needed, Agnes said quietly, 'Rosa, we'd like to say we're sorry, about, you know, speaking to you like we did. It's none of our business what you want to do and if you're happy, well, we wish you all the best, eh? Is that not so, girls?'

'Quite right,' Greta and Hattie agreed, while Mrs Banks, in the background, gave a sniff and quick nod.

'Don't worry about it,' Rosa said quickly and warmly, relieved that the atmosphere had now lightened. The others were sorry they'd spoken as they had, which made them still her friends who wished her well, and she felt a great rush of regret that she would very soon be bidding them goodbye. As she readily submitted to hugs from Greta and Hattie, while Agnes looked on, smiling, Mrs Banks remembered to find her usual nerves over dinner for the Fordyces.

'Now, are we going to get this dinner ready and the table laid or not? Greta, you and Rosa away to the dining room, Agnes be sorting out the silver, Hattie, you make a start on the tatties, eh? Time's getting on.'

All was back to normal, routine enfolding them, everyone happy, though as soon as dinner was over and the work done, Rosa let feelings of amazement again wash over her. It seemed to her, as she lay at last in her narrow bed, that she was still living a dream. Had Daniel MacNeil actually asked her to marry him? No, that was something so impossible, she hadn't even let herself imagine it. He loved Lorne; he didn't love her. How could he have asked her to marry him?

Yet he had. He had! They were to be married within a month, they were to go to Edinburgh together, Lorne was to be forgotten . . .

'Oh, Rosa, what a sigh!' cried Greta. 'I could hear it right across the room! What's up?'

'Have you been dreamin'?' asked Hattie. 'Did you just dream you were getting wed?'

'No, I did not just dream it!' Rosa snapped. 'What a cheek to say such a thing, Hattie!'

'Aye, Hattie, you just keep your mouth shut,' ordered Greta. 'You're getting far too big for your boots – remember, you're just a kitchen maid.'

'Well, I'm thinking of applying for Rosa's job,' said Hattie coolly. 'So there.'

'Looks like you know Rosa's not dreaming after all, then,'

commented Greta. 'But can we all get to sleep now? You know what time we have to get up.'

Good advice, thought Rosa, but though Greta and Hattie soon drifted off, it was some time before she herself could find any sleep at all.

Twenty-One

Once she'd convinced herself she really was going to be married to Daniel, Rosa had been looking forward to going with him to Edinburgh as his bride. But it was not to be. As soon as they met on her next half day and were settled in his van, he told her, with a darkened look, that they couldn't be married in time for her to go with him to Edinburgh. All the fault, it appeared, of the damned registrar.

'He's insisting we give at least four weeks' notice of the marriage,' Daniel snapped, 'when it need only be fifteen days if he were willing to make things easy for us.'

'But why should he not want to do that?' Rosa asked sharply. 'He can't have any reason!'

'It's because of what happened before.' Daniel lowered his eyes. 'You know, when I had to cancel . . . the previous wedding.'

'Oh.' Rosa frowned. 'Why should that matter now?'

'Because the registrar says it means they'll have to take extra care with their checks, so will need the full notice for the marriage to go ahead. A load of rubbish, if you ask me.' Daniel shook his head. 'What on earth are they looking for, anyway?'

'But we will be married?' Rosa asked quickly. 'They can't stop us, can they?'

'Of course not. They'll find out when they do their checks that there's no reason for us not to be wed. It's all arranged, anyway, as long as you don't mind that the service will be at my local church, not yours. I couldn't bear us to be married there – not after what happened.'

'That's all right, I understand. I don't want to be married there, either. Just as long as we can be married somewhere as soon as possible.'

'Darling Rosa, that will happen, never fear!'

Daniel drew her into his arms, not caring whether anyone outside the van could see in, and for a few moments they forgot their worries as they exchanged kisses and caresses, only parting when they decided to go for tea and discuss their plans.

Over the usual tea and buttered scones, they went through all that was to come, though Rosa still had the feeling from time to time that none of it was happening. Was she really sitting opposite Daniel MacNeil, discussing wedding plans? Only when she touched his hand as she passed his cup and felt its warmth and the thrill that came with it did she admit that yes, Daniel was opposite her and they were soon to be married. She was not dreaming after all.

The date for the wedding would be in late October, with Daniel coming back from Edinburgh the day before to stay with his mother as he no longer had a rented place in Kinlaine. No need for Rosa to look like that at the mention of his mother! All would be well, Daniel reassured her.

Of course, when he'd first broken the news to Mrs MacNeil that he was marrying another Malcolm, there had been the terrible storm he had expected, and he'd just had to weather it until his mother had been forced to accept something she couldn't change and gave in. With a heavy, theatrical sigh, she had said she just hoped he would not regret his folly and had agreed to see him wed, even though it would break her heart.

'Come on now, Ma,' he had said cheerfully, 'let me make you a cup of tea and you can think about baking us a nice little wedding cake.'

'If I do, it'll probably be the last decent cake you'll get!' she had cried in triumph. 'I'm sure that Malcolm girl won't know the first thing about baking!'

Having had the last word, as she saw it, Mrs MacNeil had re-trimmed the hat she'd intended to wear for the wedding that never happened, so that it was different, though only for her own satisfaction. Who would care what Daniel's mother wore for his wedding to a Malcolm girl? Why, she hardly cared herself!

'You told her it was all going to be very quiet?' Rosa asked Daniel anxiously over her second cup of tea. 'With just her and my da, Mrs MacRitchie and Agnes. It is what we said we wanted.'

'It's just what I wanted, Rosa.' Daniel gently touched her face. 'But I know girls usually like a bit of wedding fuss. Are you sure you're happy about it?'

'Daniel, all I want for my wedding is you!'

'But there's no time even for a honeymoon. I feel I'm letting you down, but I daren't ask for the time off when I've just started in the job. Later on, we'll go somewhere nice, I promise.'

'We are spending our honeymoon in our new home, aren't we? I'm just looking forward to being with you in whatever place you find for us.'

'Hope it'll be all right, then.' He pressed her hand. 'I'll do my best to find somewhere you'll like and, if all goes according to plan, the furniture should be in place too. I've made arrangements.'

'Heavens, I never thought about furniture!' Rosa cried. 'Daniel, I have none!'

'But I have! Look, stop worrying and leave things to me. You don't have to do everything yourself now.'

'How do you know I ever had to?' she asked, her eyes tender on his face, and he laughed.

'Because I know your da and I knew your sister. Things will be different when you're with me. Now, let me get the bill.'

As they left the teashop, arm in arm, Rosa asked herself again: how could her sister have spurned a man like Daniel? But thank God she had!

Twenty-Two

Even thinking about saying goodbye when she was leaving number twenty-five was hard for Rosa. After all, these people – even Mrs Banks – were an extension of her own family, and had been so much a part of her life that she could scarcely imagine how it would be without them. Of course, she would have Daniel, and that would be wonderful – but strange, all the same.

When, however, her last morning at number twenty-five finally arrived, all she could think of was that she wouldn't be having heart-to-heart talks with Agnes any more, or laughing with Greta while teasing young Hattie, or even keeping quiet while Mrs Banks worked herself through her nerves to a successful dinner. All these things would soon lie in the past, become only memories.

'Oh, but I'm going to miss you all so much!' she cried as they exchanged hugs, with even Mrs Banks joining in, and then thanked them again for the lovely pillowcases they had clubbed together to buy, which would accompany the expensive sheets already given to Rosa by Mrs Fordyce. Heavens, what other mistress would shell out for such a gift? her staff had exclaimed. But that was Mrs Fordyce for you! Whoever took over from Rosa to work for her would be a very lucky girl, eh?

But who would that be? No one had any ideas yet, except Mrs Banks, who was keeping quiet. Until, on that last morning for Rosa, she suddenly announced that there would be someone new coming, but only for Hattie's job as kitchen maid.

'My job?' cried Hattie, flushing. 'Why, what's happening to me?'

'Don't say you're still expecting to get Rosa's job!' Greta called, grinning, but Mrs Banks was shaking her head.

'No, that's going to you, Greta – you'll be upper housemaid and Hattie will working under you. Mind you keep an eye on her and don't stand any cheek.'

'Who says I'll be cheeky?' cried Hattie, looking well pleased. 'But will I be getting a rise? I should be, eh?'

'Oh, I daresay,' sighed Mrs Banks. 'But just settle down now and start on the vegetables for luncheon. Rosa will be leaving very soon.'

'Too right,' said Agnes quickly, as a great thump came at the back door. 'Rosa, I think that'll be the carrier come for your box – and you too, seeing as he's taking you to the station.'

'Oh, my, yes!' cried Rosa. 'Heavens, I must get my things together – I'd really forgotten the time.'

'Keep calm, keep calm, you're all ready – see, your case is at the door, you've just to put on your coat and hat—'

'Hattie, tell that fellow to wait,' ordered Mrs Banks. 'His passenger's just coming.'

So, this was it, then – the last farewell. With her hat and coat on and her bag and case to hand, Rosa hugged everyone again and gave a last reminder to Agnes that she'd see her at the wedding.

'Just wish you could all have come,' she murmured, hurrying to the door, but Greta laughed and asked whatever would the mistress do if all her staff disappeared? Why, she'd never so much as peeled a potato in her life, had she?

'That's not for her to do,' Mrs Banks immediately retorted. 'We all have our place in life. Hers is to be mistress and ours is to serve, so don't start complaining!'

As Greta, exchanging looks with Hattie, opened her mouth to argue but thought better of it, Rosa, from the door, was giving a last wave.

'I'll be in touch!' she cried. 'I'll tell you all that happens!'

'Aye, keep in touch!' they cried and crowded up the area steps as Rosa with her box and her case were borne away by the carrier on her first step towards her new life.

She couldn't help a few tears gathering but didn't let them fall, as the carrier, a large, cheerful man, after a quick sideways look, asked, 'You all right, lassie?'

'Oh, yes, thank you,' she told him, blowing her nose. 'I'm quite all right.'

Twenty-Three

It came at last, the end to the waiting when, on a strangely mild October day, Rosa and Daniel were married. The ceremony, in Daniel's local church in Kinlaine, was simple and short, attended only by four guests – Rosa's father, Daniel's mother, Mrs MacRitchie and Agnes from number twenty-five, though she was representing everyone there.

How nice they all look, thought Rosa, who was showing her own bridal radiance in a light blue dress with matching jacket made by the Carron dressmaker, while next to her was her bridegroom, no longer too thin but elegant in a dark suit different from the one he'd planned to wear for his marriage to Lorne. 'What a waste!' his mother had cried, and it was true he'd had to dig deep into his savings to buy it, but he and Rosa had been as one in not wanting anything from the wedding that never was to taint their own celebrations.

Though Mrs MacNeil had decided that what she wore for this wedding was of no interest, when it came to it, she still wanted to look as smart as possible and was in fact pleased with how she looked – even if no one watching her wipe away theatrical tears would have guessed she was pleased about anything. Unlike Greg Malcolm, who couldn't stop beaming, he being so thrilled that the good catch who was Daniel had not been lost to his family, but had taken on Rosa and was all set to give her a good life.

Such a lucky, lucky girl, as Mrs MacRitchie (who had asked everyone to call her Joan) described her, a thought echoed by the smartly dressed Agnes, now that she'd actually seen Rosa's bridegroom. My, wouldn't she have something to tell the girls when she got back to number twenty-five! No wonder Rosa had wanted to take on her sister's reject! Who wouldn't want such a lovely young man, then? Only Rosa's silly sister, dazzled by the attentions of somebody she considered so grand. Rosa had made the better choice, and as she and Daniel left for their little reception at the local café, everyone was wishing her well. Except, perhaps, Mrs MacNeil, even though her son's happiness depended on Rosa's, but then no one who knew her would expect Daniel's mother to be happy about him marrying another Malcolm.

The day being so mild, the small wedding party was content to be served mixed salad with slices of ham – even Greg was complimentary, though he was not usually one for cold stuff. But then there were plenty of extras – dressed-up potatoes, buttered rolls, sticks of celery and, afterwards, strawberries, before a bottle of wine was brought out to accompany the little wedding cake Mrs MacNeil had been persuaded to make. As Rosa and Daniel cut the first slice, smiling their thanks to her, she had the grace to manage a smile back before asking over the wine where had that come from and who could have afforded it?

'Was a present from Mr and Mrs Fordyce,' Agnes explained with some pride. 'They are so kind, you wouldn't believe!'

'I'm sure I would not,' Mrs MacNeil declared, taking another sip of her wine, her cheeks already bright pink. 'How Rosa will miss them, eh?'

'Maybe not,' Daniel said swiftly, his eyes on his bride. 'I hope she will have compensations. But what I want to do now is thank Mr Malcolm for giving us such a wonderful wedding breakfast – we couldn't be more grateful. Also we want to thank you, Ma, for that lovely cake, and to thank you, Mrs MacRitchie and Miss Agnes, for being with us today and acting as witnesses. A big thank you to you all.'

There were smiles and thanks and kisses exchanged, until a waitress came and whispered to Rosa that if she'd like to change into her 'Going Away', there was a little room ready for her. At which, Rosa, in spite of feeling a rush of nerves, put on a calm face and followed her. This was it, then, the time had come. She and Daniel must now leave everyone behind and set off in the van for Aviemore, where they would be spending their first night.

At least, unlike other weddings, there would be no confetti scattered over them, Rosa thought, changing into her usual grey two-piece before packing her wedding dress into a parcel for her father to take back. But she had reckoned without Joan MacRitchie and Agnes, who, as the bridal couple approached Daniel's van, produced packets of confetti, which they handed out to Greg and even Mrs MacNeil so that everyone could enjoy themselves making Rosa and Daniel look like other newlyweds, laughing and trying to escape, not really minding that they'd failed.

'Good luck!' cried Agnes, rushing up to hug Rosa. 'We're all so happy for you – both of you. But you'll keep in touch, eh?'

'I will, I promise. And you'll be getting back to Inverness all right?'

'Your kind father's taking me to the station.'

'Oh, Da!' Rosa turned to throw her arms around him. 'Take care, eh? Remember, I'll just be in Edinburgh – not going to the moon!'

'Just be in Edinburgh?' he cried, trying to laugh as Joan MacRitchie came to stand beside him. 'I'd call that the moon, anyway!'

'Goodbye, Ma,' Daniel was meanwhile whispering. 'Thanks for coming. It meant a lot to me.'

'Yes, well, you be sure to write to me, let me know how things are,' she answered, giving him her cheek to kiss, not forgetting to frown a little when Rosa came to kiss her too. 'And tell me when I can come and visit.'

'Oh, sure,' Daniel said, glancing quickly at Rosa, who was bravely keeping up her smile. 'When we're straight, eh? I'll write, don't worry, but now I reckon it's time to go – just have to get the van started.'

'Hope it does,' Greg muttered. 'Or do I?'

'Oh, Greg, she has to go,' Joan whispered, taking his arm and leaning close, everything about her sending the signal *here I am, you've still got me*, but Greg was too busy watching Daniel turning his starting handle to notice.

When the van's engine was roaring and the bride and groom had settled in their seats, there were last waves and cries of 'Good luck!' and 'Safe journey', until finally the van was out of sight and there was nothing for the guests left behind to do but sigh and prepare to go home.

'Last trip in the van,' Daniel announced as they left Kinlaine, and it seemed to Rosa that his cheerful voice sounded a little forced. Was he minding giving up the van? She decided he was not. After all, he no longer needed it in his new job and he'd be saving on the rental. Still, he appeared to be playing a part, and when she answered him, saying she'd miss their little trips, she knew she sounded the same.

'Not too far to Aviemore,' he remarked after driving for a while. 'Hope the room I've booked for us will be all right.'

'I'm sure it will be lovely.'

'It's important, our first night.' He gave her a quick glance. 'I want everything to be right for you.'

'It will be. No need to worry, Daniel.'

'I'll say the same to you, then. No need to worry – if you have been worrying—'

'I never said I was worried,' replied Rosa, who was in fact just that.

'That's good, then, because everything is going to be fine.'

'I know. Because we're together.'

'Exactly!' Daniel suddenly laughed. 'Oh, God, Rosa, shall I stop the van and kiss you?'

'No,' she said with decision, 'let's get on to Aviemore.'

'Aviemore it is, then.'

The strange thing was that when they had gone through all the motions of settling into their boarding house at Aviemore, had done their best to eat a meal and finally reached the haven of their double bed, they discovered they'd both been right. There'd been no need to worry.

'Maybe it wasn't perfect,' Daniel still felt he should say, holding Rosa close when their first ever love-making was over. 'But I promise you, it will be.'

'Wasn't perfect?' she whispered. 'What do you mean?'

'You thought it was?'

'I know it was!'

He smiled in the darkness. 'That's a relief, then.'

'You were really worrying?'

'Only for you.'

'You'd no need to worry for me, Daniel.'

'That's what's wonderful. I told you we'd be right for each other and we are – in this way and every way.'

But as they gradually moved apart and Daniel slept, for the first time on her wedding night, the thought of her sister came into Rosa's mind.

Only for a moment, for Lorne had no part in this special time – she and Daniel had never made love, so she and Rosa could never be compared. Closing her eyes for sleep at last, Rosa sent up grateful thanks that this should have been so and let the image of her sister leave her – at least for then.

In the morning, when she woke early, no further memory of Lorne halted Rosa's pleasure in watching over her sleeping husband and, as she gently bent to kiss his lips and heard him whisper her name, the thought came to her: maybe she need never worry about Lorne again?

Part Two

Twenty-Four

Grey, grey, grey.

Everything Rosa had seen since she and Daniel had reached Edinburgh appeared to be grey: the sky – what you could see of it above the tall buildings – and the buildings themselves. The roads made of blocks Daniel had said were called 'setts' – all were grey.

So much for the beautiful city Rosa had heard so much about! As they rattled along in the van over the setts and tram lines, she could not help sighing, though she knew how much it meant to Daniel that she should like her new home and wouldn't for the world upset him. Promise you won't say anything, she told herself. It can't be like this every day. And then, to her dismay, heard herself murmuring, 'But Daniel, it's all so grey!'

Now why, after all, had she said that? Maybe he hadn't heard? Of course he had.

'Seems so,' he answered, approaching a corner and slowing down. 'But it's probably only because of the haar. The city's not really grey – you'll see when we turn into Princes Street any minute now. There's the castle and the gardens, all autumn flowers – plenty of colour there.'

'What's a haar?' she asked, thinking that these towering buildings were made of tough, solid stone and were not going to change. 'It sounds foreign.'

'Does, doesn't it?' Daniel laughed. 'It's a mist, that's all, but somebody told me the name is German – meaning hair. Should have cleared by now, anyway.'

'So, where's Princes Street? That's what I want to see.'

'Coming up now, just round here – and look, it's almost clear! Just right for your first view of it. Famous street, you know.'

Thank the Lord, she was thinking, for letting it not be grey. Except for the castle, maybe, but that was very different from the buildings back in the streets she'd just seen. Truly grand, wasn't it? Quite majestic, perched on its rock over the extensive gardens where there were trees and rolling grass, flower beds and a few memorials she'd have to come and read one day. All of that was on their right, whereas on their left were the handsome facades of Princes Street's famous shops: department stores, hat shops, dress shops, even an exotic-looking fruit and flower shop.

And pavements, of course, filled with elegant shoppers who probably wouldn't have to worry about how much they might want to spend, which was something so unusual in Rosa's experience, she wished she could have seen more of this most famous of streets and the people who used it. Already, though, the van was turning right and beginning to ascend a steep hill which Daniel told her was called the Mound.

Something artificially made, it seemed, as one of the links between the Old Town and the New, formed when a large amount of earth was excavated in the creation of the New Town, which had come about when the well-to-do of the city gave up living next to the poor folk in the Old Town and built elegant homes in the new Edinburgh of the eighteenth century.

'All their houses are still there,' Daniel went on, 'built to a plan that's as good today as it was back in 1767. You'll enjoy walking around the area when we've settled in.'

'Will I?' wondered Rosa. Walking round pavements, looking at terraced houses?

She was beginning to ask herself if she could enjoy anything at all as an old, familiar pain began to build up in her chest, reminding her of how she'd suffered when she'd first left home for Inverness. Homesickness. That was its name and it was a good one. Summed it up. Sickness. Yes, it was a sort of sickness, and something else to be concealed from Daniel, who seemed to be already at home in this city he had obviously come to know quite well.

Rosa was listening to him now, pointing out the views from the Mound over the city as far as Calton Hill, wherever that was, but suddenly interrupted him.

'Daniel, when are we going to get to our flat? I want to see it.'

'I know you do,' he said quickly, 'and it's not far now. But you won't' – he gave her a quick sideways glance – 'expect it to be, well, like Princes Street.'

'What a thing to ask!' she cried. 'I'm not stupid! I know what we can afford.'

'Right, then, here we go – to our new home!'

And a determinedly cheerful Daniel and a somewhat fearful Rosa made their way through the Old Town to what was to be their first home together.

Twenty-Five

Along George IV Bridge and into Chambers Street, on to the South Bridge, then straggling Nicolson Street, into Clerk Street, Minto Street, and still keeping on – how did Daniel know so well where they were going? Rosa wondered. That she would ever find her own way about this maze of streets seemed to her impossible, and she had now given up even looking at names in the hope that one would be Ingram Terrace, relying, as she must, on Daniel to deliver them to their new home.

Couldn't be long now, surely? Oh, God, she prayed, let it be nice. May I like it and not upset Daniel. As though she would! But she was so weary, so desperate to arrive, all she wanted was to get the first sight of the flat over with, to know what she'd come to, and make, if possible, a cup of tea. But would they have a kettle?

Round and round her thoughts went, and she'd begun to believe they would never arrive, when a sudden cry from Daniel made her start and stare as the van suddenly turned right and she saw, at last, the name they were looking for: Ingram Terrace.

'This is it,' said Daniel. 'Here we are! Didn't take too long, did it? Now we want number eight, which is just here, if I remember – and there it is. Rosa, we're home!'

'Not quite,' she answered, her eyes going over the house that held their flat which, like the rest of the terrace, was tall and built of the grey stone she had already come to know, with a variety of curtaining at square windows, a front door in need of paint and steps that had never, in Rosa's opinion, ever been scrubbed.

Where were the maids to do the necessary work, then? Nowhere, of course. Tenements didn't have maids, they had tenants who had to do their own cleaning, just as Rosa had cleaned back home, but here folk had to take their turn at the communal stairs and pity help them if they didn't, so much Rosa knew, for Daniel had told her. But he'd had chances Rosa had not to talk to the landlord's agent and their next-door neighbour on the landing, who was at present holding their key.

'Come on, then,' Rosa heard Daniel say, urging her to move as he leaped from the van with their two cases and a great bag of odds and ends. 'Let's go in and get the key from Mrs Calder – a nice young woman, Rosa, you'll like her.'

And with another of their bags under her arm and her face trying not to show her apprehension, Rosa left the van for the last time and joined Daniel on the unscrubbed steps at the front door.

'But shouldn't we knock?' she asked worriedly. 'We've no key for the front door, Daniel.'

'Mrs Calder said we didn't need one – the door's never locked. They reckon there's nothing to steal. Can you manage that bag, Rosa? We're on the second floor, remember.'

'I can manage,' said Rosa, her heart sinking fast as she stepped into the hallway of eight, Ingram Terrace and breathed in the smell of a place never reached by fresh air. All she wanted to do then was to drive the walls apart and let in the air and the wind, for how she was to live here, even with Daniel, was beyond her imagination.

'There's the stair ahead,' Daniel was murmuring, moving with the cases towards it, when suddenly two boys of about eight or nine, dressed in faded jerseys and short trousers, came banging down each step as though they wanted to make as much noise as possible, and Daniel could only laugh. 'Watch out – looks like a couple of young tenants are already coming down!'

At least they've got boots even if they do make a noise, thought Rosa, remembering that she'd already seen children in the streets who seemed to have to go barefoot. But why weren't these two at school? As she and Daniel drew to one side, the boys stopped and stared, then cheekily asked in such broad Scots accents they found hard to understand, 'You coming tae stay here? Wha's your name, then? Got any weans?'

'Weans?' repeated Rosa, glancing at Daniel to see if he could translate.

'Children,' he whispered and, to the boys, gave a smile. 'No, we've no weans.'

'Och, nobody new tae play with,' one of the boys was saying when a young woman in a cotton dress and apron with her hair tied in a duster came hurrying down the stairs.

'Jackie! Donnie! You come right back up wi' me the noo! You ken fine you're no' allowed out wi' your colds!'

Pulling the duster from her head, revealing a thick and untidy mass of brown hair loosely knotted at her neck, she gave an apologetic smile at Rosa and Daniel while clutching the two boys by the arms.

'I'm aye sorry, Mr MacNeil, that you've had these laddies pestering you and Mrs MacNeil, but I've got your key already if you'll just come up the stair. Jackie, Donnie – on you go, then.'

'It's very kind of you,' Rosa murmured, grateful that this young woman who must be Mrs Calder was easier to understand than her sons. 'We appreciate all you've done.'

'Och, I've no' done much! But give me one o' your bags 'cos this is oor floor, eh? Ma door's right here – in you go, laddies, it's open – and there's you, eh, Mr MacNeil, Mrs MacNeil. Wait till I get your key.'

The room into which Mrs Calder showed Rosa and Daniel was large and, though lit by high windows, appeared dark and, to Rosa, depressing. It was well furnished from what Daniel had owned in his rented flat, some of which he'd made, and provided a spare bed for a visitor set back into the wall close to the range, where a kettle was already singing.

'Grand sound,' Daniel commented with a smile as he set down the cases he had been carrying, which it might have been, but it did nothing to raise Rosa's spirits that were already making her feel guilty.

Why did she feel as though a great cloud had descended over her? Why not look on the bright side? Because another great tide of homesickness was swallowing her up, because she felt she could never get used to this room, because it just wasn't home. Nor, it was true, had the Fordyce house been home, but that was different because it had just been a place to work, not somewhere she must welcome as her first home with dear Daniel.

'Is this not pleasant?' he was asking her as she tried to concentrate, looking round at the furnishings – his table and wooden chairs, his two upholstered armchairs, his couch with cushions, all from his flat and now being exclaimed over by Mrs Calder.

'Everything's that grand!' she was exclaiming, adding she couldn't think what the Dobsons (who'd lived in the flat before) would think of it, she really couldn't. Why, they'd never recognize it, would they?

Her broad, good-natured face, so lit by smiles, made Rosa wish she could have been smiling too, and with all her heart she longed to look happy for Daniel's sake. But he was busy thanking Mrs Calder again for all she'd done.

Why, she'd even dusted his old furniture, eh? And lit the stove, got some fuel in, as well as tea and sugar and a jug of milk.

'So how much do I owe you, Mrs Calder?' he finished, at which she smiled and said that everyone called her Molly and she wished the MacNeils would do the same. But as to what he owed her, it was nothing, for the landlord's agent had paid for it all.

'If there's anything you want, though, just say, eh? Everybody's that friendly here – you could niver have picked a better place!'

'We're beginning to see that already, aren't we, Rosa?' Daniel asked genially, at which Molly Calder smiled from his face to Rosa's but, seeing Rosa's look of exhaustion, declared that she would make them tea, and it was all Daniel could do to persuade her just to leave and let them settle in. If they needed anything, they knew she was right next door.

'Aye, right next door!' she repeated, giving them a wide smile as she left, closing the door behind her, after which Daniel sighed and smiled and said he'd make the tea, eh? Rosa must be exhausted.

'I'm all right,' she tried to say. And burst into tears.

Twenty-Six

'What is it?' Daniel cried. 'Rosa, what's wrong?'

'Nothing. I'm just tired, that's all. We're both tired, I think.'

'If that's all it is,' Daniel said in a low voice.

For a moment, Rosa met his eyes, then lowered her own. 'I'll be all right when I've had some tea.'

'Which I'm making.' After a long moment, Daniel looked away from Rosa and, fishing out his own teapot from one of the bags, rinsed it from the kettle and put in tea from the packet Molly Calder had left. 'Just need a couple of cups—'

'On the dresser,' said Rosa, rising. 'Could you pass me that jug of milk, Daniel?'

When the tea was made and poured, they moved to the couch and sat down to drink it, Rosa still in her hat and outdoor jacket, Daniel now in shirtsleeves. For some time neither spoke, then Daniel, fixing Rosa with his blue eyes, said, 'Is that all the tears were for, Rosa? Being tired?'

'What else?' she asked, setting her cup on the floor and taking off her hat.

'Maybe you don't like the flat. You haven't said.'

'I haven't seen it all yet. I've yet to see our bedroom.'

'Do you like what you have seen, then?' Daniel persisted, his blue gaze never moving from her face.

'Yes,' she answered at once. 'Well, I mean, it's fine for us as it is, but there's a lot I can do to improve it – make curtains and such.'

'You're not unhappy about being here?'

'Of course not! It's just that, well – I'm a bit homesick, that's all.'

'I know, I know.' He seemed understanding, yet his expression was as dark as she had rarely seen it, and she knew she had not convinced him she was happy about the flat he'd chosen.

'Why don't we look at the bedroom?' she asked, rising. 'I'll have to get the sheets out and make up the bed.'

'I'll give you a hand,' he told her and led her out to the one other room the flat boasted, then stood aside to watch her as she looked round.

'The bed seems fine,' she remarked cheerfully as she felt the mattress. 'And I see there's a chest of drawers. Anywhere to hang things?'

'Sure.' Daniel pulled aside a curtain, behind which was a row of hooks. 'This all right?'

'Oh, yes. That'll be perfect.'

'Perfect.' He laughed shortly. 'You don't think anything's perfect here, do you? It's not as though we're going to be here for ever, you know. It's our first place – there'll be others.'

'So why are you so upset with me?'

'Who says I'm upset?'

She hesitated, turning aside. 'It's just that I've never seen you like this, Daniel.'

'Like what?'

'Well, like I say – upset.'

'I'm not upset. Disappointed, that's all. That you're not happy with what I found for us.'

'Daniel, you said yourself, this is just our first place – it's sort of temporary – and fine for that. I'm not complaining, really I'm not.'

Still, the dark look that had taken over his handsome face lingered and she had to admit to herself that this was a side of him she had not seen before. But then she herself had not been as she usually was when with Daniel. Perhaps, as she'd said, they were both tired. Too tired to be their radiant, happy selves.

'Let me get something for our tea,' she said quickly. 'I saw some eggs Mrs Calder had left and some bacon. Then we'll make up the bed, unpack our things and get everything sorted out. We'll feel better then. In fact, I'm feeling better already.'

'Me too!' cried Daniel, and to Rosa's infinite relief, she saw that the darkness had vanished from his face and he was her own Daniel again. As he held out his arms to her and she went into them and stood for some moments, her head resting on his shoulder, she was already putting from her mind the difficult time they had been through and was wondering instead if was there a frying pan somewhere so that she could begin preparing tea.

Twenty-Seven

After the shaky start to their move into the flat, things quickly improved, with Daniel genuinely happy in his work for Mr Lang and Rosa so busy improving things, her homesickness began to fade. With a second-hand sewing machine bought through an advert in the local paper, she made new curtains for the living room as well as a bedspread, and from a length of towelling bought cheaply at one of the big stores, stitched fresh towels for use with the jug and basin that was the substitute for a bathroom. The WC on the landing was shared with the Calders, which Rosa didn't mind too much, for she did like Molly, and her husband, Ralph, who worked for the council, was pleasant, too. As for the other people in the tenement, they were still friendly faces without names, except for an older, hawk-eyed woman named Mrs Flett, who soon made herself known to Rosa to make sure she knew when it was her turn to clean the stairs.

'We're very friendly here,' Mrs Flett informed Rosa, 'but we ken fine we ha' to take our turn at what's to be done. You being a Highlander, as I've heard, you'll no' be used tae living in a tenement and stair cleaning, but you'll no mind taking your turn, eh?'

'Not at all,' Rosa assured her. 'I just want to do what's expected.'

'Aye, well, that's grand, so you'll be ready to do the stair every other Friday, eh? Washin', mind, no' just sweepin'.

'Just as you say,' said Rosa, finally escaping into her own flat and closing the door on Mrs Flett before making a cup of tea to calm herself down.

'Take no notice of her,' Molly told her later. 'Edie Flett just likes to think she's in charge. If you take your turn at the stair, you'll be fine. I think we all worry too much about it, anyway, but the main rows folk have are over the stair. Apart from when some o' the fellas drink too much on a Saturday night, o' course.'

'I don't think my husband will be drinking too much,' Rosa said quickly. 'He's not one for alcohol.'

'That lovely man o' yours?' Molly laughed.

'I'm sure he'd be too perfect to need it!'

At Rosa's slight frown, Molly patted her arm. 'Only joking, pet. Nobody's perfect, eh?'

Only a short time ago, Rosa would not have agreed, believing then that Daniel was indeed perfect, but after their recent argument she'd very slightly changed her opinion. There was, she knew now, a side to him that made him, well, more like everyone else. And that only made her love him even more.

Admiring her husband as she did, it pleased Rosa to know that others admired him too, especially Frank Lang, who owned the cabinet-making business where Daniel worked. In his late fifties, Mr Lang was a friendly, fatherly figure to the young couple from the Highlands, even inviting them to his home where his wife, Martha, was equally welcoming. It was when she was at Mr Lang's home, while Daniel was helping Mrs Lang to bring in her tea trolley, that Mr Lang told Rosa of Daniel's artistry in his work and of how he was already becoming known.

'Why, I shouldn't wonder if a chair or table of his ended up over the road from here, eh? That'd be only what he deserves.'

'Over the road?' Rosa repeated.

'At Holyrood, of course! The Palace of Holyrood House, no less, where the royals like only the best and the best is Daniel, mark my words!'

'Please make space for tea!' cried Mrs Lang as Daniel wheeled in the loaded trolley, smiling at Rosa and perhaps wondering why she was so particularly starry-eyed.

Of course, she told him when they were at home and took pleasure in seeing his eyes also light up, though he just shrugged and said he was only doing his job.

'But I'll admit,' he added after a moment, 'that I am very lucky, Rosa, to be doing just what I've always wanted to do. To feel the right wood for my pieces, to see it when it's still nothing and to make it into something beautiful! Never ceases to thrill me, make me truly satisfied.'

She gave him a long, thoughtful look from her fine, dark eyes, then shook her head.

'Yes, you are lucky,' she murmured. 'And I envy you. Because what do I do, then? Stay at home and clean the house, do the washing, the cooking?'

'Why, Rosa, darling, isn't that what women do?' Daniel drew her towards him. 'And isn't it important, making a home? Don't ever think it's not! And have you forgotten, we both said we wanted children? When they come along, your days are going to be filled and no mistake!'

'They won't be along yet a while,' Rosa said, freeing herself from his arms and flinging herself into a chair. 'And in the meantime, what do I do? It's so boring in this flat, Daniel, you've no idea. I can't keep on cleaning it!'

'Well, while you've got the time, why don't you just get to know Edinburgh?' he asked reasonably. 'Go to the galleries and the museums, learn about the city – it's the capital city, after all. There's plenty you could do.'

'Think so?' she asked doubtfully. 'It's winter, not far off Christmas. Not the best time to see places.'

'All right for the galleries if you go early before they close when the light goes. Come on, cheer up, Rosa. At least at the moment, we're free.'

'Free – at the moment? What do you mean?'

'Well, there's something I haven't told you.' Daniel had lowered his eyes. 'You know I got a letter this morning?'

'I didn't see it. Who was it from?'

'Brace yourself.' Daniel tried to laugh. 'It was from my mother. She's planning to come down for Christmas.'

'Oh, no!' cried Rosa. 'Oh, our first Christmas!'

'Well, it was that or New Year. I thought Christmas would be easier.'

'Daniel, anything to do with your mother is never easy!' Rosa sighed deeply. 'I was wondering if Da might have come, but he said it's too far and too expensive. Might as well get your ma's visit over with, then. She was bound to want to come sometime.'

'Suppose you'll have no time now to see any galleries? Daniel asked, smiling. 'Won't you be cleaning the place from top to bottom before Ma comes?'

'Whatever I do, it won't be enough. Might as well not bother doing anything at all.'

But both Daniel and Rosa knew that that was never going to happen.

Twenty-Eight

Mrs MacNeil's visit at Christmas was just as irritating as Daniel and Rosa had expected it to be, but what could they do? When she described the flat as quite unsuitable, and the other tenants not the sort of people she'd expected Daniel to be living near, all they could do was cross their fingers and keep their mouths shut. Which didn't stop Mrs MacNeil from asking why the front steps weren't cleaned, and if everybody took turns at the stairs, why did it look so neglected, so absolutely thick with dust?

'I wouldn't say it was that,' Rosa was driven to say, but her mother-in-law only sighed and asked if Rosa had eyes in her head.

Now why couldn't Daniel find a nice little house, then, somewhere away from people like the tenement tenants? What nonsense to say such houses didn't exist and if they did they'd be too expensive! Every town had nice houses – you just had to look for them.

'No point in explaining,' Daniel told Rosa. 'Ma doesn't understand Edinburgh living.'

'Doesn't want to understand anything,' Rosa retorted. 'What day did you say she was going home?'

To be fair, she had brought generous presents for Christmas – a handsome knitted sweater for Daniel, a pretty blouse for Rosa – and when these were praised on Christmas morning, she tossed her head and accepted the praise as her right. No praise, however, went to Rosa for the bed jacket she had herself knitted for Mrs MacNeil, which was described as being far too big. How on earth did Rosa expect her to wear something so huge? And what a strange colour! Could it be blue or green? Where on earth had Rosa found the wool – if it was wool!

'I'll just check on the chicken,' said Rosa, longing for Mrs MacNeil to move away from the range, but there was no hope of that. The flat was far too cold, she complained – she just hoped she didn't catch her death!

In spite of the grumbles from her mother-in-law, Rosa's first effort at cooking a Christmas dinner was a success, and when Mrs MacNeil had gone afterwards for a nap, Rosa and Daniel washed up and went out for a walk on their own.

'Sorry about Ma,' Daniel said as they stepped out together, glad to be alone. 'She's just got in the way of complaining about things – doesn't mean half she says. And she'll be gone soon.'

'Day after Boxing Day.' Rosa sighed. 'Can't say I'll be sorry.'

Yet when she had to accompany Mrs MacNeil to the station as Daniel had to go back to work, Rosa did suddenly and surprisingly feel a rush of sympathy for her. In the wintry temperature, she looked cold and thin, almost woebegone, and would, Rosa knew, be going back to an empty house where probably no friend would call round, as Mrs MacNeil had so few friends. Impulsively, Rosa gave her a hug, at which her mother-in-law looked surprised, and cried, 'Safe journey! Take care now!'

'I will, but you be sure to keep in touch and tell me all your news. About that sister of yours, eh? She still in America?'

'Yes, she's still in America,' Rosa answered unwillingly. 'Da had a card.'

'And she's still with Mr Rory? Fancy that lasting!'

'Your train's coming,' said Rosa, picking up Mrs MacNeil's case. 'I'll help you in with this.'

'I'll take it, give it here—' Mrs MacNeil landed a frosty kiss on Rosa's cheek. 'And you be sure to tell me when you've something interesting, eh?'

'Interesting?'

'Well, I'll be wanting a grandchild one of these days, won't I? Here's the train.'

As she was eventually settled into a compartment, her case on the rack and her knitting on her lap, Mrs MacNeil did at last thank Rosa for having her, and Rosa said, wondering if the heavens would fall down on her, that it had been lovely having her. Maybe she and Daniel would try to get home to the Highlands one day.

'Aye, and see your dad before he marries that widow woman next door, eh?' Mrs MacNeil cried, managing to get in a last barbed remark before the train carried her away.

Oh, my, thought Rosa. Oh, my! Thank the Lord that's over, then! Where can I get a cup of tea?

Twenty-Nine

'Be sure to tell me when you've something interesting,' Mrs MacNeil had told Rosa at the station, which meant when there was a grandchild on the way, but Rosa had never thought somehow that that would happen. She didn't know why, she just somehow couldn't see herself as 'expecting', even though it was understood that she and Daniel wanted children. Which was why she got the shock of her life when, after she'd finally got to see the doctor who saw the tenement folk if they could manage his five-shilling fee, she was told to prepare for a baby in August.

'August?' she'd cried, at which sharp young Doctor Napier had frowned.

'Aren't you pleased, Mrs MacNeil? You should be – this is the first, isn't it? Time for regrets when you've five or six at home already.'

'Oh, I am pleased!' she answered hurriedly. 'It's just that I never thought it would happen to me. I don't know why.'

'Why ever not? A fine, strong young woman like you? In my opinion, you'll sail through it. Won't need my services. You'll do well with the midwife – no need to worry about that.'

Which was true; Rosa had no need to worry about the midwife for, only two weeks after she'd seen the doctor, she lost the baby.

'Lucky I hadn't told your mother,' she sadly remarked to Daniel later, when they'd recovered a little from the shock of what had happened. 'She'd have been so disappointed.'

'I'm disappointed, too, Rosa. I'd been thinking, if it was a boy, I'd get him interested in wood carving – always good to get an early start.'

'I'm sorry, Daniel.'

'No need for you to feel that!' He held her close for a moment. 'But we'll try again. Second time lucky, eh?'

'I don't know if I feel ready for that.'

'Well, when you do, I have the feeling all will be well. Why not? Didn't the doctor tell you you're ideal for being a mother?'

'I just hope he's right.' Rosa shook her head. 'Think I'll write to Da now, and then your ma. They should be told what's happened.'

'Be sure to say we're trying again.'

She did say that, but later, after the second miscarriage which came in the early days of March, there would be no more news of grand-children, for Rosa had been given the bad news that she would never be 'expecting' again. Something had gone wrong for her after the second failure and she and Daniel must learn to give up hope of ever having a family.

'I'm sorry, Daniel,' Rosa said again, shedding tears. 'I'm so sorry.'

But of course it was nobody's fault, just one of those things, and after accepting the sympathy of Molly and all the kind-hearted folk in the tenement, they decided to get on with their lives as best they could. Daniel, after all, had work he loved and found rewarding; it was only Rosa who was left to try to find a purpose in her life which suddenly seemed so empty.

'The thing is I don't really have enough to do,' she told Daniel one evening when they'd finished tea. 'I mean, looking after this flat takes me so little time, and there's just the two of us to cook for, so not much to do there. And I know you told me to go out and look round the city, go to the galleries and such, and I have, I've done that. But what else can I do? What I really need is a job.'

'A job?' Daniel, as he threw aside the evening paper he had been about to read, appeared stunned, his dark brows drawn together, his blue eyes fixed on her suddenly as cold as winter. 'What are you talking about, Rosa? You can't take a job. No wife of mine is going out to work.'

'Whatever do you mean?' Bright colour flooded Rosa's face, rising from her cheeks to her brow, her widening dark eyes on Daniel now as cold as his. 'It's no disgrace for a wife to go to work, Daniel. Here in this very tenement, there are plenty who do. You're saying they shouldn't?'

'If their husbands can't earn enough to keep the family, of course I'm not saying that. But we're not in that sort of situation. You don't need to go out to work because we don't need the money. Thank God, I earn enough for everything and I'm not having people pointing the finger at me because my wife has to have a job.'

'This is about you, then, not me?'

Rising from her chair, Rosa was facing Daniel as though he

were suddenly her enemy, someone who would block her doing what she wanted, whose ideas were so foreign to her she could hardly calm herself enough to put her own views across.

'I thought we loved each other,' she told him, breathing fast. 'I thought you'd want what I want, would want to see me happy! What can it matter to you if I find something to do outside this flat? Why should you mind?'

Daniel slowly got to his feet, his eyes still cold but, when he spoke, his voice was quiet as though he wanted to appear reasonable, as though he had right on his side.

'We do love each other, Rosa, there's no argument about that. But I can't stand by and let you go out cleaning someone else's house because you want something to do. That's your only experience, isn't it? Cleaning?'

'Maybe I could do something different?'

'Look, I've told you, no wife of mine needs to go out to work at all. If you really want to be useful, why don't you take up charity work? Think of all you could do to help folk!' Daniel was beginning to appear excited at his own suggestion. 'So many things! And you wouldn't be upsetting me. Think about it, Rosa!'

'Charity work,' she said slowly. I suppose I could do that. But there's something about being paid that's important, Daniel, and it's not just the money. It's that someone thinks you're worth being rewarded, you see, and that makes you feel good.'

'And looking after our home doesn't?' Daniel, picking up his paper again, was making a great play of opening it out and being interested in one of the articles, while Rosa, watching him, was suddenly, painfully aware that she was again seeing a very different Daniel from the man she'd thought she'd married. Easy-going, gentle . . . yes, he was that, but when something really mattered he became conscious of his own position as husband and master and, if his wishes differed from hers, there was no question whose would take precedence.

What was she to do? Just give in, do what he wanted? And nothing he didn't?

I don't think so, Rosa said to herself. Being Daniel's wife didn't stop her having views of her own. As soon as he'd finished with that newspaper, she would take it and read the job vacancy columns. Maybe they'd be for governesses or schoolteachers but there would be posts for others, including domestic workers, that was for sure.

One day there might be something different that would exactly suit her, and if it did, she was not going to let Daniel stop her trying for it. She loved him dearly, more than anyone in the world, but she had a right to her own life as well as being part of his.

'Finished with the paper?' she asked quietly as he put it to one side. 'I'd like a quick look, please.'

'First,' he said lightly, 'a kiss. We love each other, don't we? Even if we disagree?'

'Of course we do!'

The kiss they exchanged was as long and fervent as ever, but when they drew apart, Rosa picked up the evening paper and began to casually leaf through it.

Thirty

For some time, there were no advertisements in the papers for posts that were of any interest to Rosa. Plenty for domestic workers, of course, and for the sort of work she couldn't try for, having no qualifications, but none for a job she could do that was somehow different, that would draw her attention at once. Maybe there never would be a job like that, and she must reconcile herself to being a housewife and try to satisfy her longing for something different with treks round the city, looking again at what it had to offer.

It was not until one bright morning in late April when she turned to the jobs page in *The Scotsman* that she at last saw something of interest. Not because it offered especially interesting work, but because the person wanting help in his flat was an artist and to work for an artist would be something new for Rosa.

Though she had never done any painting herself, she had done drawing at school and been good at it. In fact, she could still remember the teacher's praise for her and how it had been thought she might eventually find work in some sort of artistic sphere, but of course that hadn't happened. Jobs of that sort were not available for someone without real qualifications and Rosa had none, which meant that when the time came to leave school and take a job, going into service was all that appeared suitable for her. She hadn't minded, hadn't expected anything else, but here, years later, was a job which would bring her into contact with a real artist. And if she would only be cleaning his flat, wouldn't that still be something different?

Very carefully, she read the advertisement again, noting that it was guaranteed to cause interest from its very first words, which were *Help Wanted for Artist*, set apart on a line of their own, followed by a question: *Would any kind person be interested in the care of an artist's flat at eight, Kirby Gardens, following the retirement of the lady who previously did this work? Good wages will be paid to the successful candidate, who will be looking after four rooms and two studios. If interested, please write including one reference to Mr Jack Durno at the address given before 20 April.*

Here the advertisement ended and Rosa, having read it through yet again, lowered the newspaper and sat for some time, motionless. Her thoughts, however, were scurrying round, making her believe that she really would be writing to Jack Durno, and that however many other 'kind persons' or people like herself were in for it, she would strain every nerve to do all that she could to get it.

All she had to do now was compose her letter, find a stamp and post it. And then tell Daniel. Or should she tell Daniel first? That might make him more willing to be happy about what she was planning, though she knew that he was not going to be happy anyway.

For what was she proposing? To look after an artist's flat, which would of course involve cleaning and being paid wages, the very things Daniel had said he would not accept for his wife. Almost certainly, though, there would be several people fancying this post and probably Rosa would not be successful, which meant that there would be nothing for Daniel to worry about. Should she tell him, then, what she was planning? She was sorely tempted not to, but as soon as they'd had their meal that evening she placed a cutting from *The Scotsman* beside his cup of tea.

'There's something here I'd like to apply for,' she told him, her voice sounding to her quite artificially bright. 'Though I'm sure I won't get it.'

'Apply?' Daniel repeated, his face taking on the look she had come to know, the look of disapproval. 'You mean for a job? I thought we'd decided that you wouldn't be trying for any work, Rosa?'

'If you read the advert, you'll see it's from an artist wanting help looking after his flat. Something a bit different, then.'

'An artist wanting help looking after his flat?' Daniel stared, then gave a short laugh. 'Since when have you ever heard of an artist caring about how his flat looks? All he'll want to do is paint.'

'Maybe he's different. Or maybe the flat isn't his and he has to please the landlord.'

'After all I've said about not wanting you to go out to work, you're still set on it?' Daniel asked, not listening to her. 'Don't you care what I want any more, Rosa?'

'I do, I do, but I am interested in this job and I think you shouldn't mind if I apply. There'll be others in for it anyway. I probably won't get it, but I'd like to try and see what happens.'

'Listen, you don't know the first thing about this artist – he could be some crazy old man not knowing what he's doing. It's not for you, Rosa.'

'Don't worry. If I get as far as an interview, I'll know whether I want to work for him or not.'

'You know I'd rather you didn't get involved at all, Rosa. After all we've said, you shouldn't be thinking of it.'

'Look, I won't make you unhappy, I promise, but I would like to apply for this job and see what happens. Say you don't mind me at least doing that?'

'And if I say I do mind?'

She hesitated. 'Well, if you do, of course I'll let it go. But I can't think why you would. I mean, you want me to be happy, don't you, Daniel?'

'I want us both to be happy, Rosa.'

'Oh, well then . . .' She took his hands. 'Look, I've lost the chance of children. Won't you let me try to put something else in my life? Just as you have work you love, I'd like to have another interest too. I'm not saying this artist's job would be it, but at least let me try for it, won't you?'

For some time he gazed into her large, pleading dark eyes, then shrugged and sighed. 'All right, you do what you want,' he said, finally turning away. 'But tell me exactly what happens all the way. Keep me informed.'

'Of course I will, Daniel!'

They separated; Daniel to take a chair and pick up the evening paper, Rosa to wash the dishes she'd already stacked, her heart beating fast after what had seemed not a battle, more a little skirmish. One it appeared she had won – only, though, if Daniel was happy about it.

Thirty-One

It occurred to Rosa that before she sent in her application to work for the artist, it might be useful to know more about him, or at least what his work was like. In fact, if he was to know she took an interest, it might count towards his taking her on. Where to start in seeing his work? She didn't think he would be important enough to be in the big galleries, but there were large numbers of smaller places in the centre of the city that she might try. When she did, she was in luck with the very first one.

'We've just the one Jack Durno,' a friendly young woman assistant informed her in a quiet little gallery in Dundas Street. 'He's a bit too new for us yet, but we'll probably be taking more – his abstracts are becoming more popular, as you probably know.'

'His abstracts?' Rosa repeated.

'Yes, not just his portraits, which are of course conventional, but I've none of those to show you at present. If you'll just come this way, the painting's on the back wall.' The assistant gave a little laugh. 'You can't miss it!'

She was right about that, thought Rosa, having been brought face-to-face with a large framed picture which was nothing like she'd ever seen before. Where was there something to recognize? Where was a face, or an object, that was in the least familiar? Where was there a face or an object at all?

All Rosa could see were blocks – blocks of heavily painted strokes of colour, which must mean something but nothing that she could recognize, and as the assistant sensed her bewilderment, she smiled again.

'Has quite an impact, hasn't it? But maybe you're not familiar with Jack Durno's style here? Maybe you know his portraits better? They're his bread and butter, of course. Pictures like this one are not at present to everyone's taste, and they're quite expensive.'

'Does it have a price?' Rosa asked nervously.

'*Summer Circles*? That's the picture's title. Jack's joke, of course, as there are no circles in it. But yes, it has a price – two hundred pounds.'

Rosa stared, her dark eyes so wide, the assistant had to give another smile.

'Seems a lot, I know, but it's quite unique, you see. And in the future it will definitely fetch its price. I'm sure Jack's work of this type will soon catch up with his portraits. Is there anything more you'd like to see now?'

'Oh, no, thank you very much for all your help,' Rosa answered quickly. 'It's all been very . . . interesting.'

'Not too much of a shock, I hope?'

'No, no.'

Astonishing, really, the money involved as well as the actual work, Rosa thought, hurrying home. To think of anyone paying so much for a picture of blocks was incredible, and if there was not a great market for that type of artwork as yet, it could only be understandable. One thing was for sure, though. To work for a man who could produce such art would not – could not – be dull and as, later, she set to work on her application, Rosa found herself keener than ever for it to be successful. Thank goodness she could truthfully say she had found Mr Durno's work 'interesting' – in fact, she had never been so fascinated by any artwork before.

As for Daniel, the only thing that amazed him was, as Rosa had guessed, the amount of money this artist fellow could command. Well, not command, exactly – more like ask. If his pictures were as crazy as the one Rosa had seen, would anyone cough up good money for them?

'When I think of all the work I have to put into my cabinet-making, it makes me think there's something not right with the world,' Daniel remarked, fixing Rosa with his direct blue gaze, but she smiled and pressed his hand.

'I wouldn't swap your work for anything of Mr Durno's,' she told him. 'There's no comparison.'

'You're still determined to apply for his job, though?'

'Just to just see what happens, Daniel.'

'And you've sent off your application?'

'This afternoon. But I don't suppose I'll hear anything.'

'Couldn't suit me better if that turns out to be true,' said Daniel, to which Rosa made no reply.

Thirty-Two

Every morning, Rosa looked for a reply to her application and every morning had to shake her head in response to Daniel's questioning look. No, the post had brought nothing for her.

'Looks like your artist is not interested,' Daniel commented.

'Looks like it,' Rosa agreed.

'Well, there's plenty of interest in the paper anyway, with the king being so ill.' Daniel frowned. 'Wonder if he'll pull through.'

'He's been ill with bronchitis before, I believe,' Rosa murmured, but her thoughts, she was a little ashamed to admit, were more on her own future than the king's health.

A week later, however, a badly typed letter arrived for Mrs Rosa MacNeil, requesting her to call at eight, Kirby Gardens at three o'clock the following Tuesday. The signature was illegible but probably read J. Durno, as Daniel agreed, having studied the letter passed to him by Rosa.

'Hope this fellow doesn't expect you to do his typing as well as everything else,' he said with a laugh. 'But at least you've got what you wanted, Rosa.'

'It's just an interview, Daniel, not an offer of a job.'

'Anybody'd think he was appointing the prime minister or some such, not just a cleaning lady.'

'Folk have to be careful what sort of people they let into their homes.'

'And the folk who work for them have to be careful what sort of people employ them,' Daniel retorted, as he put on his coat and cap and gave Rosa a farewell kiss. As soon as he'd gone, she went at once to study their street map of Edinburgh to find Kirby Gardens.

It was quite central, though in an unfashionable terrace of stone houses now all converted into flats. Probably quite an expensive place to live, though, which meant that Jack Durno must be selling a lot of his portraits and even the mysterious abstracts, whatever they were, Rosa thought, now longing for Wednesday to come so that she could get her interview over.

★   ★   ★

It came, of course, at last, and Rosa, wearing her best coat and skirt of brown tweed with matching brown hat, set off, glad that Daniel's goodbye kiss had been just as warm as usual.

'You don't mind too much about me going for this?' she had asked him, and he had reluctantly shaken his head.

'I do mind, Rosa, but I've thought about it and I want you to be happy. If you want to tidy up for this artist, so be it. I won't stand in your way.'

'Oh, Daniel . . . You don't know what it means to me that you should say that! Will you wish me good luck?'

'I suppose I must.'

Then had come a more than usually passionate farewell kiss, one that Rosa was still remembering when she reached Kirby Gardens, where she found number eight and rang the top bell for 'Durno'.

Here goes, then, she thought. Let's see what sort of person I've been applying to. For everything depended on what this Mr Jack Durno was like.

Well, he seemed nice. That was her first impression when he answered the doorbell – that this big fellow, tall and broad shouldered with copper-brown hair and narrow brown eyes, was nice. Certainly, he was smiling and had a friendly manner as he spoke to her in an accent that Rosa had learned to recognize as 'well-to-do Edinburgh'. 'I'm Jack Durno. Please, come in.'

When she had stepped into a narrow vestibule, he asked her to follow him up two flights of stairs, explaining that he had the two top floors of the building.

'My studios are right at the top; the kitchen and my bedroom are on the floor below, as well as the sitting room, where we'll talk, Mrs MacNeil. Like to follow me and take a seat?'

Feeling a little dazed, Rosa followed him into a spacious, well-furnished room that could have been elegant had it not been littered with canvases, picture frames and books, all covered, like the furniture, with a thick film of dust, for which Mr Durno hastily apologized.

'You'll understand, Mrs MacNeil, that I haven't had the time to tidy all this up and since my treasure – Mrs Craddock – had to give up work because of rheumatism, well, I've had to let things go a bit. There is a Mrs Goudy who comes in every morning, but only for an hour to do the fires, which is why I need someone to help out very soon, or my mother will come over from Musselburgh and throw fifteen fits.'

'Your mother?' Rosa repeated, trying to keep track of all Mr Durno's talk, and he nodded and laughed a little.

'This used to be her flat, you see. In fact, it's where I was brought up – I slept in what is now one of my studios. But my mother made the place over to me after my father died as she wanted something smaller to share with my Aunt Vera. I needn't worry really that she'll be coming over. She said she wouldn't until I'd got someone in to help and the place had been put to rights.' He hesitated. 'Do you think you could be that person, Mrs MacNeil?'

'Yes,' she told him promptly. 'I like to set things to rights and then keep them that way. It comes from my training.'

Mr Durno was silent, studying her for some moments, then he pulled a paper towards him on a table at his elbow and read it through. It looked to Rosa to be her application and did nothing to soothe her nerves, though she could just imagine what Daniel would have said: *All this fuss for a cleaning job? What's so special?*

Maybe she was being a little silly and had just got carried away because Mr Durno was an artist and therefore different from most employers? Maybe. But she knew that she had already decided that she wanted this job, and the next moment was catching her breath, for Mr Durno, looking straight at her, said, 'Mrs MacNeil, I think I can tell you, you're the best. I saw three other ladies earlier today and I'm afraid they found the idea of getting my place straight just too daunting. Whereas it doesn't worry you, does it?'

'Oh, no!' she cried warmly. 'Not at all.'

'If I offer you this job, then, would you be free to take it, and soon? You say your husband is a cabinet-maker, which means he's an artist himself. Would he be happy for you to be working for another artist?'

For a long moment, the room seemed to rock. Then settled, as Rosa decided to do what she could to salvage the situation.

'I'll be honest, Mr Durno, my husband would rather I didn't work, but he knows I need to do something. I've no children and can't have any. Work is very important to me. That's all I can say.'

There was a silence, broken at last by the artist. 'That's very understandable, Mrs MacNeil – I'm sorry to hear of your problems. But you say work is very important to you. Would you like to work here, then?'

'I would, Mr Durno,' Rosa said earnestly. 'I'd be very happy to work here.'

'Shall we say weekday mornings, nine to one? For two shillings per hour? Would that be satisfactory?'

'Quite satisfactory.'

'Well, then, I don't think we need to be formal about this. I'll write to you, offering the job, but for now we can just shake hands, if that's all right with you?'

'Oh, yes,' she answered, still not believing what had happened, not yet beginning to worry about what Daniel would say as she and her new employer finally shook hands and made their way back to the front door.

'Would Monday the ninth be all right for you to start?' he asked as he opened the door, nodding when Rosa said it would be quite all right for her.

'I was thinking that I could get Mrs Craddock to look in, to show you the ropes? Would you like that, Mrs MacNeil?'

'I think it would be very helpful.'

'Good. That's what I'll do then.' He gave a cheerful grin. 'So, I'll see you at nine o'clock on Monday?'

'Nine o'clock on Monday,' she repeated.

They shook hands again, then Jack Durno held the door for her and she left quickly, hearing, after a short pause, the door close behind her.

The walk home didn't even register, for her thoughts were in such a whirl she scarcely noticed her surroundings, arriving at the door with a start of surprise that quickly turned into anxiety over what Daniel might say. Had she time to make a cup of tea before he came in? Yes, just, and while she drank it, she could be busy rehearsing what she would say when she saw him. If, that is, it didn't all fly out of her head.

Thirty-Three

'So you got the job,' said Daniel, striding through the door to the living room on his return from work, his eyes fixed on Rosa, who had jumped up at his entrance.

'How did you know?' she cried.

He shrugged, taking off his jacket. 'Because of the way you look – worried about what I'm going to say. If you hadn't got the job, you'd be putting on a good face, smiling away, free as the breeze. But I told you, if you want to tidy up after this artist guy, so be it. And I take it that's what you are going to do?'

'The kettle's boiling,' Rosa said quickly. 'I'll make you some tea.'

'Tell me about him first – this Edinburgh Rembrandt. How old is he, for a start?'

'I don't know exactly.'

'Inexactly, then.'

'In his late thirties, I'd say. But he's nice, Daniel. He's friendly, sort of cheerful, easy to get on with. Doesn't look like an artist.' Rosa laughed. 'More like a rugby player. But he doesn't do ordinary painting except for portraits; he does what they call abstracts.' Rosa shook her head. 'Don't look like anything to me, but they're the modern style. Thing is we needn't worry what he does; I won't be seeing much of him. He spends all his time in his studios.'

For a few moments, Daniel, lighting a cigarette, sat down in his armchair and studied Rosa. 'Any tea going?'

'I'll make it now.' Rosa hurried to the stove. 'By the way, when he heard you were a cabinet-maker, he said you were an artist too. That was nice, wasn't it?'

Ignoring that, Daniel asked how much the artist would be paying. And when did Rosa start?

'He's paying two shillings an hour and I'll only be working in the mornings. I said I'd start on Monday. The woman who worked for him before me is going to look in, show me around. Kind of her, isn't it?'

'Two bob an hour. You happy with that?'

'Sounds right to me. Look, I'll just make your tea, then get on with our meal. Remember, if I'm at home every afternoon, you'll scarcely know I'm at work.'

'I'll know, all right,' he said shortly.

No more was said about Rosa's new job, and by the end of the day, when they were going to bed, she was surprised to find herself thinking not of Jack Durno but her sister, Lorne. What would she have thought of Rosa's new job, looking after an artist's flat for two shillings an hour? Rosa wondered. She guessed she would not have been impressed, though who knew what she would have thought. So little was known of what she was doing. Their father did hear from her, it seemed, but only at rare intervals, and it was some time since Rosa herself had received news. As far as she could tell, Lorne was still with Rory, but there had been no mention of marriage and Rosa was pretty certain now that there never would be, which meant that Lorne would probably never return to Scotland. Lying awake, staring into the darkness, Rosa was grieved by the thought and sighed so deeply that Daniel seemed to come awake and draw her into his arms.

'Can't sleep?' he murmured. 'Thinking about Rembrandt?'

'No, my sister.'

Releasing her, Daniel drew back. 'What's brought that on?' he asked after a pause.

'I don't know. She just came into my mind. But you must still think of her, Daniel, don't you? Though you never talk about her.'

'There's no need to talk about her.'

'I was thinking, maybe we should. When you asked me to marry you, you said I would help you to forget her, but I don't know if that's turned out to be true.' Rosa put her hand on Daniel's arm. 'Tell me if you do – if you still think of her.'

'Not so much now,' he answered with something of an effort.

Not so much . . . It wasn't quite the answer she'd hoped for and, as though he sensed that, Daniel again took Rosa into his arms.

'Come on,' he whispered, 'let's get you out of that nightgown. I know the best way to stop thinking of Lorne, and so do you. And the best way to stop thinking about your new job as well. Don't you agree?'

'I suppose I do.' Though as she slipped out of her nightgown, Rosa was wishing Daniel hadn't mentioned her job. That was the way to make her think of it, and she really didn't want thoughts of Jack Durno at such a time.

But she needn't have worried that his image would intrude on their joy, for of course it didn't. As ever, nothing spoiled their moment, and by the time they were lying back, spent with wonderful effort, sleep itself claimed them both and they knew nothing until morning.

'Happy?' Daniel asked, playing with her long plait of hair as the new day broke for them, and Rosa, smiling dreamily, said she was.

'No more thinking of you know who?'

Did he mean her new boss or her sister? Either way, she'd put them both, at least temporarily, out of her mind and shook her head.

'No more thinking,' she agreed, and together they rose to wash and dress and begin another day.

Thirty-Four

Mrs Craddock, Rosa's predecessor, was a strongly built woman in her late forties with a sallow complexion and tightly pinned-up light brown hair. When they were introduced to each other by Jack Durno on Rosa's first morning in May, she was wearing, like most people, a black armband for the death of King Edward that had happened only a few days before, and was keen to bewail his passing, for who knew what this new king, George the Fifth, would be like?

'Aye, they can say what they like about King Edward,' Mrs Craddock sighed, 'but he was a jolly sort of man, eh? Just the one to cheer you up if you were down, I should think, and this new man, this George, he looks a bit more serious?'

'Maybe, but that's no bad thing in a monarch,' Mr Durno declared. 'There are some who'd say King Edward was at one time not serious enough. But I must get on. Mrs MacNeil, welcome to number eight. I hope you'll be happy here, but for now I'll leave you in the excellent care of Mrs Craddock.'

Rosa, as he left them, sure that Mrs Craddock's care would be excellent, smiled at her predecessor who, it seemed to her, looked as though she could have cleaned the whole place without getting out of breath. In fact, though, as Mrs Craddock explained, she'd had the bad luck to develop arthritis.

'Aye, is it no' terrible, then, for me to be struck down at ma time with such a thing? I should ha' been good for years yet, but just look at ma hands, then! Fingers all turned in, you ken. And ma knees! Och, I canna tell you—'

'I'm so sorry,' Rosa said earnestly, 'but it's very good of you to come in to show me round. I do appreciate it.'

'Nae bother,' Mrs Craddock declared, pointing to a chair at the long table in the kitchen where they were both standing. 'Now you sit down, lassie, while I make a cup o' tea for us. That's how I aye began ma day, you ken, and a very good idea it was.'

'Oh, then let me put the kettle on!' Rosa cried, but Mrs Craddock shook her head.

'No, no, I can still fill a kettle, eh? I make a good cup o' tea, though I say it maself, and in that tin on the table there's some shortbread pieces. Won't take but a minute to make the tea.'

When they were settled at the table with their tea and shortbread, Mrs Craddock admitted that she'd been surprised when she met Rosa.

'You're that young, you see, dear. I thought Mr Durno would've picked someone like me – same age, I mean – to follow me in the job.'

'I don't think I'm too young,' Rosa said at once. 'Mr Durno can't have thought I was.'

'Aye, I daresay, but it can be a bit lonely, you ken, working on your own. There is Mrs Goudy, the charlady, but she only stays an hour to do the fires. She's already gone today. You'll no' have to mind no' having anybody to talk to.'

'There's so much to do, I shan't even notice it,' Rosa said honestly, at which Mrs Craddock nodded.

'Aye, you're probably right. Mr Durno's a lovely man – him and his ma gave me a bit o' money when I left, so kind, you ken – but he's no company, being up the stair, and trying to keep track of all his mess is just impossible. Never worry about sorting out his studios, is my advice – well, he'd never let you anyway! But now, let us get on.'

Thirty-Five

A useful morning followed for Rosa, with Mrs Craddock showing her where everything was kept, which keys fitted which locks, and telling her not to lose heart at the confusion she found. That had only happened downstairs after Mrs Craddock had left and Mr Durno had been on his own for a time, because to leave Mr Durno on his own – well, it was just asking for trouble!

'You'll soon learn how to deal with everything, though,' Mrs Craddock told Rosa at the end of the morning while putting on her coat and large felt hat before leaving. 'Any problems, drop me a note, eh? Mr Durno's got the address.'

'I must thank you again for all your help, Mrs Craddock,' Rosa told her earnestly. 'You've been very kind. And I do hope that your arthritis improves.'

'Aye, well, I'll have to hope, too, but now I'll away – might see you again sometime. But here comes Mr Durno; he'll be wanting to show you the studios.'

'Just off, Mrs Craddock?' Jack Durno called, clattering down the stairs. 'Keep in touch, eh? My mother will be wanting to know how you are.'

And as the front door closed on Mrs Craddock, Jack turned to Rosa. 'Up the stair now, Mrs MacNeil. I want to show you where I work and what needs doing up there.' He laughed a little. 'Not that there's much you can do, as you'll see.'

The two large studios at the top of the house had been converted from the old attics, one being where, as Mr Durno explained, he worked on his own artwork, the other kept for his portrait painting.

'I'll show you that one first, Mrs MacNeil – it's where the sitters come, so it's the tidy one.'

The tidy one? Looking in at it from the doorway, Rosa supposed it could be described that way, mainly because there was so little in it. An easel, a sitter's chair, a mirror where looks could be checked, a wardrobe for outdoor clothes. But everywhere there was the film of dust she'd first met at Mr Durno's house, which only that morning had required tackling downstairs by Rosa and

Mrs Craddock, and must surely be dealt with before any sitters came to have their portraits painted.

On the whole, though, it wasn't too bad, Rosa decided, feeling relieved, until she noticed that Mr Durno's look was apologetic.

'Now for my place,' he told her, opening the next door, 'which is not quite as tidy as the portrait studio. Not that you need to worry, Mrs MacNeil. All you need do is sweep the floor now and again. Here we are then!'

As they moved into the large room filled with light where Mr Durno had slept as a boy and was now his working studio, it didn't seem too untidy to Rosa, who had been expecting something worse. Of course, it was stuffed with canvases, some displayed on two easels, some propped up around the walls, none showing anything that could be recognized, but there were also bookcases half-covered with protective drapery, sloping piles of magazines and a table with a gas ring, kettle and cups. In the corner of the room was a vast sink where brushes were stacked in jars, and a pair of paint-stained towels and an overall hung on nearby hooks.

As Rosa's dark eyes moved slowly round the room, taking everything in, they came to rest first on one of the easels with its canvas, and then the other, finally returning to Mr Durno, whose eyes had been following hers.

'Is it all how you thought?' he asked easily. 'My studio?'

'I suppose so, but I haven't much idea of what an artist's studio should look like.'

'How about the paintings on the easels? You did say in your application that you'd found my work "interesting". Are they interesting?'

Oh, my, thought Rosa, he's going to catch me out, find out how little I know. I should never have got involved, but I just wanted the job . . .

'They are,' she said at last, looking away from the easels with their pictures she couldn't understand. 'But I don't really know enough to say much more.'

'People often just say what they like, Mrs MacNeil, and don't really need to know anything. I'm glad, though, that you still find my work interesting. It has a name which I think you'll know, and that's abstract. Belongs to a new movement where artists don't paint what they see around them, only what they see in their heads.'

He suddenly smiled and began moving to the door, which he held open for Rosa. 'But that's enough lecturing – you must be wanting to get home. I'll see you to the door when I've given my hands a scrub. Never does any good but I try to show willing if I'm going out to lunch.'

When he finally saw her down the stairs, he had put on a tweed jacket and shapeless trilby hat, and it was true – his paint-stained hands didn't look much better. But as he said jauntily, there was no need to worry. They knew him at the pub where he was going, never minded how he was.

Outside the front door, which he locked, he said he hoped she'd enjoyed her first day and that he hadn't put her off by talking too much – his particular fault, as it happened.

'Oh, no, you've been very helpful, Mr Durno. I appreciate it.'

'See you tomorrow, then.' He tipped his hat as he turned right and she turned left. 'And no talk then, I promise.'

Walking fast, he was soon on the main road, making for the Dean Bridge, while Rosa hurried home, her head not only in a whirl as it had been the other day, but aching so badly, all she could think of was making a cup of tea and lying down.

By the time Daniel came home, she felt much better, her headache gone, her only worry being that he'd be expecting her to talk about her first morning and she would rather not. Why, she wasn't sure. There was nothing to hide – not really. She rather wished, though, that she hadn't had any conversation with Mr Durno.

'Well, how did it go, your first day?' Daniel asked as soon as he came home. 'Hope it was what you wanted.'

'It was very pleasant. Mrs Craddock, the lady I replaced, was there to show me round and that was very helpful. Then I got on with my work.' She smiled. 'Nothing that would interest you.'

'How about the boss?' Daniel was taking off his jacket, his eyes never leaving Rosa. 'He around?'

'Oh, yes, he showed me his studios, just to let me see what I'd have to do.'

'And what would you have to do?'

'Well, just keep them dusted, tidy – that sort of thing.'

Daniel's expression was sombre. 'And that's what you want to do, Rosa? Aren't you worth something better than that? It gets me down, having to think of you acting as housemaid to the Durno fellow when you could be here, at home, doing just what you want to do.'

Rosa was silent for a moment, then she spooned tea into the pot and took it to the kettle singing on the range. 'I'll make your tea, Daniel, and then we can talk about something else.'

'Fine by me. What'll it be?'

But neither of them, it seemed, could think of anything to say, until Rosa had prepared their evening meal and then they were back in routine, able to talk of Daniel's day and of how his work on a pair of chairs ordered by a customer was progressing, all mention of Rosa's job at last being set aside.

Thirty-Six

In the days that followed, a routine for Rosa's work at Mr Durno's house was established and worked well, with no further talking to him, except for brief moments when he opened the door for her in the morning. That suited her, giving her nothing she need report to Daniel, who eventually seemed to accept her work and not to mind it, which to Rosa brought tremendous relief, leaving her free to get on with improving the state of the Durno house, something she found satisfying.

The other aspect of life at number eight she enjoyed was meeting those who came to sit for their portraits and needed to be escorted up to the studio, for these were in themselves interesting people, the sort who didn't often come Rosa's way. Meeting them and learning to make conversation as she escorted them upstairs gave Rosa the sort of pleasant feeling one gets from being right, for hadn't she said when she first applied for a job with an artist that there would be more to it than usual? Not that she took the chance to let Daniel see that she'd been right, only relished the knowledge that she had been.

It was after she had been working for Mr Durno for a short while that she answered the doorbell one morning to an older lady – one she didn't know, yet who seemed familiar.

She was perhaps in her late fifties, very elegantly dressed in a light fawn jacket and matching ankle-length skirt, her copper-brown hair seeming plentiful under her hat, her brown eyes so like her son's she didn't need to give her name as Mrs Durno.

'I'm just over from Musselburgh for the day for a dental appointment,' she explained as Rosa showed her into the sitting room. 'My son's going to give me lunch first. But tell me, my dear, are you working with Mrs Craddock's replacement? Jack told me he'd appointed someone.'

'I am Mrs Craddock's replacement,' Rosa told her, noting the brown eyes looking round the room with interest. 'My name's Rosa MacNeil. Mrs MacNeil, that is.'

'Oh. Oh, yes, I see.' Now Mrs Durno's eyes were on Rosa,

seeming suddenly wary. 'My son didn't give me any details of Mrs Craddock's replacement, only said she was a very good worker. And if the change in this room is your doing, my dear, he's right there – you've absolutely transformed it. But – you'll forgive me for mentioning it – you're so young, you know. Are you the only other person working for my son here, then?'

'Apart from Mrs Goudy, the charlady, but she only comes in for an hour first thing. We don't really need anyone else.'

'And you're happy about that, Mrs MacNeil? Being alone here, apart from my son?'

'Oh, yes, I just get on with things in my own way. I don't see Mr Durno very often – he's always painting.'

'Nevertheless, I should have thought . . .' Mrs Durno hesitated, then went on. 'Please don't mind if I ask, but is your husband happy about this arrangement? It is unusual and not one I knew about.'

Rosa's colour was rising, a deep frown crossing her brow. 'What's so unusual?' she asked. 'My husband knows I'm just here to look after the house, which is what I do.'

'Yes, of course, but you must see the situation from the point of view of others. My son, as you say, is only concerned with his painting. He won't even think about your position – such a young person, working here with no other women. But you must think about the neighbours and what might be said. That's why I asked you what your husband thought.'

'Mrs Durno, my husband trusts me,' Rosa answered stiffly. 'I think that's all I need to say. If you would like me to tell your son you've come, I'll be happy to do that.'

'Oh, please, I'm sorry if I've upset you,' Mrs Durno said quickly, her eyes holding Rosa's stony dark gaze. 'I certainly didn't intend to. If you would tell my son I'm here, I'd be grateful.' She tried to smile. 'I really couldn't face all those stairs!'

'Surprise, surprise!' cried Mr Durno when Rosa finally reached him. 'See, I'm all ready in my respectable suit and collar and tie – and I suppose you're here to tell me my mother's arrived. Mustn't keep her waiting, eh?'

'Better not,' said Rosa without joining him in his smiles and, at her tone, he gave her a long, studied look.

'Has she said anything?' he asked quietly. 'You can tell me. She doesn't mean to upset you, she just likes to speak her mind.'

'No point talking about it. You'd better go down, Mr Durno.'

'"Mr Durno",' he mimicked lightly. 'Surely the time has come for you to call me Jack, Rosa?'

Her colour rising again, she shook her head. 'I could never call you anything but Mr Durno,' she told him. 'It just wouldn't do. I wish you'd go down – not keep your mother waiting.'

'I'm on my way. Just tell me first: will it do, as you put it, for me to call you Rosa?'

'I don't mind, if that's what you want; it's what my last employer did. But do go down, Mr Durno!'

'Follow me, then, and leave the house when we do, so that I can lock the door.' He gave a quick smile. 'And don't worry about anything my mother has said to you. She will have meant it for the best.'

'I'm not worrying,' Rosa said quietly. 'And if I'm to leave with you, I'd better get my jacket.'

In spite of what Jack Durno had said about his mother meaning well, her meeting with Rosa at the front door seemed awkward, for her gaze went immediately from Rosa to her son, as though she were seeking some sort of bridge between them. If so, thought Rosa, she wouldn't find it, for there was nothing between Mr Durno and herself. 'Strictly business' was how their relationship might be described, and perhaps Mrs Durno recognized that and was relieved, for she seemed quite relaxed and friendly when she and Rosa said goodbye and Jack had locked the front door behind them.

'So glad to have met you, Mrs MacNeil,' Mrs Durno said firmly. 'You're doing a very good job – the house looks better than I've seen it in a long while. Now, if there's anything you need for it, you must let me know—'

'Come on, Mother,' Jack said impatiently. 'If you want time for a decent lunch before your appointment, we'd better get along to the hotel now. Mrs MacNeil, I'll see you tomorrow.'

'Yes, Mr Durno,' Rosa said as he and his mother turned left and she turned right, feeling glad that her employer had had the sense not to call her 'Rosa' while his mother was with him.

But what a tiring morning it had been! No need to tell Daniel too much about it, just perhaps that she had met Mr Durno's mother. He'd probably be pleased, feeling that such a presence would add to the artist's respectability, though the good thing was that Daniel no longer seemed to worry about that. And why should he? There was no need for him to worry about anything at all where Rosa and her employer were concerned.

Thirty-Seven

Summer beckoned, a time for those who could afford it to go on holiday, one of them being Jack Durno, who was going to the south of France on a painting holiday.

'I'd just as soon stay here,' he told Rosa, 'but I've got a couple of friends who want me to go with them so I'm making the effort. Would you and Mrs Goudy take the same time off so I can close the house?'

Certainly they could, Rosa told him, relieved that she could take the break Daniel wanted. Her husband only had a week and it was a long way to go for such a short time, but they were planning to go back home to the Highlands.

'I was worrying that it would not be convenient for you to have me away,' Rosa told Jack, 'but it will be all right if you're to be away yourself, won't it?'

'Of course it will,' Jack told her. 'Things have worked out well. And don't forget, you'll still be paid even if you're on holiday. I'm a firm believer in workers' rights – everyone should have holidays with pay.'

'Why, Mr Durno, you're the only person who says that,' Rosa told him, smiling. 'Most people don't get holidays anyhow. You might believe in workers' rights, but as things stand not many have them. I think I must be lucky to work for you.'

'The luck,' Jack said with sudden seriousness, 'is entirely mine.' But at her look of embarrassment, he changed the subject, telling her she must do some drawing on her holiday. Bring him back a picture of her old home or maybe the Moray Firth – he'd be interested.

Still embarrassed, Rosa only said she must get on and with some relief left him before he could come up with any more ideas for how she might spend her holiday.

The strange thing was that, in spite of all the time she had to spend with her Da and Daniel's mother, she was still able to find herself buying a cheap, unlined exercise book at the post office and sitting down one fine afternoon to sketch her favourite view of the Moray Firth. And enjoy for a little while being alone.

Greg had said he wished he could be with her, but he had a plastering job to do for the schoolmaster, and Daniel had taken his mother to Nairn to get something or other she had to have, while Mrs MacRitchie from next door was very busy, having invited everyone to have their tea with her that day. Just typical of her, being so generous, Da had said, at which Rosa had bravely asked what was the situation between him and her? Were they still not engaged, or anything?

'Cannot understand what you mean by "anything", Greg had answered. 'Just leave us be, eh?'

If they ever did get engaged or married, Rosa would be the first to know.

'And Lorne?' Rosa had asked quietly. 'You'll have to tell her, if you can.'

'I have had no news, Rosa, not for a long while.' Greg had heaved a long sigh. 'One o' these days we might hear something, maybe good news at that, but I'm not counting on it. 'Tis a relief to me that you and Daniel are happy and settled. Which you are, eh?'

And Rosa had agreed that they were.

So, here she was with her pencil and her makeshift sketchbook, lost in admiration as usual of her favourite view of the Moray Firth. Only problem was how to draw something that she'd dare to show Mr Durno. (Jack, as she sometimes thought of him, but never ever spoke aloud).

'Come on,' she told herself, 'get on with it.' And by the time Daniel came to find her, she had at last completed a sketch that might do. If she had the nerve ever to show it to Mr Durno.

To her astonishment, he liked it. Or said he did when, with some trepidation, she showed it to him on her return to work. In fact, he was so enthusiastic, Rosa wondered if he was putting on an act, but he seemed quite genuine, even suggesting something she hadn't thought of, which was to make copies of her sketch and put them on sale.

'On sale?' Rosa stared at Jack's cheerful face. 'I couldn't put them on sale. I'm not an artist. No one would want them.'

'Of course they would! You'd be surprised. People love that part of the world you've drawn. And I could market them for you. I have an agent, I have contacts. Just leave everything to me.'

But Rosa wasn't happy. She had the feeling she was on some sort of rollercoaster that was taking her somewhere beyond her control, and what Daniel would say to her selling her drawings would not be hard to guess. When she said as much to Jack, he shrugged a little before asking, to her surprise, 'Do you have to tell him?'

Her dark eyes widening, it took her a moment to reply. 'He's my husband, Mr Durno,' she said at last. 'I should tell him.'

His colour rose as he turned away, saying quietly, 'Of course, Rosa, of course.'

Surprisingly, Daniel didn't seem too much against the idea of Rosa selling copies of her drawings, taking the view that if she must get involved with this art business, she might as well be paid for it. Not that he expected much to come of it, for who would want to buy work by an unknown young female artist? He couldn't see it working out himself, but was eventually pleasantly surprised when Rosa did in fact make a little money.

'As long as you don't get too involved,' he told her seriously. 'Remember what counts in our lives.'

'Of course I'll remember!' she cried. 'I know what matters to us, Daniel, and it's not me making a bit of pin money, as they call it.'

'Exactly,' he said firmly. 'I know that you needed something in your life after we knew we couldn't have a family, and I suppose this is it. Just don't let it go too far, eh?'

'Don't worry,' she told him confidently. 'I know what I'm doing.'

But what she had forgotten was that she wasn't the only person involved in what might be described now as her new life, and even Daniel seemed to have forgotten that too.

Thirty-Eight

Between them, Rosa and Jack Durno had contrived to achieve a very pleasant routine, with Jack continuing to balance the profitable portrait side of his work with his impressionist artwork, and Rosa taking pleasure in adding her drawing ability to her usual cleaning duties.

Sometimes Jack told her she was wasted spending time cleaning, and that they should find someone else to do all that sort of thing, at which she could only widen her fine eyes and tell him that would be foolish and not what she wanted at all. The truth behind everything was that she didn't want to have to tell Daniel if things changed, for who could say how he would react? Much better just to keep to the present routine she shared with Jack and not speak of it to Daniel.

If only they had kept to that routine! But it was only with hindsight that she could see what they should have done, and by then she'd learned that the easy routine they'd had could never have lasted. Perhaps Jack had never wanted it to, and it was only blind Rosa who couldn't see that.

The change came when, one day out of the blue, he asked Rosa if he might paint her portrait. Her portrait? She had stared at him. Make her into one of the sitters she tidied the studio for? Those she opened the door to and escorted up the stairs? The idea was absurd and, though Rosa knew that there was never any need for Daniel to be suspicious, she also knew he would have been if he ever heard about Jack's request, even though Rosa had immediately refused it. There was no way she could ever risk letting him paint her portrait and then Daniel finding out.

'I don't see why you don't want it,' Jack told her, looking mystified. 'It could be a present for your husband. Surely he would want it? He must know you are—'

'Are what?' she asked when Jack didn't finish.

'Well, worth painting, of course.'

'I just don't want my portrait painted,' she declared after a moment. 'It's kind of you but I . . . don't think it would be right . . . for me.'

'It's something I'd like to do. As I say, it could be a present for Daniel. May I call him that?'

'It would be better for him not to be involved. I try to keep my work here and my home separate.'

'If that's what you want,' Jack said, shrugging, 'I'll say no more.'

'I do appreciate your offer,' she added hastily. 'It's very kind of you.'

'Kind? Not really. I'd be doing it for my own pleasure.'

As he rested his eyes on her, there was something in his gaze that made her heart beat faster with a knowledge she'd never recognized before, though perhaps she should have done. A knowledge she did not want which she was already worrying over, asking herself if, now she'd seen it, she shouldn't at once leave Jack Durno's employment. For what she had seen in his eyes was a feeling for her that should not have been his, for which he had no right, and which to his credit he had never put into words. No, thank God, nothing had been said, probably never would be said, so maybe she could just stay on? Keep things as they were? After all, she loved her work at number eight – the improvements she'd made in the house and the new talent she had found in herself that had made such a difference to her life.

How could she give all that up? Go back to being at home all day? A housewife again and nothing else? Stifling a pang of guilt, she decided she need not leave Jack Durno's employment, at least not just yet and, answering his unspoken, anxious question, she said she must get on with her work, for soon it would be lunchtime.

'You're not . . . planning to leave?' he asked hoarsely. 'I mean, the job?'

'I don't see why I should,' she said, after a silence during which they exchanged uneasy looks.

'I'll see you out,' Jack said breathing fast.

'It's not time yet.'

'I mean, when you're ready to go.'

At long last, they looked away from each other, and while Rosa moved downstairs to continue her duties, Jack turned back to his easel and took up his brush with a trembling hand.

Thirty-Nine

Guilt. Never before had Rosa felt it as she did now when Daniel was with her, even though she tried hard to convince herself she didn't really need to feel it at all. After all, what had she done? It wasn't her fault that her employer had developed feelings for her he should not have, so she liked to reason. But the truth was that she knew very well that once she knew about those feelings, she should have given in her notice and never seen Jack or his studio again.

There came the guilt, then, for she hadn't done that. She had been happy with what she had at number eight, hadn't wanted to give it up, and as long as Daniel wasn't hurt – and he wasn't – there seemed no need for anything to change.

But the time would come and soon, when he was hurt and there was every need for change – even though Rosa herself had had no hand in bringing it about. For her, it came as a bolt from the blue when he came home from work one day and stood before her with the face of a stranger, so frightening to her that she dropped the teapot she had been rinsing and called to him, 'Daniel, what is it? What's happened? What's wrong?'

'What's happened?' he repeated, stumbling to get the words out. 'What's happened? Only that you've been deceiving me – me, your husband! Going out to that fellow's house every day without a backward glance, when all the time . . . all the time—'

'All the time what? Daniel, I don't understand what you are talking about! Tell me what's wrong!'

'When all the time he was painting your portrait, wasn't he? You were sitting for him, letting him stare and stare at you as though he was in love with you – which he is, isn't he? How can I bear the thought of that?'

Daniel, dropping into a chair, covered his face with his hands while Rosa stood where she was, unable to move, swept into a nightmare that was not of her making yet so real, so terrifying, she could scarcely speak to defend herself.

Somehow, though, she found the words and the strength to move nearer to Daniel, even to put her hand on his shoulder, at the same time, crying, 'Daniel, I never knew he had painted my portrait – I swear that is true. He asked me and I refused, so if he still painted it, I knew nothing about it. How do you know, anyhow? Where have you seen it? I don't understand—'

'You're saying you didn't know?' he asked, looking up at her with terrible eyes. 'How can I believe that? It's in one of the galleries in Dundas Street. You must have seen it, Rosa. You must have known about it!'

'I swear I knew nothing. I told you, I refused to let him paint me, so if he did, it was behind my back. Oh, please, Daniel, believe me! I love only you. Whatever Mr Durno feels, I don't return it. I don't, I don't! Please believe me, Daniel, please!'

'You're still telling me you didn't know how he felt about you?' Daniel, standing tall over her, was suddenly contemptuous. 'Rosa, that's nonsense! All women know when a man cares. It's something born in them, to know, and you'd have known. So, even if Jack Durno never said, never declared how he felt—'

'He didn't, Daniel, he didn't. He never said a word!'

'I'm saying you'd have known anyway and what I want to know is why you didn't leave him as soon as you did? Give in your notice then? God damn it, why didn't you leave him and tell me why?'

A dreadful cloud, as dark as in a thunderstorm, seemed to have settled over Rosa's bowed head as she asked herself that same question. Why had she not done it? And she knew it was because she had wanted to keep her artwork going, to be successful in something so different from anything she had ever done before. It hadn't seemed to matter that if she'd only thought about it, she'd have known she was not only being selfish but was causing damage to the most important thing of all – her marriage.

From the look on Daniel's face – still so cold, so hard – she knew it was too late now to do anything to mend what she had damaged. All she could do was what she should have done before and leave Jack Durno's employment as soon as possible. Tomorrow, in fact.

'I'll leave tomorrow,' she told Daniel, her voice low, thick with tears. 'I'll give my notice in tomorrow.'

'By letter,' he said harshly. 'Which I will put through his letterbox myself. You need not see him again.'

'I've things I need to collect, Daniel. I can't just leave like that.'

'All right, so in your letter, you must request that anything of yours in his house he must parcel up and send here by post. That's all you need to say.'

'All?' Rosa brushed the tears from her face. 'You want me to say nothing of why? Why I'm going?'

'You want to say something?' he snapped, and at the continued harshness of his voice and severity of his face, Rosa moved away, unable any longer to face him.

'I'm going to put the kettle on,' she whispered. 'I'm going to make some tea.'

'Tea?' Daniel laughed, a harsh, brittle laugh that was worse than any tears. 'That's the answer to everything, you think? A pot of tea?'

'It might help.'

'Not me, Rosa. Don't make any for me. I'm going out.'

'Where?' she asked wildly. 'Daniel, where are you going?'

'I don't know. Just out. Don't wait up for me. I'll probably be late.'

And as the door banged behind him and the kettle sang unheeded on the stove, Rosa, though she let her tears flow freely, found no relief, nor any kind of hope that relief would come.

Forty

Of course, she waited up for him, sitting in her nightgown and shawl watching the door, and when he finally opened it after midnight, had to hold herself back from running to him, throwing her arms around him and holding him tight. He, her abstemious husband, had been drinking – she could smell it on him, on his face, his hair – but at least the alcohol had done some good, for the earlier severity of his expression had changed to a blankness that gave her hope that his anger towards herself might have softened. Once they were together again in their bed, surely all would be well? Surely, then, they could learn to come through this awful patch they were suffering to find again their familiar love?

But it seemed they were not to be together in their bed, for Daniel, walking not altogether straight, was passing Rosa without even looking at her, saying he was away to his bed, and was already tearing off his jacket and tie as she ran to him and caught his arm.

'Daniel, our own bed's all ready – come to it, please, come to me. I've been waiting for you—'

He turned, then, and looked at her briefly before moving away, only saying over his shoulder that he would be sleeping in the spare room that night.

'The spare room?' Rosa's words were a cry of anguish. 'What do you mean, you're sleeping in the spare room? We've never slept apart since we were married!'

'There's always a first time,' he said carelessly.

'There are no sheets on that bed—'

'To hell with sheets, I don't need any. So, goodnight. Tomorrow, remember we have your letter to write to Jack Durno. I want him to know as soon as possible that you are not seeing him again.'

She could hardly believe what was happening to them, how it had all come about, except that she must face the fact that it was all her own fault. If she had done the right thing and left when she'd realized Jack cared for her, she and Daniel would not be as they were now. Strangers to each other, sleeping in different beds, married and yet apart. And there was nothing she could do.

While Daniel without further words took himself off to the spare room and closed the door, all Rosa could do was lie in their double bed and cry to herself to sleep, from which she woke several times before the dawn broke and finally did not sleep again.

The following day brought more trouble, even though Rosa tried to keep everything as usual, preparing porridge for Daniel, followed by fried bacon, while drinking only tea herself. He seemed to have no hangover following his night out and ate everything with a good appetite, as though he was determined now to show Rosa that he was able to cope with all she had done, but when it came to writing the letter to Jack, his fragile calm disintegrated and he refused to allow Rosa to write it herself.

'I know what you will do!' he cried. 'Write some silly kind of regret for leaving that'll have the fellow round here wanting to see you, trying to make you go back. But that's not going to happen, Rosa, so leave everything to me.'

'I made my own application for the job with him,' Rosa said stubbornly, 'and I'll write my own resignation, so that's the end of it, Daniel.'

'That's not the end of it, I tell you! If you write anything at all to him, he'll be here like a shot, and I'm not having it!'

'We don't know he'll be round – he's never been here before. Just let me write to him myself and you can read what I've written. Surely that will do?'

His blue eyes snapping furiously, Daniel held Rosa's gaze for some moments before letting his shoulders relax into a shrug and reluctantly nodding.

'Just get on with it, then,' he said curtly. 'I want to deliver it and then make some excuse and get late into work. God knows what'll be said – I've never been late before, but it's all I can do. It'd be over my dead body to let you go back to Jack Durno's place, do you understand?'

'Don't,' she answered with a shudder. 'Don't talk like that.'

'Write the letter, then.'

She made it so short and non-committal, Daniel, almost against his wishes, could find no fault. For what had she said? Only that she was grateful for all Mr Durno's help in the past but was sorry she must now, for family reasons, give in her notice, to take immediate effect.

'Perfect,' Daniel said quietly. 'I could have written something just like it myself.'

Then he surprised Rosa by suddenly taking her wrist and holding it hard. 'Tell me, on your honour, that you never loved him, Rosa. Will you do that? Will you say it for me?'

'Oh, I will!' she cried. 'Because it's true. I keep telling you – why don't you listen – that you are the only one for me, now and always.'

For a long pause, he held her gaze, then folded her letter and put it into an envelope marked only with Jack's name.

'Thank you,' he said, turning to put on his jacket. 'I'll take this round, then, and you can stay here. If he comes, you know what to do – just don't let him in. Don't speak to him or listen to him. Tell him he must go home and out of your life. Do you hear me, Rosa?'

'I hear you,' she said steadily. 'But he won't come here, not after my letter. I'm sure of it.'

'Let's hope you're right,' Daniel replied, then went out of the door with a backward glance at Rosa. No farewell kiss as usual, no last-minute hug. All she was conscious of was his banging the door and leaving her alone. Quite alone. Suddenly, she felt more alone than she'd ever been and knew that if her mother had still been alive she would have gone to her and cried on her shoulder.

But now she did not cry; she went to clear the breakfast things, which she followed by first making the double bed and then the one Daniel had slept on in the spare room.

'May he never do that again,' she prayed. 'May all go well between us now.'

But some time later there came a knock at the flat door, and with a thumping heart she went to answer it. Knowing, all the time, who would be there.

Forty-One

As she had expected, and even feared, it was Jack Durno standing outside her door. Wearing the casual and untidy clothes he usually wore, he didn't look much different, except for his eyes, his kind brown eyes, that now, as they rested on her face, held an appeal of such poignancy she had to look away. He was, of course, bewildered. Must be, for all would have been as usual for him until he read her letter, when it changed for ever.

'Jack,' she murmured, using his first name as though she always had, 'you shouldn't be here. Please, don't stay. Please, go.'

'How can I go when I don't know why you wrote to me as you did?' he cried. 'Everything was the same as usual and then suddenly, out of the blue, you send in your notice. How do you think I felt when I read it? Everything that mattered collapsing around me without warning? And now you think I can just walk away from you when I don't know why you did what you did? For God's sake, Rosa, let me come in – we can't talk here.'

'There's nothing more to say,' she whispered. 'The letter said it all.'

'No, no, it didn't – it explained nothing. But please, you must let me in, you must talk to me – it's too much to expect me just to say goodbye. Let me in; let's talk inside.'

Sighing deeply, she stood aside, allowing him to enter until, after closing the door, she turned to face him. 'You mustn't stay, Jack. I told my husband you wouldn't come here – I never thought you would – but if he were to come in and find you—'

'I don't care if he does. I'd like to see him face-to-face, have it out with him, because he's behind all this, isn't he? You didn't say in your letter to me, but it doesn't take much working out to know that he resents me now. Perhaps he always has. I didn't let myself even consider what he might think of your working for me, just as long as he didn't stop you. But now he has, after all this time, I don't know why.'

'It was the portrait,' Rosa said after a pause. 'The portrait you painted of me without telling me. Daniel saw it in the window of one of the galleries in Dundas Street. I'd said nothing about it because I knew nothing, but he couldn't believe that and accused me of sitting for you and never telling him, and all at once, he thought—'

For a moment, Rosa faltered. 'Well, you know what he thought.'

'May I sit down?' Jack asked, sinking anyway into the nearest chair and putting his hand to his brow. 'Yes,' he said wearily, 'I know what he thought. The trouble is he was right, wasn't he? I can't deny it.' He laughed a little. 'Not when I know I fell in love with you the first time I saw you.'

'Oh, no!' Rosa cried as though stung. 'No, don't say that. Don't put it into words. It's never been put into words. Never.'

'And that's why you could stay, isn't it? I had to bottle up all I felt in order to pay the price of your staying. Once I spoke, let you see how much I cared, that would have been the end of it. I'd never see you again.' Jack let his now-tragic gaze rest on Rosa's face and shook his head. 'I thought I couldn't bear that, but now it's going to happen anyway, isn't it? We'll never meet again.'

'We can't,' Rosa said quietly. 'What we had – it's over.'

'Over,' he whispered. 'Can you mean that, Rosa? Can you mean you can accept that? We had so much—'

'So much – yes. I'll never forget all you gave me, Jack. You opened up a new life for me and I won't let it go, what I've learned, I promise, because that would be wrong. To waste what you gave me.'

Slowly, Jack shook his head. 'I see you can think of the future,' he said, his voice low. 'A future without me. Because you've never felt the same as I feel, have you? Daniel is the only one for you.'

'I believe for everyone there is just the one love, Jack. I mean, one true love. It doesn't stop me caring for you in a different sort of way.'

'A nice, grateful way?' he asked shortly. 'The sort of way that means you can say goodbye and never see me again and that will be all right? How I envy you, Rosa! How I wish . . . Hell, what does it matter what I wish?'

'Jack, you must go,' Rosa said with sudden urgency. 'Please don't risk everything by staying . . . Just in case – for my sake, for yours – don't be here when Daniel comes home. If he were to see you, he'd never believe in our true relationship!'

'I believe he knows our true relationship,' Jack said flatly. 'Somehow he knows that I love you and you don't love me. It's the only reason we haven't had pistols at dawn. Or even a fist fight.'

Without warning, he ran his hand down Rosa's face, then kissed her on the lips.

'Don't deny me that,' he said quietly, then opened Rosa's door for himself and, looking back in a low voice, said, 'Goodbye, Rosa. Don't forget me.'

But Rosa's eyes were suddenly misting and, rather than watch him walk away down the stairs, she had already closed the door without saying a word.

Forty-Two

Rosa did not tell Daniel that Jack Durno had come to see her, as he had predicted he would, but if he had asked her outright if Jack had been to the flat, she would not have lied. She'd already decided that she would not, to keep the peace, ever tell lies to Daniel.

Fortunately, he had decided not to question her when he came home from work – why, she couldn't be sure, but as the evening wore on, it seemed to her that his coldness towards her was gradually thawing. Maybe his time away from her had given him the chance to think objectively on the situation that had earlier so much upset him? Maybe he'd decided that the best thing to heal the hurt caused to him by Rosa's association with Jack Durno would be to forget it? Put it behind him, think only of the future and the best one he and Rosa could make together.

So much Rosa felt he must be thinking, and she wasn't wrong. He'd already decided that there was no need to spell anything out – there'd been enough of that already. Now he and Rosa must just concentrate on being happy together, living their lives as they should be lived, he the breadwinner, she the home-maker. And Daniel was confident now that Rosa had learned her lesson – she would not want to face working away from home again. At home, she would be safe from involvement with a fellow like that artist; all she'd have to worry about would be which charity she'd like to work for. Because, of course, he understood she would want to spare some time for good causes. He'd always said that sort of work was the best for her.

'Have you decided what you'd like to give some time to?' he asked one evening when they'd finished tea. 'I mean, weren't you thinking once of charity work. God knows there's plenty of call for it in the Old Town . . .'

'Some time?' Rosa echoed. 'Well, I don't think I'll have much time, Daniel. I'm planning to take up my artwork again.'

There was a stunned silence. 'Your artwork?' Daniel asked after a moment, putting down his cigarette as though shocked. 'What artwork?'

'What I've been doing. You remember, the copies of my sketches sold really well – you were quite surprised.'

'Look, we've been through this before. We don't need the money; you needn't do that sort of work any more.'

'I want to do it, Daniel. It's not for the money, it's – well, it's my work. People say I'm talented. It would be a pity, if that's true, if I don't carry on.'

So utterly crestfallen by this resurrection of an old problem he thought had died, Daniel took up his cigarette and furiously drew on it, his eyes not as cold as they could be, but cold enough as they rested on Rosa.

'Look, we're not going to argue again about your working, are we?' he was asking. 'I thought, after all we've been through, you wouldn't have brought that up again.'

'Oh, Daniel!' Rosa went to him and, taking the cigarette from his fingers, kissed him on the mouth. 'I don't want to upset you, dearest, and I won't. I'll just do a bit of my artwork when you're at work and you won't know a thing about it. But it will keep me happy and you'd want that, wouldn't you?'

Taking his cigarette back, he stubbed it out and shook his head. 'Sometimes, I think whatever I do, you'll win,' he said quietly.

'As though there's a battle!' she cried, smiling, making him smile with her, and their moment of shared happiness was something that made them both think of the comfortable bed waiting for them and wonder why they should keep it waiting any longer. They had, in fact, both risen from their chairs, and were on their way to that same bed, when a quick, loud knock came at the flat door and both exchanged exasperated smiles.

'Now who the hell could that be?' Daniel muttered, while Rosa shrugged.

'Probably only Molly, run out of something. She won't stay long.'

'Want to bet? Just tell her we're out of everything.'

Rosa, smiling, went to open the door, all set to say hello to Molly. But the words died on her lips when she saw it was not Molly who was waiting, and though she tried to speak to the slim blonde girl who was smiling at her, it was the girl herself who said, 'Yes, it's Lorne, Rosa. Back from the dead. Or, America, if you prefer. May I come in?'

Forty-Three

While Daniel stood like one turned to stone, his face pale, Rosa could not take her eyes off Lorne, who was so much the same, still so very attractive, still the sister Rosa remembered, yet mysteriously not. Just as perhaps she, Rosa, was not the same sister Lorne would remember. How could either of them be the same after their different life experiences had worked so well to change them?

Though there was no doubt that Lorne was as smart as ever, in a dark grey jacket and ankle-length skirt. Had she done well in America, then, that country that was as far away in Rosa's view as the moon? If so, why was she here? For Rosa knew her sister too well – she would not have turned up out of the blue as she had without a reason. When would she come out with whatever it was?

Pretty soon, Rosa guessed, though at that moment she only seemed specially to want to speak to Daniel, who was still neither moving nor speaking and still very pale.

'So nice to see you again, Daniel,' Lorne was saying in her new voice that was not exactly American in accent but certainly no longer Scottish, and was putting out her hand to him and smiling at him as though, it seemed to Rosa, she had never done anything in the past to hurt him. Was that how she was going to carry off this awkward moment? Just pretend she had never left him on their wedding day? Oh, how typical of Lorne! Just as she thought it was quite all right to ask him now if he would mind bringing up her luggage she had left at the bottom of their stairs!

'The taxi man said he'd take it all the way up for me, but I knew he'd want a bigger tip and I'm practically down to my last dime – penny, I mean.' And with a brilliant smile, Lorne turned to Rosa. 'That's why I'm throwing myself on your mercy, Rosa. Will you take me in for a bit? Just till I get myself sorted out?'

'But what's happened?' cried Rosa, flushing. 'Lorne, you must tell us what's happened! Why you're here, for a start.'

'I will, of course, but it's a long story. Can Daniel bring my stuff up first?'

'I'll get it now,' he said, his eyes going at once to Rosa, as though to say he'd have to do that, at least. In fact, Rosa was then so sure he was not urging her to make any commitment to Lorne, she felt a great rush of relief seep through her being. Even though, as Daniel left them to run down the stairs, Lorne's look to her sister was knowing. All she did, though, was ask if there was any chance of a cup of tea?

'I haven't had a thing since a ham sandwich ages ago.'

'I'll put the kettle on now. But first I'll show you where you can sleep. We're lucky – in this flat, we have a spare room.'

'My, I'm impressed. You've done well, haven't you? All thanks to Daniel?'

'He's really very talented as a wood carver, Lorne. He doesn't do any carpentry now – he works for a very experienced man who has a wonderful business. Their things sell really well. But let me show you where you can sleep and put your things. Then I can get you something to eat.'

When Lorne had had a light meal of eggs on toast, and they had afterwards all settled down in the living room together, she agreed she should tell Rosa and Daniel how she came to have returned to Britain and why she was alone. First, though, she said she must have a smoke and, smiling at Rosa's expression, took a cigarette from a case and, having accepting a light from Daniel, lay back in her chair, appearing quite relaxed.

'You never used to smoke,' Rosa commented. 'Is it what all American women do?'

'Oh, no. Only women like me who don't mind a bit of criticism.' Lorne drew on her cigarette. 'Just let me put this down, eh? Got an ashtray?'

Immediately, Rosa set one before her and, having stubbed out her cigarette, Lorne at last began to tell her story.

Forty-Four

'You'll have guessed that Rory gave me the push over in the States?' she asked with one of her smiles that did not, however, reach her green eyes. 'He did, anyway. Traded me in for a very attractive young lady with pots of money, daughter of his boss at the bank where he'd been given a job.'

'I never thought Rory would work in a bank!' cried Rosa as Daniel remarked that he was rather surprised he'd been allowed to work at all. Weren't Americans very particular about allowing foreigners to work in the States?

'Oh, yes, but as soon as Rory arrived in New York, he looked up some American chaps he'd met at university and they fiddled all he needed. Next thing I knew, he was working in a bank, not as a lowly clerk, you might guess, but as some sort of boss job that paid really well, and I was so thrilled! I thought the next step would be that we would marry, maybe become Americans, have a wonderful life . . . How stupid can you get?'

'Rory didn't ask you to marry him?' Rosa asked, worriedly glancing at Daniel, whose eyes were riveted to Lorne's face, though he said nothing.

'Never did,' Lorne replied, producing no more smiles. 'And when I spoke to him about it, he seemed amazed I'd even thought of it. When I told him I'd always believed we would be wed, he just stared, and by then, of course, I didn't need it spelled out. I'd been a servant, he was the son of the house – there was never any chance that we would be married. Hadn't I understood that when we went away together?'

'Why should you have understood?' asked Daniel, breaking his silence. 'Why should you not believe you could be wed? He'd told you he loved you, hadn't he?'

Lorne laughed. 'What men say and what men do are two quite different things. Anyway, he soon brought me down to earth when he said he was going to marry Miss Bellamy. He apologized for not telling me sooner, would you believe, but said I'd be well taken care of. He would pay my fare back home and give me money as well, so that would be all right, eh?'

'The blackguard!' cried Daniel as Rosa shook her head, her dark eyes fixed on her sister's face.

'What did you do?' she whispered.

'I told him I'd accept the passage money home because I knew I'd never get home otherwise, but I didn't want anything else from him ever. I just . . . never wanted to see him again. Thank God I never will!'

After that, no one spoke for some time, until Rosa finally asked quietly if Lorne had first gone to their father's on reaching Scotland, because he'd never said. But then he was the worst letter writer in the world.

'Oh, yes, I went to Dad's and he was thrilled to see me. But not Mrs MacRitchie, his lady friend, as you'll guess, and neither were the folk in the village.' Lorne gave a contemptuous smile. 'Soon as I walked down the main street, you should have seen all the old cats pointing the finger! As though I cared! The only thing that shook me, really, was seeing Bluff House again. And then I had to get away. I didn't want Rory's folk knowing I'd come back, questioning me.'

Her smiles gone, her face bleak, Lorne was silent for a while, her eyes cast down as though she was reliving painful feelings she would not describe, while Rosa and Daniel watched and waited for her to continue.

But she had tired of talking, said she was beginning to feel she needed her bed, if that was all right? But first, making an obvious effort, she asked if they'd mind if she stayed with them for a short time. Just until she got settled?

'I'd find a job,' she added quickly. 'I could find something, pay my way. But if you'd let me, it'd be a great help for me to be with you.'

'Of course you can stay with us,' Daniel said swiftly, beating Rosa, who was still hesitating. 'No need to worry about that. Isn't that right, Rosa?'

'Oh, yes,' she agreed, even managing a smile.

'We'll be glad to help.'

'Even if I don't deserve it?' Lorne asked lightly, but neither Rosa nor Daniel would answer that, Rosa only being quick to rise to take Lorne to the spare room where the bed was already made up. The fact that, not long ago, Daniel had been threatening to sleep in that same bed, was not of course something Rosa would tell

Lorne. For nothing must ever be told to Lorne that would allow her to guess that Rosa and Daniel had had problems. They were happy – that was all she needed to know.

'Such luxury,' Lorne observed, yawning as she looked around the spare room. 'Never had anything like this at home, did we, Rosa?'

'You must have had nice enough rooms in America, Lorne.'

'I'm trying to forget America,' Lorne replied, opening one of her cases, then suddenly coming to Rosa and hugging her close.

'Rosa, you've been so kind, so good, I do appreciate it. But you were always good to me, weren't you? I didn't dare hope you'd still be the same.'

'Lorne, don't worry about talking now. I can tell you're dead on your feet. Are you sure you're all right? You're so thin, now I come to look at you.'

'I'm fine, Rosa. Just tired. I'll be all right when I've had a good night's sleep.'

'Hope so,' said Rosa, noting the great shadows under her sister's eyes and the pallor of her lovely face. Was she really all right? No doubt it was true – she just needed her sleep. Tomorrow would probably see her looking very different.

'Goodnight, then,' she said a little awkwardly, the strangeness of having her wayward sister back from America and here, in Rosa's spare room, striking her afresh. 'If there's anything you want—'

'Just want to get to bed. Goodnight, Rosa – and thanks again. For everything.'

Later, in bed with Daniel sleeping soundly beside her, Rosa lay awake, wondering how things would work out now that Lorne was with them in their home. They weren't used to having a third person to share their lives, had hardly even had any visitors, except Daniel's mother that time. And then there was the worrying memory at the back of Rosa's mind that Daniel had been in love with Lorne, would have married her if she had not run away with Rory Thain. Now that she was to be sharing his home and he would be seeing her every day, how could Rosa be sure his old love would not return and burn as brightly as it had used to?

Moving restlessly, it was not long before she woke Daniel, who suddenly put his lips to her face and asked her if she couldn't sleep.

'You might guess I can't sleep,' she answered, sighing. 'Is it surprising? When my sister comes back out of the blue and is sleeping in my house instead of America? Why aren't you lying awake too?'

'You've no need to worry about me, Rosa. I'm not going to be losing sleep over Lorne.'

'Is that true?' Rosa whispered.

'Of course it's true. Look, you needn't worry about me and your sister. My feelings for Lorne – they don't exist. They're dead. You're my wife. I only care for you.'

'But when you see Lorne every day—'

'It will make no difference, I promise. We'll do what we can to help her get settled, then let's hope she moves out to her own place. Can't stay with us for ever.'

'Daniel, you don't know how much better I feel to hear you say that.'

For some time, they kissed and caressed, until Rosa said she thought she might sleep after all, at which Daniel sighed and asked if she was sure that that was what she wanted.

'Yes,' she answered firmly, pushing him away. 'Tonight I need my sleep.'

And finally, sleep came to both of them. While they slept entwined together in their double bed, in the next room, in her single bed, Lorne slept too, though not as peacefully. Dreams she would never remember persisted through the night and though, in the morning, she woke feeling she must be refreshed, she really didn't feel like getting out of bed. Only when Rosa brought her a cup of tea did she rally and put on her act again, which was enough to set Rosa's mind at rest.

Forty-Five

It didn't take long for the people of the tenement to notice the attractive young blonde woman staying with the MacNeils, and speculation was rife concerning her. Was she just a visitor or had she come to stay permanently was the question, easily solved by Molly Calder, who simply asked Rosa outright on the stairs one morning, and on being told she was Rosa's sister and might be staying a while, expressed even more interest.

'Why, is she no' the one who was in America then?' she asked at once. 'Why ever did she leave? Don't folk say it's the land o' milk and honey?'

'I think she just wanted to be back in Scotland, Molly. And she's got no ties; she's free to do what she wants.'

'No' married, then? Was there no fella in America wanting her to stay?' Molly asked with interest, but at the closed look on Rosa's face, apologized for seeming 'nosey'. She knew it was none of her business to be questioning Rosa about her sister.

'But she's a lovely girl, eh? Though no' like you, Rosa, and you're lovely too. But all the fellas here are talkin' about her, and no' just the ones that are single.'

'I daresay they are, but Lorne won't be interested. She's wanting a job. She's out now, as a matter of fact, answering an advertisement for someone needed in a dress shop. She'd be good at that; she always looks good in what she wears.'

'Awfully thin, though.'

'They like thin girls for that sort of work.' Rosa turned to leave and said she'd best get on, at which Molly hastily said she must go too. Maybe, she added, she could meet Rosa's sister some time? Just to wish her well, eh?

'I'll arrange it,' said Rosa, relieved to be taking leave of Molly, someone she liked to talk to, though not about her sister. Why was everyone always so interested in Lorne? Somehow, she drew folk without lifting a finger, and could usually get them to do her bidding. Not Rory Thain, though, for after the first mad falling in love, his holding himself apart probably came down to class. Lorne was good enough to run away with but not to marry. How foolish of her not to realize that! If she had, though – a little shiver ran down Rosa's spine at the thought – she would have married Daniel. And where would Rosa be now?

Thank God Lorne had turned him down! Thank God he was Rosa's to make happy. And when he'd said he had no feelings now for Lorne, he'd been quite definite. His feelings for her did not exist. They were dead – his very words. May they be true, always true, Rosa prayed, as she went about her duties, and then was happy to have her mind occupied with something else when Lorne came back, all agog, to say she'd got the job and was to start on Monday.

'Oh, I'm so relieved!' she cried, looking flushed and excited. 'They don't pay much – shops never do, but I'll be getting enough to pay for my keep and have something left over. What a relief!'

'I never wanted you to be worrying about paying anything,' Rosa declared. 'We're family, we do what we can for each other, and that's the way it should be.'

Lorne's smile was suddenly rueful. 'I didn't always live up to that, did I? I seemed to remember I – well, used folk. Used you, Rosa.'

Rosa hesitated, unable to deny Lorne's words and feeling again something she'd felt since Lorne's reappearance – that she was very different now from the Lorne Rosa remembered. What had changed her? Leopards didn't change their spots went the old saying, and Rosa had always thought it true, yet Lorne did seem to have turned over a new leaf since she'd returned from the States. Why should that be?

Maybe because for once she hadn't got her own way, had had to come face-to-face with rejection and learn how to accept it? Or maybe she'd just grown up and found the world not quite what she'd thought it?

Whatever the explanation, she was much easier now to talk to, much more thoughtful than she'd ever been, and if she wanted to stay in Edinburgh for some time, well, Rosa could accept it. Daniel seemed to think that Lorne should find her own place to live, but Rosa was now becoming quite reconciled to her sister's company, and with Daniel's promise that his old love for her was gone, why shouldn't they all three be happy for a while sharing the flat?

'I'll put the kettle on, shall I?' Rosa asked, putting aside her thoughts. 'Tea's not exactly much of a celebration, I'll admit, and you were probably used to something much more exciting in America—'

'I wouldn't say that,' Lorne said quickly. 'Later on, when Rory's friends got him the bank job, things were easier, but in the early days when we first went off together, to be honest, it was tough. They stopped his allowance, you know, his folks, and seeing as he couldn't have a proper job, I was the one who had to earn some money doing what I could find.'

At the expression on her sister's face, Lorne nodded.

'I can tell you're surprised I wasn't living the grand life over there in the States. But that's the way things were and I didn't mind because I did love Rory. I did think one day we'd be wed.'

For some time, the sisters were silent, Lorne seeming lost in thought and Rosa wondering if she would ever mention Daniel. Didn't he come into her mind at all, then? Didn't what she'd put him through matter to her? Or had she just forgotten him?

Slowly raising her eyes, Rosa found Lorne's green gaze fixed on her, and as though some sort of telepathy existed between them then, heard her quietly ask, 'Rosa, are you thinking of Daniel?'

'How did you guess?'

'Maybe because I'm thinking of him too. I know you're wondering why I don't talk of him, but the truth is I just feel too bad about him to say anything. It was only when Rory gave me up, you know, that I realized what I must have put Daniel through. Do you believe me?'

'All I know is you left him, Lorne. I've no idea what you think about him now.'

'I daren't think of him because I know he must hate me.' Lorne heaved a great sigh. 'It was awful cheek of me to ask you to let me stay for a bit, but I just had to hope he wouldn't mind me being here. Do you think he's forgiven me?'

It was Rosa's turn to sigh. 'I don't know, but he was happy for you to stay with us, so I suppose he must have done. Look, let's not worry about it any more. You're here until you want to go and we'll just leave things like that, shall we?'

'Oh, Rosa,' said Lorne, shaking her blonde head. 'What would I do without you?'

Forty-Six

As time went on, it seemed that all was working out well for the threesome in the MacNeils' flat. Lorne's new job at the dress shop suited her perfectly and she had already been told that the owners were delighted to have her, while Rosa, rather self-consciously, had taken up her artwork again and was doing well selling her drawings with the advice of the agent Jack had recommended. As for Daniel, he had said no more about Lorne's finding a place of her own and appeared to have accepted her presence in the flat without complaint, which was a great relief for Rosa.

Sometimes, Rosa couldn't believe how smoothly her sister had fitted into her new life. They got on really well, taking turns at cooking and enjoying exciting news in the newspapers, when they followed, among other things, features on the trial of Dr Crippen, who had been found guilty of murdering his wife and running off with a young woman, for which he'd been hanged, vying for the headlines with the news of the suffragettes clashing with the police when protesting over having no votes.

'I mean, it's so ridiculous that we can't vote in elections when we know as much as any of the men!' Lorne would cry, and Rosa, though not politically minded, didn't hesitate to agree, while Daniel looked on politely, saying nothing. He didn't argue with the women, perhaps because he didn't want to upset Lorne, Rosa thought, being happy if that were true, for her main hope was that the two would get on, even after all that had happened in the past. Certainly, so far, the sharing of the flat had worked out well. Daniel must have meant what he said about his lack of special feeling for Lorne; maybe it was time to believe him.

She could never pinpoint when the change came, but suddenly it dawned on Rosa that Daniel was no longer looking at Lorne when they had occasion to speak. Being very polite, yes, but always when she turned her face to him, not meeting her gaze.

What did it mean? Rosa asked herself. Why shouldn't he want to look at Lorne? She didn't mind looking at him, but when she talked to him as they'd talked in the past, Daniel's fine eyes were always somewhere other than on her face.

She wouldn't mention it, Rosa decided, wouldn't ask why Daniel should no longer want to look at Lorne. Had he taken against her? No, Rosa didn't think that was it. He was just somehow ill at ease in her presence, which he hadn't been when she'd first arrived.

Was it something to worry about? Rosa couldn't decide whether it was or not. Daniel had never said anything to her that might explain his new reaction to Lorne, and indeed, the last time he had discussed her sister, it was to say that his old feelings for her were quite dead. What a relief it was for Rosa then to remember that! In fact, so increased was her confidence, she decided she needn't ask Daniel why he had somehow changed in his attitude towards her sister, and was beginning to feel happier in herself. Until the next worry surfaced: Daniel was spending too long at work.

So long, in fact, that by the time he came home he appeared exhausted and only wanted something to eat, which he usually didn't finish, before going early to bed.

'Goodnight, Lorne,' he would say very formally, still not looking at her before retiring to bed, leaving Lorne one evening to exchange glances with Rosa and ask if she thought Daniel was all right. Perhaps he was overdoing things? Needed a tonic from the doctor? Like me, she added, lying back in her chair, while Rosa, for the first time in weeks, put Daniel from her mind and looked at her sister.

Why, she's thinner than ever, she thought. There's nothing to her; she could be blown away on a puff of wind. Why haven't I noticed how she's begun to look? Because I've been thinking of Daniel, only Daniel. But here was Lorne looking so thin she could only be unwell.

Overcome by remorse, Rosa asked at once how Lorne was feeling. She'd lost weight, she didn't look well, had she thought of going to see the doctor?

'Good Lord, no!' Lorne replied. 'I don't need any doctor. I've been thin for years – it's natural for me. Nothing to worry about.'

'I don't agree, Lorne. At least see Doctor Napier for a check, just to make sure. He's very kind, very sympathetic.'

'Maybe, but should I see him if I feel all right? What's wrong with being thin?'

Rosa, unwilling to say she'd been reminded of their mother's loss of weight in her last illness, shrugged and said all she wanted was for Lorne to see the doctor for a check. It would be worth his fee if he could set their minds at rest. Why shouldn't Rosa go with Lorne to his surgery the following evening? Get it over with, eh?

'Anything to have you give up nagging,' Lorne said, adding that she felt a bit tired, she'd be away to her bed.

'And tomorrow we'll see the doctor, eh?'

'I've agreed, Rosa; what more can I do?'

Alone, Rosa felt no easier in her mind over Lorne's health, even though there was the prospect of her seeing the doctor. In fact, looking back on what Rosa now saw as her neglect of her sister, she again felt guilty and vowed to do better. It was true, perhaps, that Lorne, because of her past behaviour, didn't qualify for such attention, but in Rosa's view, her sister was her sister and, whatever she'd done, now that she needed attention, she should have it. As for Daniel, Rosa had only just begun to think of him when the door opened and he appeared, a coat over his nightshirt, his face pale, his eyes on Rosa red as though he needed sleep but could not get any.

'Aren't you coming to bed?' he asked. I thought I heard Lorne go some time ago.'

'I'm just coming, Daniel, but I thought you'd be long asleep.'

'I can't sleep, wish to God I could. But Lorne's gone to bed, has she?'

'Yes, you heard her, you said. But she's not well, Daniel. I'm taking her to the doctor's tomorrow.'

'Not well?' Daniel's eyes sharpened. 'She always says she's just thin. And she's right, isn't she? Being thin doesn't mean she's ill.'

'She reminds me of my mother,' Rosa said, after a pause. 'The way she looks now.'

'Your mother? No, Rosa, don't say that! Your mother – that was consumption, wasn't it? Lorne hasn't got that. It's like she says, it's just that she's thin.'

For some moments, the husband and wife exchanged looks, both hard to read, then Rosa said quietly, 'We'd better get to bed, Daniel. You'll have to try to get some sleep, with work tomorrow.'

'If you're with me, it'll be all right, Rosa. Things are always all right when you're there.'

Her dark eyes now sorrowful, she shook her head. 'Wish that could be true.'

Slowly, finally, they put out the gaslight and made their way to their bed, where Daniel at last fell asleep and Rosa lay awake for she didn't know how long, her eyes staring into the darkness but seeing only faces – Daniel's and Lorne's.

Forty-Seven

When Daniel returned from work the following day, Rosa and Lorne were already back from Dr Napier's surgery. Everything appeared normal, with Rosa preparing the evening meal and Lorne glancing through the evening paper, but Daniel, expert in sensing undercurrents, knew at once that the news from the doctor had not been good.

Both Rosa and Lorne were keeping their faces blank but, when Daniel asked how things had gone, Lorne only shook her head irritably, while Rosa's face, bent over a pan of potatoes, almost crumpled and she had to fumble for a handkerchief to wipe her eyes.

'Oh, don't take on, Rosa!' Lorne cried while Daniel sprang to Rosa's side. 'We don't have to believe that doctor! He might be nice, but does he know what he's talking about? I don't think so! I mean, he says I've got what my mother had and I haven't even got a cough!'

'He did say he'd send you to the infirmary,' Rosa said, sniffing. 'To make sure, he said.'

'Well, maybe we should wait till I've been there before you start getting upset. Even if I *do* have what Ma had, it doesn't mean I'll . . .' she faltered a little before finishing, '. . . go like her. I feel well. I really am all right.'

'You don't look it!' Rosa cried. 'As thin as a rail. Is it any wonder I'm worried?'

Daniel, whose face was now as expressionless as a mask, turned aside to pick up Lorne's discarded evening paper. 'Perhaps Lorne's right,' he said carefully, opening out the paper. 'We should wait to see what the infirmary says before we do anything else. Did you get an appointment?'

'They'll be sending one,' Lorne answered stiffly, moving nearer to Rosa, who had taken up a fork and was prodding the vegetables cooking on the stove. 'I'll set the table, shall I?'

'Thanks, that would be a help,' said Rosa. Adding, though she didn't believe it, 'I'm sure we could all do with something to eat.'

* * *

It was only after the meal was over, the washing up done and Lorne was using Rosa's sewing machine in her bedroom that Rosa was able to go into Daniel's arms for comfort.

'It's no use not facing facts,' she murmured. 'Cough or nor cough, Doctor Napier is pretty sure Lorne has consumption and so am I. I remember Ma too well.'

'Let's wait to see what the hospital says,' Daniel said, releasing Rosa and moving to his chair. 'There has to be hope.'

Wiping her eyes, she looked across at him and at the desolate expression he could not hide, and felt not just her old fear that his old love for Lorne would return but a certainty that it had. In a way, she felt almost sorry for him – he had done his best not to give in to the return of his love for Lorne and did not want to hurt her, Rosa, so would never speak, never spell anything out. There was, after all, nothing to be done to change things for him. He was a married man. He could never marry Lorne, for divorce wasn't an option for people like them – and maybe she wouldn't want to marry him anyway. She hadn't wanted to before.

Poor, poor Daniel. Not only was he suffering from a love he couldn't reveal, there was now the new anxiety that Lorne herself was mortally ill.

Mortally? The word that had come into Rosa's mind struck like an arrow, and for a moment she wavered under it. For if she was sorry for Daniel, she must be even more sorry for her sister, staring into the abyss.

I must be strong, thought Rosa. I must try to find the hope Daniel talked about. After all, some folk lived quite long lives with consumption. Why not Lorne? Yes, why not? No way would Rosa admit that, for Lorne, the diagnosis of her illness might have already come too late.

Forty-Eight

When the doctors at the Royal Infirmary confirmed Lorne's consumption – respiratory tuberculosis as they called it, which meant TB of the lungs – she took it very badly. Not surprising, of course, yet she'd been so stoical about all other bad news recently that when she reacted with anger over what she saw as the unfairness of it all, Rosa was deeply affected. Until the infirmary's diagnosis, Lorne had seemed confident that she wouldn't go the same way as her mother, but when the doctors told her she would have to give up her job and accept a place in a local sanatorium, she wept angry tears and said at first she wouldn't go.

'No fear!' she cried to Rosa and Daniel the evening after she'd been told what she must do. 'I'm not going to lie in bed and be ordered about by some bossy nurses. Never! I'm going to stay right here and take the medicine they give me and pull through on my own. It's my life, my illness, I'll do what I want to do and that's that!'

'Oh, Lorne, you know it's no good talking like that.' Rosa sighed. 'Your best hope is the sanatorium. Folk do get better there, the doctors told us, so just go along with it.'

'Rosa's right,' Daniel said, looking away as usual, after which Lorne stared at him, though she must by then have realized that he would not look at her. 'You have to do what the doctors say to have any hope of cracking this thing, Lorne.'

'That's what my mother thought, and look where it got her! And I don't care what anyone says, I'm not as bad as Ma. Think of the cough she had! Well, you wouldn't know, Daniel, but Rosa does. You remember it, eh? I haven't even got a cough, have I?'

'You'll still do better with the special care at the sanatorium,' Rosa said wearily. 'You can't stay here – it's a risk for other people. I don't mean Daniel and me, we're not worried, but, well, there are others to think about, aren't there?'

After a long, mutinous stare, Lorne bent her head and gave a hopeless sigh. 'I think I'll have an early night,' she said, rising. 'Get out of your way.'

'Oh, don't talk like that, Lorne!' Rosa cried and ran to put her arm round her sister. 'All we want is for you to get better – we don't care about anything else. I wish I could look after you here but if I can't, Daniel and me will visit you as often as they'll let us. We'll be with you all the way, I promise, Lorne!'

'I know, I know,' Lorne said quietly. 'I know I'm lucky to have you – both of you. Don't think I'm not grateful—'

'Don't be talking about being grateful – we're family, Lorne. Families stick together when there's any trouble, eh?' Rosa hesitated for a moment. 'Which reminds me – shouldn't we get in touch with Da? He could come down to see you.'

'Leave it till I go to this sanatorium place. But tell him, if he does come, not to bring Mrs MacRitchie. I'm not having her fussing around me like some old hen, and that's for definite!'

'Never mind her now. Come on, I'll give you a hand to bed—'

'As though I need it!' Lorne cried, before politely saying goodnight to Daniel. When, for once, he fixed his fine gaze on her face and pressed her hand.

'Goodnight, Lorne. It'll be all right, I'm sure of it. They've caught it in time. You're not going to go like your ma.'

Silently, she again stared at him, her lip trembling, then she smiled and said, 'Thank you, Daniel. It cheers me up, what you say, because I know it's true.'

He nodded and stepped back as she turned away and followed Rosa to her room for the early night she wished she needn't have.

'You've talked of hope,' Rosa murmured to Daniel when she'd left Lorne. 'Do you think there is any?'

He didn't answer for some time, only sat in his chair, his face turned away, finally saying he thought there might be. It was true what he'd said – Lorne need not go like her mother. The doctors could have caught the disease in time.

'She certainly hasn't got a cough like Ma's,' Rosa said, sitting down to take up some mending. 'Hasn't got one at all, has she?'

It was only later, when Rosa and Daniel were preparing to go to bed themselves, that they discovered Rosa's words were no longer true. For the first time and as clear as though it was with them in the same room, they heard Lorne begin to cough. Over and over, over and over, as Rosa stood transfixed, knowing she must run to her, take her something . . .

'Like Ma's,' she whispered. 'Oh, Daniel, it's just like Ma's.'

'No, no, Lorne isn't like your mother. Hang on to that, Rosa, hang on.'

For how long? wondered Rosa, hurrying with cough mixture, finding strength to be with her sister, knowing she would always find it. Somehow.

Forty-Nine

So absorbed was Rosa in her sister's problems, she would never have believed there could be anything else occupying her mind – until, quite by chance, she saw Jack Durno again. He was just ahead of her, walking down George Street, and at first, because she hadn't seen him for a while, she wasn't even sure that the casually dressed man looking in a bookshop window was Jack himself. But then he turned his head, his eyes met hers and a great smile lit his tanned face as he swept off his hat and took her hands in his.

'Rosa! I never thought to see you since I got back, though you can guess it's wonderful – I mean, for me – to meet you like this, with no planning, no expectation! Just what I'd have asked for – if there'd been anyone to ask – that we might just bump into each other and be quite blameless, and that nobody need be upset – but, oh, God, I'm rambling, eh? So taken aback to see you, you see, and to know you're not immediately running away—'

'Back from where?' Rosa asked faintly, pulling her hands from his and searching his face, which seemed to her thinner, yet with its bronzed look, particularly attractive.

'I've moved there – the south of France, I mean. I'm only back to see an agent about letting the house while I'm away. Up to now, I haven't bothered about it, but my mother's right, it will deteriorate, not being lived in. Never mind me, though – what's the news with you? Tell me, are you still doing your artwork, as you did when you were with me?'

'Not just now. Maybe some time in the future.'

'I hope you mean that, Rosa. You have real talent, remember. Don't just let it go.'

When she only smiled and shrugged, he bent his head, looking long and seriously into her face. 'You're as lovely as ever,' he told her in a low voice. 'I haven't forgotten. But there's something wrong, isn't there? Are things not good for you, Rosa? Can you tell me about it?'

Looking up the wide street and seizing Rosa's hand again, he said they must have a cup of coffee at the George Hotel – it was just up the street, wouldn't take a minute.

'Mr Durno – Jack – you know I can't have coffee with you. I'm glad to have seen you but I can't spend time with you. I'm sorry, but that's the way it is.'

He was silent as the wind blew around them, finally saying he understood very well that she couldn't spend time with him and the last thing he wanted was to make any trouble for her. He just wished she could tell him what was worrying her, but if it was something private, he would not try to intrude.

'It's not private; it's my sister, Jack. You remember, the one who was in America? Things didn't go right for her over there and she came back to be with us, but now' – Rosa's voice shook a little – 'now she's been told she has consumption. TB, the doctors call it – and we don't know . . . we can't know . . . how long she's got.'

'Oh, God, Rosa, that's terrible!' Jack shook his head. 'For her, and you – for all of you. What can I say? I wish I could say something . . . do something . . .'

'No one can do anything. We're in the hands of the doctors.'

'Well, they're good, Rosa. Very good. And there's always hope—'

'So Daniel says. All cases are different. Lorne might live quite a long time yet.'

'That's true.' Jack looked down the long street, then again at Rosa. 'If you have to go now, may I walk a bit of the way with you?'

'Better not. I think I must hurry.' She quickly touched his hand and gave him a last smile. 'I was glad to see you, Jack, to know you were all right and doing well – painting away in the south of France, it sounds ideal.'

'Not altogether,' he said quietly. 'But I'm grateful for having seen you again. I'll be thinking of you – and your sister. I suppose you couldn't keep in touch, could you?'

'No, it's not possible. But it's good to see you – I mean that, Jack, and I'll wish you all the best for the future.'

'Of course, I'll wish you the same.' Jack touched his hat and tried to smile, but the smile did not reach his eyes. 'I suppose we have to say goodbye now?'

'Nice to have met, though.' She slipped off her glove and put out her hand. 'Goodbye, Jack.'

He took and held her hand until she removed it, his eyes on her face, taking his time before he too said goodbye.

She left him then, walking quickly away down George Street, battling the wind as he remained where he was, watching her slender

figure in a navy blue jacket and ankle-length skirt until he could
see her no more.

Would she tell her husband about their encounter? He was pretty
sure she would. And she did.

'Daniel, I met Jack Durno in George Street today,' she announced
almost as soon as Daniel had set foot in their door after work. 'Quite
by chance, but I had to speak to him, you know, to be polite.'

'Had you?' Daniel, looking pale, had sunk into his chair and was
lighting a cigarette. He seemed not to be too interested in her news.
'I was hoping he'd moved on somewhere.'

'He has, really. He works in the south of France now, was only
home to see about letting his house.'

'That's a relief.' Daniel gave Rosa a long, weary stare. 'So, what
did you talk about – when you were being polite?'

Rosa hesitated. 'Lorne, as a matter of fact. He said I seemed to
have something on my mind and I told him about Lorne's illness.
He was . . . very sympathetic.'

'As though he could understand! He has no idea, no idea at all,
of other people's troubles. When's he ever had to suffer?'

Rosa, at the stove, moving the kettle to bring it to the boil, was
shaking her head.

'Let's not talk about him any more, Daniel. He belongs to the
past and we have other things to think about now.'

He stared at her, his eyes showing the pain he could no longer
hide. 'We have,' he answered. 'Oh, Rosa, we have.'

He stubbed out his cigarette and rose to take her in his arms,
holding her close against his chest, but if he thought he was comforting
her, she knew he was in fact searching for comfort for himself. And
that the time he might find it was so far away, it couldn't yet be
thought of.

Fifty

Within a short time of Lorne's diagnosis, she was given a bed in a sanatorium some miles out of Edinburgh, where she claimed that all she'd dreaded about being in hospital with a boring regime and strict nurses had come true, and all she wanted to do was to go home again.

'You know you can't do that, Lorne,' Rosa told her earnestly on one of her afternoon visits without Daniel. 'You have to stay here; this is where you will get better.'

'I'm sure I don't know how,' Lorne snapped. 'All I do is lie in this bed while the doctors talk about collapsing my lung and I don't know what, and the nurses bang about, making as much noise as possible. Some people stay in these places for years, you know, but how they stick it, I don't know.'

'Lorne, you're being very unfair. All the nurses are very patient and kind – and doing a very difficult job, you have to admit. Just try to accept things – it's the only way.'

Lorne, still unsmiling, lay back against a pillow, trying to conceal a cough while Rosa, studying her, felt her spirits plummeting as they always did when visiting her sister. Even in the short time she'd been in the sanatorium, Lorne seemed to have changed, to have wasted away a little more, her face, now so very narrow, seeming to be just prominent cheekbones and huge eyes still sharp when she gazed around the ward at the patients lying still, the nurses hurrying, always hurrying, and one of the cleaners sweeping up something spilled on the floor. Finally, she brought her eyes back to Rosa and managed something of a smile.

'Sorry, Rosa, I know I shouldn't go on – they're doing their best in here. It's just that it's all so . . . unfair! Why should this happen to me? I've always been healthy; I've never done anything to deserve being struck down.'

'Lorne, you're going to get better!' Rosa said urgently, holding one of Lorne's frail hands. 'That's why you're in here – Ma never went anywhere, never had much treatment, but you're going to be all right, I'm sure of it!'

Lorne gave a tired smile. 'You know what the best thing here is for me? It's you and Daniel coming to see me. I know it isn't easy, you've to take two buses, but it makes all the difference, I can tell you.'

'We'll always come to see you, Lorne, and I've a piece of good news to tell you as well. Da's coming down next week. I got his letter today!'

'Da's coming all the way from home to see me?' Lorne's eyes were wide. 'And on his own? No Mrs MacRitchie?'

'No Mrs MacRitchie.'

'That's grand, then. You know how Da sometimes got on our nerves, going on about what he could do? Well, now I just want to see him!'

But Lorne was tiring, her colour had faded and as the bell went for visitors to leave the ward, it seemed clear she very much needed her rest. Leaning forward, Rosa whispered that Daniel would be coming with her the next day, but for now, she'd just say goodbye. She could not, of course, kiss Lorne's cheek, but pressed her hand again.

'Have a good rest, Lorne – we'll see you tomorrow.'

'Tomorrow,' Lorne murmured, not opening her eyes and, after a moment, Rosa moved quietly away.

'Oh, Mrs MacNeil,' the ward sister called to her as she reached the door. 'May I ask – are you coming in tomorrow to see your sister?'

'Yes, probably with my husband. Did you want to speak to us?'

Rosa was looking anxious, but the sister only gave a brief smile and said that one of the doctors would like to have a quick word. Would Rosa let her, the sister, know when she arrived tomorrow?

'Oh, yes,' said Rosa. 'Of course.'

And then, at last she was leaving the sanatorium and making for the bus stop which was conveniently outside the gates, her spirits lower than usual. Why did the doctor wish to speak to her and Daniel? Was it just routine? Or not? All the way home, Rosa kept thinking about what he might say, and when Daniel came home, immediately began to discuss what it might be. Which, as he said, was a waste of time.

'We'll just have to wait till tomorrow,' he told Rosa. 'Thank goodness it's Saturday and I can be with you.' He hesitated. 'But how was Lorne, then? Any improvement?'

'No, and I don't think there will be.' Rosa shook her head. 'Not until they've given her treatment. Collapsing one of her lungs, or whatever it might be.'

They were silent then, until Rosa began preparing their tea and Daniel, lighting a cigarette, took up the evening paper. Whether or not he read it, Rosa, preparing the fish they were to have, could not be sure.

Fifty-One

It appeared that the doctor who wished to speak to Lorne's relatives was Dr MacKail – a tall, dark-haired young man Rosa had first met on Lorne's admission, serious and caring in his manner and someone Lorne herself had not afterwards actually criticized. If they had to have a talk from a doctor, both Rosa and Daniel were relieved he should be the one, for from him they'd get something they could understand, which they could only hope wasn't bad news. When he called them into a small private room off the ward, they each searched his face, hoping though failing to read what he might say, but in any case he didn't keep them waiting.

'Mr and Mrs MacNeil, it's good to see you.' He gave them a brief smile. 'As you may know, we like to keep relatives up to date with the progress of patients, and I believe you are closest to Miss Malcolm?'

'Yes, well, because our father's in the Highlands,' Rosa explained. 'But I've just heard that he is coming to see my sister very soon.'

'I didn't know that but I look forward to meeting him.' Dr MacKail hesitated for a few moments, rolling a pencil in his fingers. 'I must tell you both, though – and eventually your father – that Miss Malcolm's case is presenting some problems.'

'Problems?' Daniel repeated curtly. 'What sort of problems?'

'Well, the fact is, she has come to us a little late. Her illness is so far advanced, there is no question now of an operation. It is no one's fault. Possibly because she didn't develop a serious cough as is usual, she didn't think to go to her doctor earlier—'

'She never wanted to go!' Rosa cried. 'So I'm to blame. I knew she should go, she was so thin. But I gave in, I should have made her, been more firm—'

'No, no,' the doctor said quickly. 'No one is to blame. You mustn't feel guilty, Mrs MacNeil – you did everything you could, I'm sure of that. The question now is how much can we do for your sister?'

'How much?' asked Daniel. 'What do you mean, how much? Even if Lorne can't have an operation, there are things you can do, aren't there? Medicine, pills . . .'

'Of course, I can assure you we'll do all we can for Miss Malcolm,'

Dr MacKail said gravely. 'My seeing you today was to make that clear. But you must . . . prepare yourselves . . . that it may not be enough.'

After these words a silence fell, when the eyes of Rosa and Daniel met once then moved away. It was only when the doctor rose to his feet that they too struggled up from their chairs and stared about the room as though they were waking from a troubled dream. For a long moment, he waited, giving them time to be ready to hear him continue.

'You know now what I wanted to tell you,' he said quietly, 'though I don't wish to alarm you. We must see how your sister progresses, and it may be that she will do better than we hope, but it's best in the circumstances that you are, as I say, prepared . . . for what may happen.'

'The worst?' asked Daniel, his voice very low.

'That she . . . may not win her fight.'

Another silence fell in the little room while Rosa and Daniel gazed at the doctor, who eventually asked if they would like to stay where they were before visiting their sister. But Rosa shook her head.

'It's very kind of you, Doctor, but I'd like to see my sister now. Thank you for telling us . . . what we had to know.'

'Yes, thank you,' Daniel muttered, turning to the door. 'We appreciate . . .' His voice trailed off and he too shook his head, as though he could find no further words, opened the door and dazedly passed through.

'He's . . . very upset,' Rosa told Dr MacKail. 'He's known Lorne a long time.'

'And you've been very brave, Mrs MacNeil. But before you visit your sister, would you like to take a little time to think over what I've said? Maybe go to the canteen? Have some tea?'

'No, I don't think so,' Rosa answered. 'Lorne will be waiting for me, wondering what has been said—'

'You won't . . .? No, I needn't ask that.'

'I won't tell her anything.' Rosa put out her hand and, as the doctor shook it, she murmured her thanks again.

'Any time you need to speak to someone, don't hesitate,' he told her, opening the door for her. 'Remember, we're here to help relatives as well as patients.'

'I'll remember, and thank you.'

★　★　★

Out in the ward, she looked for Daniel but could see no sign of him and, taking a deep breath, she progressed towards Lorne's bed, the magazine and the fruit she'd brought now at the ready, a smile brightening her face.

'Lorne, how are you? I think you're looking a little better today.'

Fifty-Two

George the Fifth, the king who had come to the throne in 1910, was eventually crowned on a June day in 1911 to great rejoicing throughout his kingdom. Except for us, thought Rosa, for it was on the king's special day that Lorne had finally slipped away. There had been no fuss, no relatives at the bedside, for she had died in the small hours, very peacefully, without pain, and by the time Rosa and Daniel had arrived, looked like the young girl she had once been, which seemed to them to make it all the harder to say goodbye.

Somehow, they made the arrangements, or at least Rosa did, for Daniel didn't seem to want to be a part of any of it, leaving the sanatorium very soon afterwards 'to walk somewhere', he told Rosa, and was not seen again until the evening.

'You might have helped me,' she felt driven to say to him when he finally returned home. 'You know there are formalities that have to be done, and we've got the special arrangements to make for . . . my poor Lorne.' The tears came afresh as she said her sister's name, but she kept talking as best she could. 'I mean, for what Da and me want, taking her home.'

'Taking her home,' Daniel said softly. 'Yes, it's a good that she'll be going back to Carron. I'm glad we discussed that when your da was here. I know it's expensive, what we're doing, but it's what she wanted, isn't it? She'd never have wanted to be' – his voice trembled – 'buried here.'

How terrible it is that he can't admit how he really feels, Rosa thought, the pain of her own grief being made worse by her recognizing his, as well as knowing how he was trying to conceal his love for her sister. He'd never admitted it, never would. All there could be was secrecy, which he seemed to think would be best for Rosa and perhaps was. But it didn't stop her pain.

Some days later, it was all arranged. Using every penny of his savings, Daniel had paid for the last trip home for poor Lorne, her coffin being transported by the same train on which her sister and brother-in-law would travel to Carron themselves. Very soon afterwards, the local funeral Greg had organized would take place and Lorne would be laid to rest next her mother in the little Carron churchyard. All that remained then would be for Rosa and Daniel and everyone to take up their ordinary lives again, though how that was going to happen, Rosa still couldn't imagine. Ordinary, normal lives didn't seem possible for her or Daniel at that time. Would things ever be ordinary and normal for them again?

On the long journey home, very conscious of her sister being carried somewhere else on the train, Rosa's thoughts went again and again to Lorne herself. Her sister, her little sister, had gone, and whatever she had done had been put aside, for she would do no more; her short life was over.

There was no doubt that Lorne had been no saint, had never wanted to be, and that what her father had once said of her, that she only thought of herself, was certainly true. Yet she had been Rosa's sister – her only one – and already Rosa was missing her. Missing those shared memories, those good times they'd had, gossiping, laughing . . .

Was she seeing Lorne through rose-tinted glasses? Probably, for think how badly she had behaved towards Daniel! How she had coolly cast him aside for someone she thought better, leaving him with a broken heart. Rosa had never thought she could forgive her sister for what she'd done then, but somehow – when she'd turned up again from America – she'd seemed different. As though she had learned her lesson, had suffered and had come through, and was not quite the Lorne she'd been before.

Clearly, Daniel had forgiven her, and Rosa knew she had too. Would give – oh, what would she give – to see Lorne's green eyes lighting up her face again? To see her dressmaking, cutting out material, smiling with a mouthful of pins? To go with her to their mother's grave, to lay spring flowers or to exchange smiles with Rosa when Da went on about all that he could do.

'Oh, Lorne,' Rosa murmured, leaning her head back in the railway carriage, fighting back her tears, for there were strangers around.

'Like a cup of tea?' asked Daniel. 'We could go along to the refreshment car?'

His face was as stricken as ever, but his simple request warmed Rosa's heart, and when she rose and went with him in search of the refreshment car she felt, for the first time since Lorne's death, just a little better.

Fifty-Three

The day before the funeral, Rosa was standing alone, in her black dress and coat, looking out over the Moray Firth, as she so often used to do before she left the Highlands. Gazing out over the vast expanse of water, she felt again something of the calmness the view had brought to her in the old days, when she had had no need to think of Lorne and knew things could never be the same as that again. Would never be the same, even though the views were unchanged, for now the remembrance of her sister brought bitter-sweet emotions to the one who was left, and for a while the waters before her blurred as though with rain, when no rain was falling.

She turned aside and walked a little way, wishing Daniel would have wanted to be with her, but he had gone to see his mother and she hadn't really wanted anyone else at her side. Not even Da, who was looking so forlorn, and certainly not Mrs MacRitchie – Joan, as she kept reminding Rosa to call her. Anyway, she was far too busy, making refreshments for folk to have after the ceremony, for which Rosa was truly grateful, and felt a little guilty for not helping. Perhaps she should go back now? Show willing? She turned back to go to Joan's cottage when a man came hurrying towards her, his smile uncertain but his looks known to her. This was, of all people, Rory Thain, who should be in America. What was he doing back at Carron, this tall, handsome son of Bluff House, so clearly wanting to speak to her?

And why should she speak to him after the way he had treated Lorne?

'It's Rosa, isn't it?' he asked, taking off his hat. 'Mrs MacNeil, I know, but Lorne talked of you so much, you are Rosa to me. May I speak to you for a moment?'

Her dark eyes met his grey gaze without flinching as she said clearly, 'I see no reason why you should want to speak to me, Mr Thain. My family has nothing to say to you.'

'Please, don't say that, Rosa. Let me explain – this trip from the States was made to see my family, I'll admit, but when I heard what had happened to Lorne, I couldn't believe it. It hit me like a blow, yet I thanked God I was here so that I could pay my last respects. That's what I wanted to speak to you about – to ask if you'd have any objection to my attending the funeral.' He hesitated, swallowing hard. 'I loved her so much,' he said in a low voice. 'I don't know how she put it to you, but she was the love of my life, she really was, it was just that—'

'Just that she wasn't suitable to marry?' Rosa asked coldly. 'Now that you are engaged to someone else, are you really thinking we'd want to see you at my sister's funeral? Please don't come, Mr Thain – you won't be welcome. And I'm sure your family will be relieved. If you'll excuse me, please?'

Moving quickly past him, Rosa took pleasure in not looking at him again and, as he made no move to stop her, kept walking at speed until she was at her father's cottage. As for Rory Thain, she had no idea what he did. All she knew was that she hoped she would never again see the man who had made her sister so unhappy. True, it might be said that Lorne was only discovering how others felt when discarded, but it had been a hard lesson and, now that she was gone, Rosa wished she had never had to learn it.

Thank heavens, anyway, that Rory Thain had asked if he might come to the funeral, not just turned up for it. At least they had been spared the sight of him arriving for it out of the blue . . .

'Rosa, there you are!' her father cried as she let herself into the cottage and took off her hat and jacket. 'Joan wants us to go to her place for our tea. Now all we need is Daniel. Any idea when he'll turn up?'

'No idea at all, Da,' Rosa told him, noticing again that her poor father was looking handsome still, yet years older than before he'd lost Lorne. He might have liked to criticize her, but she was his daughter and, like Rosa, beloved. Now he was loaded down with grief again, for even when she had been in America, so far away, she was all right, she was alive – one day he could see her again. That was the thing about death: there never any seeing again, whatever the spiritualists said.

'Come on, Da, let's go next door. Joan will be waiting for us,' Rosa said, trying to sound brisk. 'We needn't wait for Daniel. His mother will be keeping him.'

As Rosa scribbled a note for Daniel to tell him they would be next door, Greg said thoughtfully, 'Taken it badly, hasn't he? I mean,

Lorne's death. She was always special to him, our Lorne, in spite of what she did.'

'Always,' Rosa answered, putting her note with the clock. 'But we don't talk about what she did, Da. There's no point. It's all over now.'

'For her; maybe not for Daniel.' Greg's look on Rosa was sombre. 'You told me once things were fine between you.'

'They were – they are.'

'And Lorne's coming back, that was all right with you?'

'Da, don't be worrying.' Rosa firmly took his arm. 'Let's go to Joan's, eh? And just remember, everything's fine between me and Daniel.'

'If you say so,' said Greg.

Fifty-Four

'Grand refreshments,' folk were commenting after Lorne's funeral. 'Thanks to Joan MacRitchie – still hoping to get wed to Greg one o' these days, eh?'

But a good crowd anyway to see Lorne off. For Greg's sake – or maybe Martha's, Lorne being Martha's daughter, though there weren't a lot who liked her. So pleased with herself, she always seemed, just because the men were always round her like flies, but look what she did to Daniel MacNeil! Chucked him over for Mr Rory, the silly lassie! Now wouldn't she have been better off with Daniel? But he had had the sense to marry Rosa, such a lovely girl. Pity there were no children, eh?

So the talk went on, while Rosa and Daniel helped Joan to pass around the sandwiches and sausage rolls, the sponge cakes and shortbread, while Greg moved through the mourners talking of everything but the deceased now laid to rest, as was the way at funerals.

When will it all end? Rosa thought, her eyes often seeking Daniel, who was so pale but doing his best to circulate, while his mother gave grudging praise to Joan's refreshments. Did any of these people care tuppence for Lorne? Would her passing make the slightest difference to anyone? Only to her da and her sister – and Daniel, of course, but Rosa moved her thoughts on from Daniel.

Until in passing he touched her arm and whispered, 'Courage, they will go. Eventually.'

'And then I must pack. Seeing as we have to leave first thing tomorrow.'

'I shan't be sorry to get back.'

She noticed he didn't say 'home', but what did either of them think of as home? And how would it be, returning to the flat where they would never again see Lorne? As a small, dull pain tightened in Rosa's chest, she was still able to heave a sigh of relief, for people were beginning to come up to shake hands, to thank Greg and Joan, Rosa and Daniel, to show sympathy again. Soon Lorne's family would be alone, and already Joan was worrying about their tea. As though they needed anything!

'Well, you must take some of this stuff back with you,' she told them when Rosa and Daniel said they couldn't eat any more. 'I'll make a picnic for you, eh? It's a long way you're going, remember.'

'You'll come down and see us again, Da?' Rosa asked him the next morning when they were waiting to leave. 'You know you're always welcome.'

'Aye, we'll see you in Auld Reekie,' he said, smiling strangely. 'Might have some news for you then, and all.'

'What sort of news?'

'That'd be telling.'

'Well, tell then!'

'There's no details fixed.' Greg looked around at Joan, who was packing up what seemed a huge amount of food for the train journey, then turned back to Rosa. 'But the thing is – well, you must have wondered when it was coming, eh?'

'When what was coming?' cried Rosa, guessing anyway, at which Greg smiled and called Joan over.

'I'm just going to tell 'em, Joan. Didn't want to come out with it before, with the funeral and everything.'

'Oh, get on with it!' laughed Joan, red spots appearing on her cheekbones. 'We're engaged, that's the thing. If it does not sound too silly for folk of our age—'

'Engaged?' cried Rosa, smiling. 'Daniel, do you hear the news? Da and Joan are engaged.'

'Congratulations!' he said, producing a smile. 'That's grand news. When will the wedding be?'

'Oh, not for a while.' Joan hesitated. 'We want to wait a bit, you know, after poor Lorne's passing. After all, we're in mourning. But by the time we see you again I think we will be wed.'

'Taxi!' cried Daniel, hearing the rap at the door. 'We must go. But we couldn't be more pleased, could we, Rosa?'

'Couldn't,' agreed Rosa, remembering how she and Lorne had rather dreaded the possibility of this engagement but knowing things were very different now. Very different, as everything was, really, without Lorne.

Fifty-Five

At least Daniel had managed to show polite interest in her father's news, Rosa thought as they embarked on the long train journey back to Edinburgh. Wrapped in thoughts of his own, Greg's engagement probably meant nothing to him, but he had concealed that well, for which Rosa, who knew how much he was grieving for her sister, was grateful. Was even glad, in a way, that now he was on the train with just herself, apart from strangers, he needn't try too hard to hide his feelings.

He might not realize, because of course, nothing had been said in so many words, that Rosa knew exactly what he was feeling and therefore he needn't struggle to hide it. But he would know, as Rosa knew, that for them to continue living together in their usual way, things should not be spelled out. The less things were made clear, the more quickly Daniel could get over a love that could never mean anything now. And come back to her, to Rosa.

So she argued to herself as the train went on its clickety-click way from the Highlands, though she knew that many women would not agree with her. They'd be all for having things out in the open, so that a husband and a wife knew where they were, but 'least said, soonest mended' was the motto Rosa was following. Once words had been said, they could hang for ever between people and could never be unsaid, which was why Rosa took no credit for herself in letting Daniel keep his feelings private. It was the best thing to do, for him, for her, for their future.

'Shall we start our picnic?' she whispered as other people in the compartment were opening out packets of sandwiches and sausage rolls and, after a shrug or two, Daniel said that though he wasn't hungry, they'd better have something to eat. It would be a long time till they got back to Edinburgh, and he'd also like to tell Rosa something he'd have told her earlier, had it not been for circumstances.

'Is it something important?' she asked anxiously.

'Sort of, but nothing to worry about. Let's pack the picnic stuff away and go into the corridor. Stretch our legs.'

The corridor was cold and draughty but empty of people, and as they clung on to the brass railing beneath the windows, swaying with the motion of the train and only briefly aware of the scenery as it flashed by, Daniel seemed to think it wasn't too noisy to talk.

'We could walk a little way, if you like,' he offered, and Rosa agreed that that might be better than letting their fellow passengers in the compartment watch them talking.

'But I wish you'd tell me your news, whatever it is,' she told him as they paced the corridor. 'I'm getting nervous.'

'It's good news, in a way. The thing is Mr Lang is doing well and opening up a new shop and workshop over in Fife – Kirkcaldy – and he wants me to manage it.'

'In Fife?' Rosa thought for a moment how this could affect their life in Edinburgh. 'You could travel there on the train, couldn't you? That wouldn't be too difficult.'

'I don't want to do that,' Daniel answered, his eyes looking past her down the corridor. 'I do long hours; I don't want a late journey home. It would be better for me to stay over in Fife during the week.' Still keeping his gaze away from Rosa, he quickly added, 'But I'd come home at weekends.'

'Weekends,' she repeated slowly. 'Just weekends? We've never been separated before, Daniel.'

'I know,' he answered, his tone uneasy. 'Things would be . . . a bit different from what we're used to.'

'Are you happy about that?'

'No, but you have to think of the good side, Rosa. There'd be more money coming in. We could save to buy a cottage or a house instead of a flat. And I'd have more responsibility. I'd be training people to do what I can do, as well as creating my furniture as before.' Finally, Daniel brought his blue gaze down to her. 'I really think these changes are going to be good for us, Rosa. In the long term, I mean.'

'With me on my own during every week?'

'You could take up your artwork again. You've always wanted do to that.'

'And you've never wanted me to, have you?'

'I've always been proud of your work, Rosa. It's true. I mean it. Anyway, I've told Mr Lang I'm happy to go along with his plans, and when you've thought about it, I'm sure you'll be happy about the changes too.'

And you'll be able to lead a different life where you never knew Lorne, thought Rosa as tears pricked her eyes and her lip began to tremble. But she decided she would say nothing. If this was Daniel's way of coping with a grief he could not name, so be it, she would go along with it, and maybe one day, when time had done its work, he would come back to her. For weekends or not, with the future he'd worked out he was not going to be with her as he'd always been before. Let him see how his new life suited, while she – oh, God, what would she do during the long weeks when he was over in Fife?

Her artwork? She couldn't think of it. Only that as well as losing her sister, somehow she had lost Daniel too.

'I'm going back to the compartment,' she told Daniel and, because she couldn't cry in front of the strangers in their compartment, had to bite her lips and find a hankie to wipe her eyes before she met their looks. Could they see she was holding back tears? It didn't matter if they did. They could see that she and Daniel were both in black, that they were in mourning, which was only true. But now it seemed to Rosa that they were mourning more than the loss of Lorne.

Part Three

Fifty-Six

Time went by. Days, weeks, months, which gradually became years, and by early 1914, what had been a new routine for Rosa and Daniel, bringing them together only at weekends, became the norm. What Daniel thought of it, Rosa never asked, but it was not something she herself could ever be happy about. Seeing each other as ships that passed in the night – how could that suit a husband and wife who had at one time never known separation? Not well, surely? But neither suggested returning to earlier ways. Somehow, they just accepted that things were different now. Mainly because of Lorne's coming into their lives again and then so tragically leaving, Rosa believed, but this was something she and Daniel never discussed.

After Daniel had first begun work in Fife back in 1911, Rosa, in need of sympathy, had told Molly Calder, and Molly's sympathy, as Rosa had known it would be, was generous.

'Och, pet, what a shame!' she cried when they were standing together on the stairs one morning. 'All this to be happening, eh, and just when you're grievin' for your puir sister! 'Tis terrible for you, Rosa, 'tis too much!'

'These things happen.' Rosa sighed, wearily leaning against the wall. 'I know Daniel's job must come first, we have to fit in with that, but I have to admit, it's all getting on top of me.'

'Aye, but you're too good at puttin' up with things, eh, Rosa? If twas me, I'd be creatin' such a fuss they'd hear me at the castle!' Molly laughed, then laid her hand on Rosa's arm. 'But listen, eh? If you iver want a bit o' sympathy, you'll come over tae me? Promise?'

'I'll be glad to, Molly.' They hugged hard before Rosa drew back and said she had to tackle Lorne's things, all that she'd left, waiting now for Rosa's decisions. Had to be done some time, deciding what to do with everything, but finding the will to do it – that was the problem.

''Tis hard, Rosa, very hard,' Molly said. 'I'd 'gie you a hond, but I ken fine you'll want tae sort your sister's stuff yourself. Come and have a cuppa when you're ready, eh?'

'I will, Molly, and thanks.'

*   *   *

Later, in what had been Lorne's room, surrounded by her posses-
sions, Rosa had begun well, sorting everything into those that were
to be given to folk in the tenement, or to charities, or to be kept
by Rosa herself.

That green jacket for instance, that Lorne had liked so much
because it brought out the colour of her eyes, Rosa would keep in
her wardrobe, away from upsetting Daniel. And the suit she'd worn
when she'd first come to the MacNeils' door, asking if she might
stay – oh, that must be kept, it brought her back so well!

But in the end it was all too much for Rosa, who suddenly
bundled everything away into cupboards, deciding she'd wait for
Joan, now married at last to Greg, who would be visiting Edinburgh
soon on a belated honeymoon. Yes, best to leave Lorne's things to
Joan and get on with something else. Always plenty to do, wasn't
there? And, like so many afternoons, Rosa's ended in tears.

Gradually, though, as the weeks went by, her grief for her sister
didn't hurt quite so much, and with the help of Joan, everything
was sorted out and life took on its new routine. Even Daniel
began to improve, to come back to normal. Still no words passed
on Lorne between him and Rosa, but Rosa didn't try to change
that. Better not, she had long ago decided.

That was in 1911. By early 1914, Rosa had not only sorted out
her new life, she had taken on new work, having met Bob Brewer,
Jack Durno's agent, who had persuaded her to take up her artwork
again and had sold many of her drawings of Edinburgh, and even
the few watercolours she had attempted, much to her satisfaction.

True, she still missed seeing Daniel, except at weekends, but you
could get used to anything, it was said, and Rosa had got used to
all the changes that had come her way. Had, in fact, prospered, as
her looks showed, and as Jack Durno told her when he saw her
again, quite by chance as usual, in the Royal Botanic Gardens where
she was sketching winter branches. And this time when he asked
her to go for coffee in the Botanics café, she did not say no.

Fifty-Seven

He was looking older, which was not surprising – he *was* older than when they'd last met, and so was Rosa, but she had not, she believed, changed. Hoped so, anyway. Perhaps she was wrong? Perhaps it was difficult for those looking in their mirrors to see what was really there rather than what they believed to be there? Perhaps, but Jack greeted Rosa with such effusion, exclaiming that she hadn't changed at all, that she felt relieved the days of strain and sorrow had not, it seemed, left their mark.

'I can't believe I'm seeing you!' Jack was exclaiming again, holding her hands until she let go of his. 'I can't believe you're here, in front of me. I thought when I came back that sometime, somehow, we'd meet again, but of course, as I couldn't get in touch with you, all I could hope for was a lucky chance meeting like this, and here we are then, you looking so lovely, so much the same, it's as though time has stood still—'

He shook his head wonderingly, perhaps at his own good fortune, while Rosa, quickly managing to get a word in herself, asked him when he'd come back and from where.

'From New York, only a couple of weeks ago. I had an exhibition there – very successful – but the way things were going here, I knew I had to come back. But look, we can't talk here. The café's just five minutes away – can you for once have coffee with me?'

'Oddly enough, for once I can,' Rosa said, smiling, feeling glad she'd taken the trouble to wear her best dark blue skirt and matching cape, though she'd thought she'd only be walking by herself. Never had she dreamed of meeting Jack Durno in the Botanic Gardens.

'That's wonderful,' he said in heartfelt tones, as though she'd said something important.

'This way, then. Let's see if we can find a table and have some good Scottish scones.' He laughed and Rosa saw again the laughter lines around the eyes that she remembered so well. 'Can't tell you how much I missed Scottish baking in the States. They've terrific things themselves – doughnuts and flapjacks and stuff, but nobody can make scones like the Scots!'

Oh, yes, thought Rosa, walking at his side to the café, Jack might be looking older but he had the same vitality about him, the same way of getting the best out of things. Except perhaps when in the past he'd tried to convince her of his love, but she wouldn't think of that now. Like so much, it was all in the past.

Settled into window seats in the café, they ordered coffee and the scones Jack so much admired, and while Rosa undid her cape and touched at her hair beneath her hat, Jack sat, leaning forward, his gaze always on her as he followed her every movement.

'I don't want to question anything about this meeting,' he said softly, 'but how is it you can be with me having coffee when you've never permitted it before? Has anything changed?'

'Nothing important, Jack. It's just that Daniel has to work in Fife during the week, so I'm not having to rush to shop for meals except at the weekend. I have just myself to think about.'

'But you'll tell him about this chance meeting?'

'Of course. I tell him everything.'

They were silent as their coffee arrived with a plate of scones and butter and jam. It was only when they were sipping their coffee that Jack ventured to ask how things were with Rosa.

'I heard from Bob that you had a bereavement some years ago. Your sister? I was very sorry to hear it.'

'Yes, that was Lorne,' Rosa answered, looking down at her plate. 'It was very hard, what happened to her. I mean, she was so young to go, just like my mother. Took me a while to get used to it and sometimes it all comes over me again, though I suppose we're used to losing her by now, Daniel and me.'

'Rosa, you have all my sympathy.' Jack seemed to be concentrating on his scone, until he looked up and said quietly that he too had lost someone. 'My mother, Rosa. You'll remember her?'

'Oh, yes, Jack, and I'm so sorry to hear she's gone. Was that recent?'

'Two years ago. Her heart gave out suddenly. She really wanted me to come back and live in the house again, and I suppose, if I get the chance, that's what I'll do.'

'How do you mean – get the chance?'

'Well.' Jack shrugged. 'A lot depends on what that crazy man does over in Germany. The talk is that he wants war.'

'You mean the Kaiser?' Rosa's eyes were large on Jack's face. 'You say he wants war? Why should that be?'

'It's the way he is; he's dying to have us all fighting and him winning. If, as most people think, war will eventually be declared, chaps will have to volunteer. I may be getting on—'

'Jack, don't be silly!'

'But I think the army will still take me. I'm fit enough, that's for sure—'

'Look, let's not talk of this any more.' Rosa, finishing her coffee, was thinking of Daniel. If this German Kaiser did start a war, would Daniel be volunteering?

'This has been lovely, Jack,' she said at last, 'but I must go now – I've a few things to do.'

'We could go to a gallery or something?' he asked, beckoning to their waitress to bring the bill. 'I mean, if there's no hurry for you to get back.'

'Thank you, Jack, but I really think I must go.' Rosa, rising and fastening on her cape, was certain now that she must leave him. Even having the coffee had been perhaps something she would find difficult to explain to Daniel. She'd better not risk spending any further time with Jack, innocent though that time was.

'I'll see you on your way,' a now-subdued Jack told her, having paid the bill. 'I do understand that you have to go. I've been lucky to have had time with you.'

'There's no need for you to come with me, Jack. I'll be getting the tram in Inverleith Row – that's out of your way.'

'I'm seeing you to your tram,' he said firmly. 'Don't deprive me of my last bit of time with you.'

Outside the Botanic Gardens, walking towards the tram stop, Rosa felt strangely vulnerable, as though exposed to the view of someone she knew who would see her with Jack, although there was no one around like that. And, of course, Jack, being so attuned to her feelings, knew that she was minding now being seen with him.

'It's all right,' he told her quietly, 'I'm pretty sure there's no one who knows you round here.'

'What if they do?' she asked lightly, pretending she wasn't worried. 'We're only walking to the tram stop.'

'And here it is,' he said sadly, standing with her in the small queue of people waiting. 'We haven't much time, Rosa, but I want to ask – I suppose there's no way we could meet again, is there?'

'No way.'

'Then I'll quickly ask: would you like me to do a portrait of Lorne for you?'

'A portrait of Lorne?' Her eyes were sparkling. 'Jack, that would be wonderful, oh – I'd love it!'

'I could do it from a photograph, if you could send one. Could you do that? Send one to the house?'

'Yes, oh, yes, I will!'

'Well, here's your tram.' Under the eyes of those at the stop, Jack, smiling as though he didn't mind her going, shook Rosa's hand and stepped back as she boarded the tram. When the tram moved off, he waved and so did she, after which he turned aside and slowly began to retrace his steps.

Fifty-Eight

As soon as Daniel came home the following weekend, Rosa prepared herself to tell him about her meeting with Jack.

'Pure chance,' she said, as Daniel, looking weary, sank into his chair. 'We met in the Botanic Gardens, right next to the café, so we just had a coffee and chatted a bit. He was looking older, said he'd been in New York, but now he was back. Thinking of volunteering if there was a war.'

Daniel stared, his blue eyes shadowed, his face very pale. He lit a cigarette.

'You met Jack Durno and "chatted" about a *war*?'

'He seemed to think the Kaiser would start one.'

'And that's what you talked about while you were having coffee?' Daniel shook his head. 'Hard to believe, when Jack Durno's in love with you?'

'That was a long time ago. I'm sure if it was ever true, it's not true now.'

'You think people can give up loving because time goes by?' Daniel's face showed such sudden pain, Rosa had to look away while he stubbed out his cigarette and sat staring into space.

'Can't help feeling sorry for your Jack,' he said, almost to himself. 'To love and not have your love returned – that's hard.'

'Let's not talk about him,' Rosa said desperately. 'Promise me that if there ever is a war, you won't volunteer to go to it, will you? I can't bear to think about it. Ordinary men never used to go to war; they left that to men already in the army, didn't they? The professionals.'

'There's talk now that if war comes, it will be different from any other war we've had before. There are airplanes now, there are bombs. Civilians will be involved.' Daniel rose. 'But let's leave talk of all that for now. I'll go and wash. Might freshen me up.'

'And I'll start tea,' said Rosa, watching Daniel depart with his small weekend case. She was thinking that he had taken the news of her meeting with Jack better than she'd expected. Not that he wasn't interested, she felt sure, but clearly it didn't worry him as it might once have done. Because he had something else to think about now? Another person, perhaps? A person now dead?

Jumping to her feet, Rosa decided she must stop her thoughts always turning to Lorne. Her sister was dead; she could not, surely, still be occupying Daniel's thoughts? Oh, but why not? She had never returned his love, which meant that it was of himself he'd been thinking when he'd said that to love and not have your love returned was hard. For me too, then, thought Rosa. And for Jack. As she finally made herself begin to prepare the evening meal, it occurred to her that the love that everyone wanted was far too often only the means of bringing heartache. She must put it out of her mind – at least for the time being.

Over the meal, she remembered to tell Daniel that Jack had offered to do a portrait of Lorne from a photograph, and hoped Daniel would be happy that she'd accepted.

'A portrait?' Just for a moment, Daniel allowed himself to look pleased. 'Well, why not? As long as it's not in his modern style.'

'It will be what we want, I'm sure. He knows our tastes. I'd like to have it, anyhow.'

'Me too.' Daniel suddenly laid his hand on Rosa's. 'It's good of Jack to offer it. We must give him that credit.'

'When I send him Lorne's photograph, I'll tell him you're happy about the portrait, then.'

'Yes, tell him that,' Daniel agreed.

Yet it seemed to Rosa, as she began to clear the table, that though Daniel said he was happy about the portrait, he could not be said to be happy about much else.

Can I not be of any comfort to him? Rosa asked herself. Does my love mean nothing now?

No, she didn't believe that. They'd been very happy, very content, before Lorne had come back into their lives. One day, things would be between her and Daniel as they'd used to be. She must just wait for that.

And so she imagined herself doing, as further time went by, but she had reckoned without the momentous events that came to a head in August of that year. An Austrian archduke had been assassinated by a Yugoslav national, causing Austria to declare war on Serbia and, in the chaos that followed, Germany invaded neutral Belgium, only to have Great Britain supporting Belgium and declare war on Germany herself.

At once, large numbers of young men began volunteering for army service, declaring that it might all be over by Christmas and they wanted to have a crack against Germany before that. And one of these volunteering young men, to Rosa's despair, was Daniel.

Fifty-Nine

She had taken so much, accepted so much, it might have seemed strange that this latest action by Daniel had been the last straw, but so it came about. No sooner had news come that his country was at war than he had hurried down to enlist and now was gone, away to the Black Watch regiment in which his grandfather had once served, and it was goodbye, Rosa – he would write when he could and she was not to worry. So came that last straw, leaving her not just eaten up by anxiety but also angry. Yes, anger that she couldn't remember feeling before. Now she was beginning to wonder if she would ever be at peace again.

For he hadn't needed to go – that was what she couldn't accept. Men were not being called up – though there was talk of that coming in the future. For now, it was left to them to decide if they wanted to go to war or not. So, Daniel need not have gone. If he had cared for Rosa as she cared for him, he would have stayed with her, wouldn't he? Other men were doing that.

Of course, though, she had to swallow her anger and forgive him, for she couldn't even be sure that he would return to her. Must see him off at the station where other men were parting from women who must stay behind and from which the train was about to depart, uncaringly bearing off loved ones while those left behind had to turn away.

'I'll get leave,' Daniel had said. 'I'm not going away for ever.'

'You don't know what you're going to,' Rosa had whispered into the handkerchief she'd pressed against her face, but Daniel had heard her and repeated that he would get leave. She'd see him again, no need to worry about that. They were meaningless words that did nothing to cheer her, but she'd tried to pretend she wasn't crying when Daniel had to kiss her and leave her. Then the guard had blown his whistle and the long train began its journey, oblivious of both cries from those left behind or smiles from the brave.

Rosa, who did not try to be one of the brave ones, just kept on waving with tears on her cheeks until she could no longer tell whether Daniel was waving too, for the train had gone too far – oh, much too far – was out of sight, in fact, which meant that there was nothing else to do but turn away and go home. Home. Home just for herself? Rosa couldn't bear to think about it, was still standing still on the platform with tears misting her eyes when she heard someone say her name. And it was Jack.

Brushing the tears from her eyes, she tried to focus on him, saw indeed that he was in uniform – nothing she recognized – and was smiling, beaming, at finding her, even though one look at her face must have told him how she was feeling.

Jack being Jack, of course knew at once that she'd been seeing Daniel off on the troop train and should be left alone with her sadness, yet couldn't resist being with her. Perhaps he could expect nothing from a meeting at such a time and should try to make nothing of it, but how could he do that when he'd been so lucky to find Rosa? When he could at least try to comfort her?

'You look exhausted,' he said softly. 'Come on, let me get you a cup of tea so you feel up to going home – I was just about to have one myself. God knows why I came so early – my train's not due out for some time – but I'm glad I did.'

'You're joining up?' she asked, letting him take her arm and feeling suddenly as exhausted as he said she looked. 'What regiment?'

'Artists' Rifles.' He smiled. 'Yes, it exists. Artists want to do their bit too.'

'Do their bit,' she repeated drearily. 'That's what it's called, is it? Throwing away their lives for nothing?'

'Come on, that's too hard! Anyway, this will all be over in no time. Chaps are just hoping they'll get a chance to see some action. But let's go and have tea.'

The tearoom was crowded but they were lucky to find a table a young couple were just leaving and Jack, as usual, turned on his magic and found a waitress to bring them tea and cake.

'I'm not at all hungry,' said Rosa, wiping her eyes, but Jack was masterful, making her drink the tea and even eat a mouthful of the slice of Madeira he put on her plate.

'You'll feel the better for something,' he told her cheerfully, but when she gave him a tragic look from her dark eyes, he bit his lip and looked down at his plate.

'You'll have to forgive me, Rosa. I know I'm being unbelievably crass, talking to you when you've just said goodbye to Daniel, but I get so few chances to talk to you at all, you mustn't blame me.'

'All the same, there's no point in you talking to me, Jack. What good does it do? You can't change anything, however much you want to.'

'I can at least let you know my feelings for you are the same and always will be. I know now isn't the time to think about the future, with Daniel on his way to war and me soon to follow, but if there is one and we all meet again, maybe there will be changes, Rosa. Who can say? Promise me we'll keep in touch. That's not too much to ask, is it? At least let me write to you from wherever I find myself. You needn't reply. Just let me write.' Again, he looked down at his plate. 'As long as I can, anyway. They won't be love letters, Daniel needn't worry. Just . . . notes from a friend.'

When she looked at him as he rose to pay the bill and made ready to leave – for war, as Daniel had done – Rosa's heart drummed with pain and she feared for him as she feared for Daniel. Two men going to war, facing the unknown, perhaps never to return. How was she to accept such a situation, to live with it for who knew how long into the future? Seemed she must accept it, in just the same way as the two men were accepting it, taking about what came their way. How could she even compare her own situation to theirs, she, a woman safe at home, while they . . . She stopped her thoughts there, unwilling to dwell on what the men must face.

'I'll have to go,' Jack was saying as they stood on the platform. 'I see some of my chaps arriving – it's nearly time we have to be off.'

His eyes, meeting hers, were suddenly as tragic as hers, though of course he was not allowed to shed a tear or two as she could do. He did, though, briefly brush her cheek with his lips – surely nothing Daniel could mind?

'Oh, take care!' she cried as he began to move away to join his fellow soldiers. 'Take care, Jack! And come home!'

He smiled, waved his hand and was drawn into a different company from hers, one that was already setting him apart, as Daniel's future had set him apart. And in moments, he was gone, on his way with his fellows, while Rosa was left alone on the platform, a silent witness to heartache.

Sixty

Over by Christmas? So some had prophesized, but Rosa had never believed it. Maybe the soldiers themselves would be glad to be free of a war not of their making – they'd been happy once to fraternize between trenches with the Germans – but the German leader was the Kaiser and everyone knew that all he wanted was war. And on the one time Daniel had been able to come home on leave, he'd warned Rosa not to hope for any quick ending to the conflict.

'Three years it will take, at least,' he'd said, his face darkly serious as it so often was. 'Four, maybe – yes, I'd say it will be four years before we see an end to it.'

And which of us will be around to see it? he had thought, though of course didn't put the thought into words for fear of upsetting Rosa. Too late, she was already in tears, wondering how she would cope with her worries for Daniel's safety for what would probably be years, when every time she opened the newspaper there would be casualty lists bringing heartache to somebody – some mother or father, some sweetheart or wife.

I don't think I can bear the parting! she wanted to cry, but worse for her was that she guessed Daniel might be able to bear it very well. She wasn't sure, of course, but it did still seem to her that he was different now from other people in his acceptance of loss and suffering. He hadn't always been so, and she thought she knew when the change in him had begun but she didn't want to think that it had only developed since the death of Lorne.

Of course, she didn't expect him to tell her everything about his life of danger in the trenches, yet if they could have shared their love and anxiety at this time, how different things would have been! But his leave passed and it was time for him to return to his unit. When she went with him to the station and waved goodbye alongside all the other wives, he did seem to melt a little, to kiss and hold her before boarding the train that would so soon bear him away.

Would she ever see him again? It was the same thought that was present in the minds of all the tearful wives waving goodbye and not something they could avoid. The only way to accept their situation was to believe strongly and truly that they and their menfolk would meet again, and that everyone would be together in the new, wonderful world without war that must surely await them all.

'What are you going to do with yourself now?' was one of the last things Daniel had asked before his train pulled out, and Rosa had been going to say she didn't know, except that it came to her suddenly that she might take an assistant nurse's course she'd seen advertised at the infirmary.

'That'd be excellent,' Daniel had said when she'd told him of it. 'A great idea.' And then surprised Rosa with a smile and a little mock salute as his train began to move away, which was why Rosa was able to get home without crying all the way, rather surprising Molly, who was coming down the stairs as Rosa arrived and whose sympathetic hug did bring the tears at last. Especially as poor Molly herself had just been through the same ordeal of saying goodbye to her husband, who had left the day before to join his regiment.

'They say it's worse to be the one who's left.' She sighed as she and Rosa hugged, but neither she nor Rosa could be sure if that were true. At least they could make a cup of tea, and if there were tears shed as they drank it, nothing needed to be said.

Sixty-One

Four years, Daniel had prophesized for the duration of the war, but he was not to see those years, nor was Rosa really surprised that he did not. Ever since she'd made that last goodbye to him at the station, she'd had the strongest feeling that she would never see him again. The comfort that should have come from that last meeting was not there, for in spite of all her efforts, she could not lose her desolate certainty that she would never see Daniel again.

She never told anyone of this premonition, for she knew they would have tried to cheer her out of having it. After all, it wasn't sensible, was it? Even though it was true there was the possibility that Daniel would not survive, which was the risk for all men fighting in the trenches, it was also true that he might be one of the lucky ones who 'made' it. For lucky ones there were.

So it seemed, but Rosa's belief that she would never see him again remained with her – her own terrible secret, darkening her life, when others had no suspicion. Wherever she went – to her assistant nurse's job or visiting Molly – she managed to keep her feelings secret and played along with the belief that there was always hope. Hope that Daniel would come through.

But then, in July 1916 came the battle of the Somme which, with almost 60,000 casualties being recorded for the first day alone, had some of the worst-ever infantry casualties. Of these, it had to be that some would be from the Black Watch, though it would be some time before news of the only casualty that mattered to Rosa would come to her via the dreaded telegram.

"'We regret to inform you . . .'" she began to read after opening it with shaking fingers. Then started crying, 'No, no!' And again, 'No!'

It didn't matter how much others might try to comfort her – all she was conscious of were those terrible words sounding the knell in her brain . . . *Regret to inform you* . . . *Regret to inform you* . . . Words which so many young women had already had to accept and which she must herself accept now.

There was unexpected comfort when the private letter that Daniel's commanding officer wrote to her brought praise of Daniel, who had been, it appeared, just as she'd expected, an exemplary soldier. One who lived 'by the book', as the officer wrote, not because it was officially 'the book', but because it was right. She, who had been Daniel's wife, could be truly proud of him and the contribution that he had made in the great struggle they were all enduring, a contribution that would never be, as the officer wanted her to know, forgotten.

And she did know it, and was truly proud, of course she was. Yet she would have given all the pride she felt in Daniel's achievements in the army for a love from him that might have been hers, had things in their lives been different. It was too late now to hope for what might have been if he had lived, too late for him ever to have come to love her as she loved him. All she had now were her memories of those early married days when there had been just the two of them and she had been so radiantly happy. Only memories, perhaps, but she would become like so many women and live on them. Live on her memories, yes, and be thankful.

Sixty-Two

Among the several condolences letters Rosa received was one from Jack. Not quite what she'd expected, in that it was the same sort of letter others had written, detailing all of Daniel's good points and stressing the sort of loss he must be to Rosa, whereas she'd been sure that if Jack got in touch it would be to outline a future for Rosa and himself now that Daniel had gone.

Of course, he might only be trying to be tactful, writing as he did, but he had never been known for his tact, and she couldn't help thinking that something must have changed in his feelings towards herself. That was fine, as far as she was concerned, but it was all rather mysterious and she might have wanted it explained had she had room in her mind for anyone but Daniel. In any case, she made no contact with Jack, who had only given her his home address anyway, and it was unlikely he would have been there.

As the weeks went by and she gradually began to come to terms with Daniel's death, she came at last to accept Molly's suggestion that she should visit his mother and her own father in Carron. Travelling wasn't easy with the war still being on and train services much reduced, but Molly thought Rosa would surely feel better once she'd seen her relatives.

'I don't know that I'm up to it,' Rosa sighed but, at Molly's frown, knew she was just making excuses and, within a week or two, found herself making the long journey to the Highlands, sad because she was alone but looking forward to seeing her father again and the place that had once been her home. Only seeing her father again turned out to be quite a shock, for it was immediately obvious that he was ill.

Why had Joan never told her? There he was, sitting by the range, so thin, so changed, Rosa scarcely recognized him, and all the while, as he described it himself, 'coughing his head off', giving thick, painful gasps that signalled only too well the state of his lungs.

'Da, you shouldn't be smoking!' Rosa cried, at which he tried to laugh.

'Bit of a cough, it's nothing,' he said as Rosa turned her dark eyes, full of reproach, on Joan.

'Why didn't you tell me?' she whispered when her father had gone early to his bed. 'Why didn't you tell me how bad he was? That's not just an ordinary cough he's got, is it?'

'Well, it's not the consumption!' Joan, swift in her own defence, said sharply. 'Just bronchitis, the doctor says.' Her eyes slid away from Rosa's. 'Chronic, he calls it, chronic bronchitis, but it's not, you know, serious. I mean, not fatal.'

'Just means he can't get better. And can't go to work, eh? Oh, Joan, this is terrible – I mean, how are you managing, then?'

'Oh, not too badly. No need to worry. I've got my sewing machine and I've taken up curtain-making again, or dressmaking, whatever folk want. We're all right, we pull through.' Joan hesitated for a moment, then took her turn to ask how things were for Rosa now that Daniel had gone. It was grand that she'd been able to afford the trip home; it had cheered her da so much.

'Well, I manage, too,' Rosa told her. 'Daniel left me a little and I'm earning money myself, so I was able to come home and see how you and Da were faring. You will keep in touch, Joan, now I've seen you and Da. Promise me you will?'

'Oh, I will, I will. I only didn't tell you before because I thought you'd enough on your plate, but things'll be different now.'

Unlikely to be better, thought Rosa.

Sixty-Three

Though the memories were at times bittersweet, it did Rosa good to see Carron again.

When she pictured her mother, playing with herself and Lorne, she found herself shedding tears, yet was happy she could remember the good times and not just the dark days when their mother had left them.

The memories of Lorne were strangely selective too, for being sister to the attractive blonde who seemed to break hearts wherever she went had not been easy. How easily, though, Lorne had twisted Rosa around her little finger! How she could always wheedle her into doing things she didn't want to do! Best not to think of all that, Rosa decided, looking out at the Moray Firth again and breathing in the sea air she so loved.

Best to remember Lorne at her best, playing hopscotch or running races at school, her yellow hair flying, her green eyes laughing. Oh, yes, they'd had their good times, the sisters, and it was only the good times that Rosa intended to revisit. Even to remember Daniel here was not something she wanted to do, for all that came back to her was his love for Lorne, which brought Rosa no consolation. Both were gone now, her sister and her husband, with Rosa the only one left, and it was partly to forget her situation that she was willing to meet Daniel's mother and listen to whatever she wanted to say.

Strangely enough, Mrs MacNeil, who was known for making a fuss about everything in her life, when it came to dealing with the true tragedy of the loss of her son made no fuss at all. It was as though she needn't, for there had been no tragedy, and what had happened to Daniel had never actually happened, so his mother believed.

At first, this to Rosa was of course disconcerting, but gradually she did what Mrs MacNeil wished and talked of Daniel as though one day he would undoubtedly come home, even rather accepting it herself while she was with his mother.

'It has been lovely to see you, Rosa,' she was surprised to hear

Mrs MacNeil remark. 'I used to think you would never make a
good wife to him, you know, but now I believe you are just right.
When he is back, you must come again to see me and we will all
be together again. Now be sure to do that, Rosa. Be sure to come
again.'

'Of course I will!' Rosa cried. 'I will come again!'

'Both of you, of course, when you can,' Mrs MacNeil added
comfortably. 'Both of you come when this war is over and the
laddies are home. Now, promise me you will, Rosa.'

'Of course I promise,' Rosa said fervently, and Mrs MacNeil smiled
and kissed Rosa's cheek. 'That's settled, then. Now take another
drop scone, my dear, and I will give you my recipe. You must be
sure to make some for Daniel – they're his favourite.'

Oh, poor woman, Rosa thought when out in the fresh air, making
for home. Poor Mrs MacNeil, unable to face the awful truth that
she would never see Daniel again. Who could blame her for choosing
to live in a world of her own, then? May she never move out of it,
Rosa prayed, until she was strong enough to face reality.

Almost back at her father's cottage, Rosa was surprised to see a
woman ahead of her, making, it seemed, for Bluff House, home of
the Thain family. She was dressed in a black jacket, ankle-length skirt
and small, fashionable hat, but when she turned her head to look
back at Rosa, whom she must have heard, her face didn't match her
smart clothes, for all Rosa could read there was the grief she had so
often seen elsewhere. And who, Rosa wondered, could she be grieving
for, this young Mrs Thain, mistress of Bluff House, wife of Greg's
landlord? For though she was much changed – thin, pale, and lines
around the eyes and mouth – Rosa had recognized the young lady
who had once been Lorne's employer. And Mrs Thain, it seemed,
recognized Rosa, for, holding out her hand, she said, 'It's Rosa, isn't
it? Rosa Malcolm? I believe your father has one of our cottages?'

'Yes, I'm here from Edinburgh to visit him. But I'm not Rosa
Malcolm now – I married Daniel MacNeil. Perhaps you remember
him?'

While Mrs Thain frowned a little, trying to place him, Rosa, her
lip trembling, said, 'I'm afraid he's gone now. He died on the Somme.'

'The Somme?' Mrs Thain gave a shudder. 'That terrible, terrible
place, the battle where my dear stepson, Rory, also lost his life. It
was so cruel, so very cruel.'

'Cruel,' Rosa whispered. 'Yes.'

Mrs Thain dabbed her eyes. 'Rory's widow is with us now, helping to comfort my husband. He took Rory's death very hard, you know.'

'I'm so sorry.'

Mrs Thain, lowering her handkerchief, fixed Rosa with her reddened eyes. 'But you must have heard about Rory's death, Rosa?'

'No, I never heard.'

'Because your poor sister is dead, too? She would have told you. Such a pretty girl, you know.' Mrs Thain sighed. 'No wonder Rory lost his heart to her. My husband could never understand, but I knew – I always knew – how much Lorne meant to Rory. And now they are both gone . . .'

For long moments, the two women were silent, until Rosa said she must say goodbye and Mrs Thain asked her if she might come again soon to see her father. Perhaps come back to live? Was there anything to keep her in Edinburgh now?

'Only my memories,' Rosa answered and held out her hand, which Mrs Thain shook. 'I think I must stay on in Edinburgh.'

They exchanged sad smiles and shook hands again, after which Mrs Thain turned to her home and Rosa continued on her way to her father's cottage.

Sixty-Four

'I met Mrs Thain just now,' Rosa told Joan as she took off her coat. 'In mourning for Mr Rory. She looked so sad, so much older. But how easy she is to talk to . . . treats you like an equal, I mean.'

'Which of course you are,' snapped Joan, who was heating an iron on the stove ready for pressing a dress she had made for sale. 'All that's different about the so-called gentry is that they've got more money.'

'I wouldn't say that about them all, Joan. Mrs Thain, for instance . . . Like I said, she treats folk as if they're the same as her. Catch Mr Thain doing that! He thinks his servants belong to an inferior world, nothing to do with him. Still, you can't help feeling sorry for him. Mrs Thain says he can't get over the death of Mr Rory.'

'I daresay, Rosa, but after the way Rory treated Lorne, I'm not sorry he's gone and I'm not pretending otherwise.' Joan finished her pressing, her face dark with her thoughts, then hung up the dress and said she'd make some tea. 'Your da will be getting up soon – he's had a good sleep this afternoon. Should be feeling better.'

'I'm so glad I've seen him.' Rosa hesitated for a few moments. 'I wish I could be nearer to you both.'

'Why couldn't you be?' Joan asked, giving her a sharp glance. 'I mean, what's to keep you in Edinburgh? I was thinking you could go back to doing that drawing you used to do – sell it up here to the visitors. It'd go like hot cakes. Ask that artist fellow who got you started. What's his name again?'

'Jack Durno. He's in the army – I don't see him now.'

'He'll get leave, eh? You get in touch with him, see what he says. You might both think about working here. If your da could see you, it'd make such a difference to him.'

'Mrs Thain said the same,' Rosa admitted. 'Thought it would be so easy. But it's Daniel, you see – he's so real to me, where I am now. His flat is still his home, as I see it . . I know he's never coming back, but all the memories of our marriage are in Edinburgh.'

'Oh, well, then, I understand. I'll make the tea now and then go and see how your da's feeling. I thought I heard him just now.'

'Let me see how he is,' Rosa said quickly. 'I'll help him down the stair.'

'If he's up to it. He'll feel better for seeing you, anyway.'

But as Rosa made her way up the little stairs to see her father, and Joan made a pot of tea, the faces of both women showed a sadness they could not hide.

Fancy Joan remembering Jack! thought Rosa as she prepared for bed that night, after having seen her father settled with Joan hovering about him as though he were a child. Showed how bright Joan was, though, didn't it, that she tried to use Jack as an attraction for Rosa's return? If only that could happen!

But of course it wasn't possible. Not only was he away in the army, he seemed to have lost touch with Rosa, for she couldn't remember when she'd last heard from him. All those letters he used to write were indeed just a memory, though she'd enjoyed every one and still had them somewhere. It seemed that Jack had finally given up hope of a relationship with her, even though Daniel was dead.

Or worse, it suddenly came to her – Jack might be dead himself. She was not his next of kin; she wouldn't have been told if anything had happened to him. She tried to stop thinking of him and settled herself for sleep, finally succeeding in putting him out of her mind, allowing the dear face of Daniel to come to her as it always did just before sleep claimed her.

It was when morning came at last that the idea came to her to try to find out, when she returned home, just what had happened to Jack. Someone, somewhere, would know. But now she must hurry up and wash and dress before she went to see how her father was. There weren't many days of her stay left, and she must spend as much time as possible with him before she had to leave.

When the time finally came for her return to Edinburgh, the wrench was terrible, with Rosa feeling so bad to see how forlorn her father seemed, and how Joan, though she said nothing, showed all too plainly how she disapproved of Rosa's going home.

'I'll be back in no time,' Rosa declared earnestly just before the carrier came to take her on the beginning of her journey. 'You'll see, Da. I'll be with you again before you've missed me going away.'

As she kissed and hugged him, he only sighed deeply, and Rosa's eyes on Joan saw the disapproval that her stepmother was making no effort to hide.

'It's true,' Rosa whispered to her. 'I will be back soon and, if Da gets worse, you've promised to tell me, eh?'

'You know what would be best,' Joan said quietly. 'Have another think about it Rosa, because your Daniel will be with you wherever you go is my thinking. You needn't stay where he used to live.'

'Maybe not,' Rosa said hurriedly. 'I'll see how things go.'

'And don't forget to try to get in touch with that artist fellow again to help you with your drawing. It'd be a shame to waste your talent.'

'I will try,' Rosa said to please her. 'But I don't hold out much hope of getting in touch with Jack soon.'

'Well, see what you can do. You never know how you'll do till you try.'

'True,' Rosa agreed, sadly aware that she must make her last farewells, for the carrier was at the door and she must go.

With more tears and sighs, hugs and final kisses, she managed to get on her way with last waves as she was borne away, filled with regrets – remorse, even – that she was leaving the sad couple at the cottage door.

I will come back soon, she told herself, her handkerchief to her eyes. I've promised them I will.

But the journey back to Edinburgh, even though it was to the home she shared with Daniel, had never seemed so dismal, and her arrival back at the flat would have had her in tears again, except that Molly was so pleased to see her and had brought in so much that was needed, Rosa felt she must put a good face on things.

No one could be as welcoming as Molly and it helped that her husband had just written, saying he was all right and might be getting leave soon, which meant that Molly was so happy, Rosa even managed to share her feelings for a little while.

Alone, of course, darkness returned to hover over Rosa, though it was true she was able to turn her thoughts to Daniel and feel his presence. There was comfort in that, but for a long time after she went to bed, she could only think of her da and how soon there might be a call from Joan telling her she must return at once, her da was worse.

As for Joan's urging her to seek out Jack, that was not something

Rosa thought was at all worthwhile. He would be away with his Artists' Rifles, even if she'd wanted to get in touch, which she did not. It seemed more and more likely to her that Jack had dropped his interest in her and there would be no point in trying to meet up, which, with all her anxieties, did not matter to her anyway. He was no longer a part of her life, as she was not part of his, her only regret being that she didn't actually know that he was safe. Who would know if he was? she idly wondered, and no one could have been more surprised than she was when, crossing Princes Street one afternoon, she suddenly saw him in civilian clothes and, gathering her wits about her, managed to call his name.

'Jack, Jack! Wait, it's Rosa!'

And as he turned to look back, she finally understood why he had not been in touch, for though his left arm in its sleeve appeared to be normal, the right arm of his jacket revealed all too clearly that it was empty. Jack had lost his right arm.

Oh, God, thought Rosa, her hand to her lips. Jack had lost his painting arm. He hadn't wanted to tell her, hadn't, perhaps, been able to face what had happened, poor Jack, poor Jack . . .

Even now, she could tell that he didn't want to see her, but she ran to him anyway and, throwing her own two arms around him, held back her tears, while Jack looked as if he might shed a tear or two of his own.

Sixty-Five

'Why didn't you tell me?' she asked as she took a step away from him, keeping her eyes on the face that was still recognizably his though so changed, so sad and cold as she had never before seen it.

'Tell you what? That I'd lost my right arm? My painting arm?' Jack's mouth twisted. 'I could scarcely believe it myself – how could I have told you?'

'It must have been terrible,' she whispered. 'Terrible. How . . . how did it happen?'

He shook his head, then took her arm. 'We're right outside Logie's; let's go in.'

For tea? As though this was just an ordinary meeting? Allowing him to lead her through the swing doors of the well-known store, Rosa could scarcely take in what was happening. That she was back with Jack as she'd so often been before, yet with everything seeming so different, so dream-like. Thank God he would be able to tell her what had happened to him and how he was managing after what must have seemed to him to be the worst blow to hit him in the world.

Oddly enough, as they ordered tea and scones at a table in the tearoom where they'd so often met before, Jack almost echoed her own thoughts.

'The worst thing I could have imagined was what happened to me,' he told her. 'Apart from losing my sight, which thank God I still have, to lose my right arm was the worst punishment, something I couldn't bear to accept – even though thousands of fellows have had much worse things happen to them.'

'I can't think what it must have been like for you,' Rosa murmured as she poured the tea the waitress had brought and tried not to watch as Jack clumsily used his left hand to accept his cup. Passing him scones, she wondered if she should offer to butter one for him, but knew he wouldn't accept, and in fact he didn't take a scone at all.

'My favourites,' he muttered. 'When I used to care about such things. What the hell does it matter what you eat? Nothing matters to me now if I can't paint.'

'You still have your left hand,' she ventured, at which he frowned and shrugged.

'And when did you ever see me using a paintbrush in my left hand?'

'But you could try it, Jack. You'd get used to it. I mean, isn't it the brain that controls these things? I'm sure I read that somewhere.'

'Aren't you the knowledgeable one!' he exclaimed, at which she flushed, making him shake his head and reach across to take her hand.

'Sorry, Rosa, sorry. You see what's happened to me? I'm not worth bothering about. Something hits me and it seems I can't take it. God, when I think what's happened to some of the men I knew, I am ashamed. Forgive me, Rosa. I want to be as I used to be but words keep coming that are wrong and I end up just feeling sorry for myself—'

'You're not to blame!' cried Rosa. 'You've a right to mind what's happened to you. But tell me about it, Jack – maybe it would help to talk about it.'

'There's not much to say. I came out of a trench, a sniper fired, he hit my arm, the wound festered and – well, I lost the arm. Was sent home, invalided out of the army – and have been brooding ever since.'

With a sudden, quick reminder of the old Jack, he smiled at Rosa, drank some tea and said he thought he might have a scone after all.

'You were right, Rosa,' he said softly as she took a chance and buttered and passed one to him. 'It helps to talk. Especially to someone as sympathetic as you. I haven't let you say one word about yourself, so tell me how you are and what you've been doing.'

'I'm well, just doing my usual jobs. But I have just lately been up to Carron to see my father, who's not well. He and my step-mother would like to see me move back to be near them, but I don't want to leave Edinburgh.'

His expression bleak, Jack nodded as he drank his tea. 'Memories?' he asked quietly.

'Memories. Yes.'

'Of course, you think of Daniel.'

'Oh, yes.'

'Only to be expected.' Jack raised his left hand to summon the waitress. 'I'll get the bill, Rosa, and walk you home.'

'Thank you, Jack, but I've some shopping to do.'

Rosa said no more until the bill was paid and they were once more in Princes Street, when she turned to Jack and told him how much it meant to her to meet him again, how much he would be in her thoughts.

'I suppose,' she finished hesitantly, 'I couldn't come to see you at home, could I? Would that be all right?'

'It would be all I'd want, Rosa. Let's fix a date, shall we?'

When they'd arranged for her to call one afternoon the following week, Jack smiled a little and told her she wouldn't find his place too untidy. He had a tough housekeeper who kept him on a short rein, even forcing him to keep his studio tidy, not that he spent much time in his studio any more.

We'll see about that, thought Rosa, making no remark to him, only shaking his hand and then leaning up to brush his cheek with her lips. 'Till next week, Jack.'

'I'll be counting the days.'

They parted, Jack to wave that sad left arm before walking fast homewards, she to catch a tram to take her to the shops near her flat. But her thoughts were so agitated, so churning in her brain, she could hardly remember what she needed to buy.

Sixty-Six

A tough housekeeper, Jack had said he now employed, who kept him on a tight rein, and when Rosa arrived at his house on the day they'd arranged, she quite understood why he'd described his Miss Ferguson as he had. A particularly thin woman, in her forties, with pale brown hair scraped into a bun, she had piercingly clear grey eyes that seemed, as they swept over Rosa, immediately to find fault, though at the same time managing to be perfectly polite.

'Mrs MacNeil?' she repeated in cold Scottish tones when Rosa had introduced herself. 'Please come in. Mr Durno is expecting you.'

Though why he should be was not to be understood, she seemed to convey as she led Rosa up the familiar stairs to Jack's studio, her back wonderfully straight, her head held high, reducing Rosa to a bundle of nerves longing only to see Jack and be out of Miss Ferguson's presence.

'Mrs MacNeil, Mr Durno,' the housekeeper announced, at which Jack, in a casual sweater and flannels, came forward eagerly to shake Rosa's hand.

'Rosa, how good to see you! You remembered the way all right?'

Still holding Rosa's hands, he turned his head to Miss Ferguson, indicating that she might leave them but perhaps bring them some tea later on?

'Certainly, sir,' she replied, her manner still so frosty it seemed that winter had come to the studio, but finally she withdrew and Rosa, shivering, freed herself from Jack's grip and stood gazing round at the studio that was tidier than she'd ever seen it.

'Oh, heavens, Jack,' she said in a whisper. 'How do you stand that housekeeper? She puts the fear of God into me!'

'What, Miss Ferguson? That's her manner – she's all right, really. Likes everything shipshape, of course, but that's a good thing, isn't it? Still, I don't want to talk about her. I just want to thank you, Rosa, for coming to see me. I feel so much better for seeing you – just like I did after we met the other day.'

'I'm glad to hear it, Jack, and it's grand to be here again.' Rosa paused, then said with emphasis, 'Where you did your painting. And where you'll paint again.'

Jack's smile faded. He shook his head. 'You know I won't do that, Rosa. Don't you realize painting is over for me? My hand's gone, my arm's gone. Gone, Rosa, and that's that.'

'Your right arm's gone, Jack. You still have the left one.'

'We spoke of this the other day. I can't paint with my left hand. I can't do anything with it, never could.'

'I saw you using it the other day,' Rosa said quietly. 'And I think, if you were to practise, you'd find it could be a substitute for the right one.' She looked around the studio, so strangely empty. 'Couldn't you try now? Just to please me?'

'It's no use, Rosa. I have tried it – a bit, anyway, and I got so damned frustrated I felt like tearing the canvas apart. You've no idea what it's like to try to do something and fail when you used to have no problems.'

'I know, I know, it's hard, but if you were just to persevere, Jack, I'm sure you'd get somewhere.' Rosa smiled cajolingly. 'Why don't we find some paper now and you have a go? Or on canvas, maybe? Yes, let's set up one of your easels, find some paints and begin.'

'I'd much rather get you started painting again, Rosa. You've real talent and I have the feeling I'd be good at guiding you—'

'Jack, never mind me. Just let's see what you can do with your left hand, eh?'

Heaving a great sigh, Jack one-handedly pinned some paper to one of his easels and took up a pencil, saying he'd just attempt drawing for the moment.

'Not that I'll be any good, Rosa. I'm just going to let you see for yourself how little I can do.' He stared at the paper in front of him and shook his head. 'The thing is what can I draw? There's scarcely a damn thing in this studio any more.'

'Draw me,' Rosa suggested. 'Just my face. I'm right here.'

'So you are. Maybe you could take one of the chairs – sit a little distance away.'

'This do?' she asked, seating herself on one of the studio chairs and smiling, suddenly feeling nervous.

'That'll be perfect.'

For some moments, Jack hesitated, then slowly with his left hand began to draw Rosa's face, scarcely seeming to breathe as he concentrated hard, while she, also holding her breath, watched him as he watched her and felt a great longing that whatever he was producing would make him happier. Please, God, she prayed, let him have some success this time. Let him have some hope of a future.

For some time, Jack worked on, the real Rosa apparently forgotten as he tackled her likeness, until she finally cried, 'How's it going, then? You seem to be making that left hand work harder than you thought you might.'

'I'm certainly having better luck than before.' Jack gave her a sudden grin. 'You're bringing me good luck, Rosa. I've never used that left hand for as long as this before.'

'I'm so glad, Jack, so very glad!'

'I tell you, you're bringing me good luck.' Suddenly he downed his pencil and went to her, taking her in his arms and hugging her hard. 'I never thought I could get so far until you came and I want to thank you. Really, really thank you. I'd given up, you see. I'd lost heart. But now . . .'

Still holding her in his arms, he put his thin face close to hers as though he might have kissed her, except that the door to the studio suddenly opened after a single knock and Miss Ferguson appeared before them holding a tray packed with tea things. Teapot, hot water jug, cups and saucers, dainty little sandwiches, a fruit cake already sliced and a plate of Scottish girdle scones. It seemed that the housekeeper could do what the Scots were said to do best, which was to provide the wherewithal for tea.

She took one look at Jack moving away from Rosa as Rosa moved away from him, then set down her tray on a chair near him and, with a contemptuous look from her wintry grey eyes, left the studio, banging the door behind her. Not a word had she said.

'Oh, Lord,' groaned Jack. 'She's upset, but why the hell should she be? What are we supposed to have done?'

'I expect she doesn't need an excuse to be upset.' Rosa sighed as she poured tea from the full teapot Miss Ferguson had left them. 'Come on, Jack, we might as well have the tea now it's here.'

Taking one of the housekeeper's sandwiches, Jack muttered, 'As soon as we've had this, I'll take you home before she starts playing up – if that's what she's planning.'

'You think we'll meet her at the door?'

'Oh, she'll want to see you, I expect. I must admit I've been surprised, the way she's behaved.'

'I haven't,' said Rosa.

Sixty-Seven

Luckily, when they eventually reached the front door, ready to leave, there was no sign of Miss Ferguson and, like a couple of truants escaping school, they hurried away, Jack insisting on taking Rosa home.

'You really don't need to, Jack,' she protested. 'I know you're dying to get back to your studio.'

'How little you know me,' he said with a laugh. 'And it's dark already. You think I'd let you go home on your own in the dark?'

'As though I don't go home in the dark nearly every day!' she said with a smile.

Yet she was glad he was with her when she arrived back at her flat, for a telegraph boy had just reached her door.

'Telegram for MacNeil?' he asked, looking sympathetic.

'Yes, I'm Mrs MacNeil,' she told him as Jack stood by, looking worried, and with a puzzled look she took the telegram. She'd already had the telegram that had caused her so much grief and dreaded to think what this new one could hold.

'Want to see what it says?' asked Jack, but she shook her head, saying she would read it herself, and with trembling fingers tore the message open, her eyes quickly running along its few tragic words . . .

Regret Greg passed away Tuesday Stop *Funeral Saturday if all right with you* Stop *Be in touch* Stop

'Any answer?' asked the telegraph boy, who had already been given sixpence by Jack.

'No – yes – I don't know—'

Rosa, shaking, took the hand that Jack held out for her. 'Jack, my father's dead. I must go to the funeral on Saturday, look up trains, let my stepmother know—'

'Right, we'll send a reply to her via this boy. You'll want to go tomorrow?'

'Yes, tomorrow – oh, but I can't believe it, Jack. He's dead, my da's dead—'

'You go up to your flat and I'll give the boy a reply to take for us. What's the address?'

In a daze, she gave him Joan's address, then after Jack had paid for a reply and the boy had cycled off with it, Rosa and Jack, hand in hand, slowly mounted the stairs to Rosa's flat.

'Of course I'll go with you,' said Jack while Rosa took off her hat and coat. 'There's no way you can go all that way on your own. I'll go out now and get the tickets.'

'No, Jack, it won't do. You didn't know my father, you don't know Joan or anyone up there – there'd be no point.'

'I'd be a support, Rosa, which is what you need. There must be some pub or somewhere that'll put me up.'

But at her expression, his eager flood of words dried and he sighed and shook his head. 'You don't want me to come, Rosa? I thought I'd be a help.'

'It's good of you, Jack, and I appreciate your offer, but I'd be better on my own, and I know the journey so well I'll be all right.' She touched his hand. 'You could see me off, if you like. I know there's a train that leaves at eight and I'll just get my ticket tomorrow morning.'

'No, I'll get it. I'll come round here by taxi, which we can keep for the station.' Jack smiled a little. 'If you'll just let me do *something*.'

'You're doing plenty, but now – I think . . .'

'You want to be on your own? Sure you do.' He quickly kissed her cheek, then went to the door. 'I'll see you tomorrow morning, then – early.'

'Till tomorrow. Thank you, Jack, for everything.'

He only smiled and let himself out, while she sank into a chair. She sat there for some time before finally collapsing into tears, not just for her father, but also for her mother and Lorne, for Daniel and even for herself. She was, of all of them, the only one left.

Sixty-Eight

Another long journey to Carron, then. But this time, as she again travelled alone, leaving a sad Jack behind, Rosa's thoughts had to be with Greg, who had never meant so much to her as he had in recent years. Had her mother lived, Rosa knew they would have been very close in the sort of way she would never have expected to be with Greg, but in his last illness she liked to think they'd shared a new affinity. After all, with her mother gone and Lorne, too, there'd been just the two of them left from the original family, herself and Greg. And now there was just herself, travelling again to Carron, to pay her last respects as his chief mourner after his wife, who would need all of Rosa's sympathy now that she was alone.

At least, neither Joan nor Rosa could feel alone at Greg's funeral, for the whole village turned out for him, along with many of his old customers from afar and even Mrs Thain, Greg having worked for the family from the big house, though it was not expected that Mr Thain would appear, and he did not. Rumour had it that he was still not over the death of Rory, perhaps never would be, and had become quite a recluse, as much a victim of the war as any who had suffered in a conventional way.

Joan, now Greg's widow, had been almost pathetically grateful to have Rosa with her, not only to share her sorrow but to help arrange the funeral and the reception afterwards that was held in the village hall, although of course there were plenty who would help there.

'It's been so grand having you here, Rosa,' Joan told her when they were at home, the funeral over, their tears over too, at least for the time being. 'I was so dreading this day, I don't mind telling you, saying goodbye to Greg, seeing him, you know, buried.' Joan sniffed a little. 'Going where I could not follow. That's what you feel at funerals, eh? That the person you loved has left you for ever?'

'No, Joan!' Rosa cried. 'That's not true! Their body's gone but we can still remember the way they were as a person. Don't you feel that, Joan? Oh, you must!'

'Maybe.' Joan sighed, putting her handkerchief to her eyes and rising to move the kettle on the stove so that they might make some tea. 'I don't know what I feel yet, I suppose. Except that I'm alone.'

'You've still got friends, Joan. You've still got me.' Rosa put her hand on Joan's. 'And I was thinking, Joan – you could come down to stay with me when you're sorted out, you know. You'd have a change of scene; it would do you good.'

'Rosa, I'd like that,' Joan answered quickly. 'When I've sorted things out, as you say. Oh, yes, as soon as I can, I'll come to Edinburgh, if you're sure you want me.'

'Of course I want you! As soon as you feel like coming, be in touch, eh?'

'And I won't be getting in the way?' Joan, preparing the teapot, smiled a little. 'Won't upset the artist, will I?'

'Joan, the only man I'm interested in is Daniel,' Rosa said quietly. 'Still.'

'Of course,' Joan agreed quickly. 'Of course, Rosa.'

All the same, it was good to have Jack meet her train – the third time he'd tried to find the right one, he admitted – and to be aware of his sympathy and practical help as well as his pleasure at welcoming her home. Finding a taxi, carrying her bag, even declaring his intention of boiling her kettle and making her tea (except that dear Molly was already on the scene, ready to do that for her), he couldn't have been more thoughtful.

'Molly – Jack – you two must meet each other,' Rosa declared. 'Jack, this is my good friend and neighbour, Mrs Calder. Molly, this is Mr Durno, the artist I told you I once worked for.'

'Also a good friend, I hope,' Jack said easily. 'Mrs Calder, I've heard a lot about you – all of it good.'

'I'm very pleased to meet you,' she told him, clearly pleased at meeting the famous artist at last. 'If I go to the galleries, can I see your paintings?'

'Only if you like modern art,' Jack said with a laugh. 'Rosa here has only just got used to it and still isn't sure about it, isn't that right, Rosa?'

But when he looked across to her, she was lying back, looking so weary, his face changed as he took on anxiety for her and he rose to touch her hand and say he must go, she needed to rest.

'Oh, she does,' cried Molly, rising hastily herself. 'I must go and all, but let me know if you need anything, Rosa. I've left some things in your larder, anyways.'

'You're so good, Molly – I'll just get my bag, settle up with you—'

'Nae bother, Rosa – don't want you worrying about that now. You just get some rest and knock on ma door when you feel better. Mr Durno – it was grand meeting you. I'll no' be forgetting to see your paintings when I can, eh?'

'And forgive me if you find 'em too crazy.' Jack, shaking Molly's hand, laughed again, then was serious as he thanked her for all she'd done for Rosa.

'I can tell Rosa has a good friend here,' he said earnestly. 'Isn't that so, Rosa?'

'Och, I'll be going!' Molly cried, blushing as she made for the door. 'Rosa, you'll come round, eh? Soon as you feel like it?'

'So goodhearted,' Rosa murmured when she and Jack were alone. 'I don't know what I'd do without her. Or you, Jack.'

'I only wish I could do more. You're looking so sad, Rosa – not surprising, of course, in view of the present circumstances.'

'It's not just my circumstances, Jack. I saw a newspaper headline on the train – so many killed at the battle of Cambrae, I can't stop thinking about it. So much useless slaughter . . .' Her voice trembled. 'So many young men gone, like Daniel.' Raising her great dark eyes to Jack's concerned face, Rosa whispered, 'When will it end, Jack? When will it all end?'

Sixty-Nine

When will it all end? Rosa had asked. It was the question on everyone's lips and only answered on the eleventh day of the eleventh month in 1918 when, after Germany had been defeated on the Western Front, an armistice was declared between Germany and the United Kingdom. Now, at last, as the poets put it, the guns could fall silent. Casualty lists were no longer needed and, after four long years, loved ones were no longer at risk.

Even so, it took a long time to accept that hostilities had ended, that the war was really over, that there would be no more killing. In fact, for some, the truth had to be faced that the armistice had come too late, that their loved ones would not be coming home at all.

Jack, watching Rosa one dismal November afternoon, knew that the truth was being faced by her and that her thoughts were not on her present drawing of autumn leaves but with Daniel, for whom the armistice had come too late. And with the knowledge of her sorrow, Jack's own feelings of anger could only deepen.

'Why didn't it happen before?' he demanded, pacing his studio. 'If it could happen now, why not Christmas 1914 when some were actually predicting that the war would end?'

His thin face flushed with anger, his blue eyes snapping at the thought of the generals he blamed for wasting so many lives, Jack seemed so unable at that moment to find calm that Rosa left her easel to go to him.

'Jack, Jack, settle down,' she told him. 'It was wrong that the war should ever have been allowed to happen, but now, at last, it's over.' She paused, her eyes filling with tears, and sighed. 'And no one else, thank God, will have to face those telegrams.'

Gently shaking his left arm, she gave Jack a long, sympathetic look, hoping he would listen to her and stop working himself up into a rage which would do no one any good. After all, she was nursing heartache herself, knowing that Daniel's death might have been avoided if the top brass on either side had just got together and talked, as it seemed they'd been talking now. How many lives might have been saved? How many would have been spared blindness and disfigurements, or nightmares they would never forget? How many wives would have been spared widowhood and their children the loss of their fathers?

'Come on, Jack,' Rosa said gently. 'You've every right to feel bitterness that this armistice has come too late for you, but let's be glad other men will be saved from going to war. So, we'll just get on with our painting, eh? You're supposed to be giving me a lesson, don't forget.'

'Feel more like going to a pub and drowning my sorrows,' Jack said with a sigh. 'But you're right – we have to be glad for what's happened, even if it should have happened long ago. Don't ask me to celebrate, though. There's been too much sadness for that.'

As Rosa made no reply, only looked away, her eyes still full of tears, Jack took her hand.

'I know what you've been through,' he said awkwardly, 'believe me, I do. Losing the love of your life. I know what that must have meant. I only have to think of how I would feel if . . .' He shook his head. 'If anything happened to you.'

'Nothing's going to happen to me,' Rosa said uneasily, aware that Jack seemed to be leading them away from their usual easy-going talk towards somewhere she wasn't sure she wanted to follow. She knew he loved her, he had told her long ago, but somehow he had kept the intensity of his feelings to himself and they had remained on friendly terms, which was easier all round. For some time there was silence between them, only eventually being broken by Rosa, who suggested that Jack might like to look at her drawing, then she must be thinking about going home.

'Not before Mrs Milner brings our tea,' he said quickly. 'She'll be here any minute.'

'Mrs Milner,' Rosa repeated, considering Jack's kindly and easygoing housekeeper. 'What a difference to Miss Ferguson, isn't she? So easy, so calm?'

'Like you, Rosa. So easy, so calm. But come to think of it, I used to be pretty calm myself, can you believe it? Now that the war's over, maybe I'll get back to being like that again. There'll be changes anyway, won't there? Now that we only have to worry about picking up the pieces.'

'Changes? For us? I don't see why. I don't see why anything should change.'

'You don't?'

'Well, no. Do you?'

Jack, studying her intently, seemed to be considering his reply with particular care when the door opened and Mrs Milner appeared with their tea tray.

'Oh, Mrs MacNeil, there you are!' she cried. 'I've put some of my sultana scones out for you – I know you like them, eh? You too, Mr Durno – you always seem to know when I've made a few because there you are behind my back, sneaking one or two before they've even cooled out of the oven! Oh, but they can count as a celebration for our grand armistice, eh? I'd never heard that word before but I know what it means now – it means peace on earth, eh? Just like in the carol. But I'd better go and leave you to your work. Enjoy your tea, now!'

Away she went as Jack and Rosa helped themselves to scones, exchanging smiles at the housekeeper's flow of words, which Jack said didn't bother him in the least.

'She knows not to talk when I'm working, walks about as though she's on tiptoe, but I let her talk when I'm not doing much. She's so good-hearted, like your friend, Molly. I know I'm damn lucky to have found her.'

His gaze fixed on Rosa's face, and Jack reached forward and took her hand. 'And you,' he said quietly, 'I'm lucky to have found you. You may not realize it, but you pretty well saved my life after I lost my arm.'

'Don't, Jack, don't talk of that. You were never going to . . .' As Rosa hesitated, he laughed.

'Do away with myself, do you mean? Well, I don't know that I'd ever have actually done that. Just felt like it sometimes.'

'Jack, please don't speak of it.'

'It's all right, it didn't happen.' Jack shrugged. 'And won't now, I promise you.'

Still holding Rosa's hand, he looked long and seriously into her face before saying in a voice so low she could scarcely hear it, 'Now that I've begun to hope, I mean.'

'Jack, let's not—'

'What? Not talk of the future, you mean? Everyone's got to have hope for their future, Rosa. You can't go on without it.'

'I know, but I don't think we should – you know, be getting involved now . . .'

'Too soon?'

When she did not reply, he shrugged, then somehow found a smile.

'Yes,' he said quietly. 'Forgive me, Rosa, it's too soon. I do understand, believe me. I know we have to wait. Just don't give me up while we're waiting. Promise me.'

'I promise, Jack.'

Gently pulling her from her chair, he kissed her briefly and told her he would take her home.

'I'm glad we talked, Rosa. It's good that we did. For me, anyway.'

'Next time, you must look at my drawings,' she told him. 'I know I've still a lot to learn.'

'Rosa, you're very talented. I mean it. You've a successful future ahead of you.'

But Rosa only smiled and said maybe, but for now she'd like to get home. No need for Jack to come with her, she certainly knew her way.

'You know it's my pleasure to take you home, Rosa. Just wish . . .' Jack sighed. 'Just wish you needn't go.'

'I must, I'm afraid.'

'I know, I know. Don't mind me. Sometimes I lose my head. Think how it would be, you know, if it wasn't too soon to say . . . what I want to say.'

He looked so woebegone as her eyes went over his face, she felt a sudden strange wish to make him happy as she knew only she could. Dear Jack. They'd been through so much; each in their way had faced such heartbreak – was it time at last to look for happiness? Not the happiness she'd shared with Daniel, that couldn't be expected, but the sort of love that came from giving, from opening the heart to another's longing . . .

'What would you like to say?' she heard herself asking in a whisper, and felt Jack's start of surprise as his eyes widened and his hands on her arms tightened, and couldn't help smiling that he, who was never lost for words, could find none now to tell her what she already of course knew. He loved her. What more could he say?

Only what men usually said, or rather asked, after they'd declared love.

'Rosa, will you marry me?' he asked, still holding Rosa's arms, his hands trembling. 'Not now – it's like we said, too soon, and I'm not asking that you'll love me the way you loved Daniel. It's to be understood that that love was different. But I promise you that I'll do all I can to make you happy. It'll be all I want to do, I swear, if you'll be willing to accept me.'

Still in wonder at her sudden intention to make him happy, she went willingly into his arms and, as they clung together, Jack, after looking long and deeply into her face, asked, his lips against her cheek, if she would make him the happiest man in the world? To which she made no reply. Somehow, it didn't seem necessary.

Seventy

Of course, life didn't just change overnight because a four-year war had ended. There'd been difficulties caused by that war, not just the tragedies of loss that so many had had to endure, but continuing shortages, for example, particularly of food, and they lingered on for months, not only in defeated Germany and other parts of Europe, but also in victorious Britain. It was just as well, the British people said, that they'd grown used to queuing and going without during the war, when in a way the fact that they were the victors made it harder to accept the difficulties.

'As though they matter!' cried Jack. 'We should think ourselves lucky we're at peace. That's all that matters.' But then he shook his head as he and Rosa patrolled the Botanic Gardens on a summer's day in 1920 and gave a wry smile. 'Not quite all,' he amended. 'There are other things that matter. To me, anyway.'

'Your painting,' suggested Rosa. 'That's a first for you. I think it's wonderful that you are doing so well. Everyone says so.'

'You're doing well too. Quite successful, aren't you, these days? With your postcard work?'

'Amateur stuff, Jack. It's not to be compared with what you do. If I can make a bit of money with it, that's all I want, but you're one for the art books, aren't you? And people want you for lecture tours and all sorts of things, don't they?'

'The most recent offer is for a tour of America.'

'America?' As they approached a bench, Rosa pointed and said they should sit down so he could tell her all about his offer. 'I didn't even know about it, Jack. Were you keeping it a secret?'

'In a way, because I know I should accept and I don't want to.' As his eyes rested on Rosa, Jack's face had taken on the sort of look she knew went with something serious and she braced herself to find the right thing to say, at the same time becoming aware that she was anxious for him not to leave her. These days, they were such loving companions, what would she do without him?

'What are you going to do?' she asked after a silence. 'Shall you go to America?'

'Not without you, Rosa.'

She laughed. 'Well, I can't go!'

'Can't you?'

'Why, whatever would they think? The two of us going there together?'

'If we were married, there'd be no problem.'

'Yes, but we're not married, Jack, are we?'

She had been looking down but raised her eyes to him and saw that he was suddenly looking anxious and caught her hands.

'Could change that,' he whispered. 'Could change that very soon. Because it's not too soon now, is it? Remember that the time when we said it was? Tell me it's true, Rosa. Things are different now, aren't they? Please, for God's sake, tell me they are!'

'Yes, of course they are. But I can't forget Daniel.'

'I know, I understand. That love is special; you could never love me in the same way. But I'm not asking that you should. I'm a different man from Daniel. My love for you is different from his, and what you feel for me will be different too. Not so strong, maybe, but it's there, isn't it? Your feelings for me?'

She did not hesitate. 'Yes, Jack, it is. I think it has been for some time, only I didn't realize it.'

'I was just dear old Jack?' he asked lightly. 'Someone you were used to?'

'Someone I cared for.' Rosa hesitated, searching for the right words. 'Someone I know now I cared for . . . very much.'

A long, long silence fell, so long it seemed neither could break it, but Jack at last took Rosa in his arms and, smoothing back her hair, asked quietly, 'Cared enough for to be my partner, Rosa?'

'As you'll be mine, Jack.'

He gave a long, blissful sigh. 'Will you marry me, then? You never have answered me on that. If you do you won't regret it. I swear I'll do all I can to make you happy. And I'll never expect you to think of me as another Daniel. Dear old Jack will do.'

'No,' she told him with decision, 'it won't. You'll never be just dear old Jack to me. Perhaps you were once. Not now. We'll be what you said we'd be just now – partners.'

'Partners in art, partners in love. We'll be married as soon as we can arrange it?'

'So that I can go to America with you?' Rosa's laugh was a little nervous, but Jack shook his head.

'So that you can spend a lifetime with me. That's what I'm offering, my dearest.'

'That's what I'm taking then,' she replied.

And they went into each other's arms.

Seventy-One

A registry office wedding was arranged with only Molly and her husband as witnesses and Joan and Jack's agent Terence Roy as guests, after which Rosa and Jack hosted a small reception at a city hotel and left for their honeymoon, not in America as Jack had planned, but in Carron – Rosa's choice.

'You don't mind, Jack?' she asked him. 'I know Carron is not a place you know well but it means a lot to me. I'd like to see it again before we go abroad.'

'Of course I don't mind,' Jack told her quickly. 'As long as . . .' He hesitated. 'As long as it doesn't bring back too many memories to upset you.'

She gave him a long, clear look of understanding. 'I'm not going to be thinking of Daniel all the time, Jack. Please don't believe that.'

'I won't, of course I won't. I know you just want to be where your family were before we have to depart and I'm happy about that. As long as we can make our own way there and not have to travel with Joan – much as I like your stepmother.'

'Of course we won't be travelling with Joan!' Rosa told him, smiling. 'I want just to be with you, Jack, as Joan will know. After all, we are on our honeymoon.'

'Thank God,' he said quietly. 'I still feel I'm living in a dream. You know, none of this is happening.'

'Me too,' said Rosa, thinking all the same that the situation was easier for Jack than for her. He didn't have to think of someone else at this time, someone who couldn't be asked to give his opinion, who was lying in a soldier's grave too far away even to be visited. Would Daniel have minded if he could have known that his widow was marrying again? Over and over again, Rosa had asked herself that and the truth was that secretly, never put into words, she knew that she would have liked Daniel to have minded. It would have been a sign, wouldn't it, that he had loved her as much as she had loved him? But he hadn't; she had long ago learned to face that and now – now that she had Jack – she need never face it again.

'Jack,' she asked quietly. 'Do you love me?'

'Now, why do you ask that? You know I do.'

'Just checking,' she said smoothly, though looking into Jack's eyes she knew there was no need for any checking. Daniel's eyes had been beautiful but their gaze had rarely been solely for Rosa. How different it was with Jack.

Everything was different with Jack. Especially back in Carron, where they stayed with Joan and Rosa took a strange pride in introducing him to all the people she knew. Some might have minded that she had a new husband while Daniel was in his grave, but nothing was said, and Jack was so pleasant and so worthy of sympathy over the loss of his arm in the war that Rosa could only sigh with relief that things seemed to be working out so well.

Mrs Thain, in fact, was immensely impressed with Jack, not only with his friendly nature but also that he was a well-known artist, a man of achievement.

'I'm so pleased for you,' she whispered to Rosa when Jack was studying what pictures the Thains had, most of which were traditional but still of great interest, as he politely claimed. 'I think you'll both be wonderfully happy, and to meet happiness these days . . .' She sighed. 'Well, it's rare.'

When Rosa asked after Mr Thain, who had said very little to the visitors before excusing himself to be alone, locked in his own world of grief, the shadows returned to his wife's face as she explained that there had been no change in him and probably would be none. Although they still had Hugo, he was now based in Edinburgh where he was studying at the university as a mature student, and though of course he came over as often as he could and did cheer his father a little, he wasn't his brother, who would never cheer his father again.

'Poor chap,' Jack said softly of Mr Thain. 'Wish there was something we could do.'

'I think you may in fact have done a lot of good,' Mrs Thain told him. 'At least my husband was talking to you a little. I'm very grateful for your visit – you will come again, won't you, before you leave?'

'We will,' Rosa promised as they took their leave but, outside the house, her smile was a little wry.

'You know, Jack, at one time I'd never have been entertained by the Thains as I have been today. Mrs Thain was always pleasant and treated staff well, but Mr Thain thought they were scarcely human.'

'Has other things to think of now, it seems.' Jack sighed. 'Can't help feeling sorry for him, and his wife, of course. But where to now for us? Another walk by the sea wall?'

'I think, if you don't mind, Jack, I'd like to go back to the graves. It's my chance to see them again before we leave.'

'Sure it is. I want you to do just what you want while you can.'

There they were, the graves of Rosa's family, in the churchyard in the High Street, her parents' and Lorne's. Flowers had been placed by Joan in memory of Greg, but the beautiful lilies on Lorne's grave had been put there only yesterday by Rosa. And though she had shed tears then, she shed them again now as she bent to straighten the flowers a little, feeling that every time she contemplated her sister's death the tears would fall.

'She died too young, you see, Jack – she should have had years still to come. We were sisters together, after all, Highland sisters making our way in the world – it doesn't seem fair that she should have already been taken.'

'There's nothing fair in this world, Rosa,' Jack said sadly. 'All I know is that we're lucky; we're facing a wonderful life together. Isn't that what matters?'

She raised her dark eyes to his as they stood together by Lorne's grave, Jack's one arm encircling her, her right arm round his waist, until at last they turned away, both so sad yet at the same time filled with hope for a future shared together. There would be problems, of course. Things might happen that didn't seem fair, as they both knew. But there would also be memories – some sad, others beautiful – and the future that had been denied their loved ones would be theirs. For that they must be grateful.

As they traced their steps away from the resting place of others, Rosa, so conscious of being the remaining Highland sister, made a silent vow to make the very best of the future she had been granted with Jack, as well as keeping alive her memories of those who had left her.

'I'm so glad,' she murmured to Jack, 'that I've had this chance to see where my family lie before we have to go away. And to know that Joan will be looking after them.'

'Of course she will, but we're not going away for ever, Rosa.'

Jack pressed Rosa's arm in his. 'We'll be back, you know. I want you to be happy, you see, and I know it will make you happy to remember that.'

'That we're coming back? Yes, it's good to know. But what really makes me happy, Jack, is to be with you.'

'You mean that, Rosa?'

'You know I do, Jack.'

'I'm a lucky man, then.'

'Let's say we're both lucky,' she said quietly.

And together they left the family graves to step into their future, the solitary Highland sister and the man who loved her. It would be a good future, they would make it so, but the past with its memories would not be forgotten. Even when they were far away, for Rosa especially, this place she called home, and the sister and others who had shared it with her, would be with her always.